LETHAL WEAPON

WARNER BROS. Presents
MEL GIBSON • DANNY GLOVER
A SILVER PICTURES Production
A RICHARD DONNER Film
"LETHAL WEAPON"
GARY BUSEY
Music by ERIC CLAPTON
and
MICHAEL KAMEN
Written by SHANE BLACK
Produced by
RICHARD DONNER and JOEL SILVER
Directed by RICHARD DONNER

A NOVEL BY
JOEL NORST

BASED ON A SCREENPLAY BY
SHANE BLACK

A JOVE BOOK

LETHAL WEAPON

A Jove Book / published by arrangement with
Warner Bros. Inc.

PRINTING HISTORY
Jove edition / March 1987

ISBN: 0-515-09179-0

Jove Books are published by The Berkley Publishing Group,
200 Madison Avenue, New York, NY 10016.
The words ''A JOVE BOOK'' and the ''J'' with sunburst
are trademarks belonging to Jove Publications, Inc.

PRINTED IN THE UNITED STATES OF AMERICA

CHAPTER 1

"Do you want—?"

Then she remembered that she was alone.

She closed the door to the medicine chest. Its mirror quickly panned reflections of the rumpled bed, the two empty wine glasses on the polycarbonate night stand, and finally halted before her face.

She smiled at herself disdainfully. Then she lightly touched her bare breasts with her fingertips and struck a pose that nearly made her laugh. Laugh except for one thing—she had forgotten why she'd come into the bathroom. And that is exactly what she had done: She'd padded in here and opened the medicine chest, only to shut it again.

Mentally, she retraced her steps since lying in bed.

"Oh yes," she whispered with the same unhappy smile. Pleasure. Warmth. Unexpected closeness. All followed by an abrupt parting that had left the apartment as still as a tomb.

But even before that, she reminded herself, something had disturbed her as she lay across her bed, waiting. Her guest was in the bathroom. The water was running loudly from the tap, but still she heard the medicine chest door click shut.

This confused her: Why would her guest want to open it? *Everything* was here, within easy reach of the bed. But then she put this out of her head and glanced down at the oval hand mirror balanced on her pillow. Its reflection was duplicating a snowy little peak into an opaque diamond. Pretty. And wedged into the wooden handle was a single-edged razor blade. She reached for it but changed her mind. Instead, she moistened a finger, then buried it to the first knuckle in the snowy pile. The residue that clung to her skin she gently rubbed onto her gums.

Then her guest came back to bed. The hours became minutes. And all too soon, her guest was dressing, talking a bit nervously, then hurrying out the door.

And she was alone in the silent apartment.

It was then that she'd decided to check the medicine chest, which had been opened by her guest without explanation. More so than any of the many who came and went from her bed, she trusted this guest with her passion—but not with her prescription supply of secobarbital. She would need those capsules to come down, to sleep in the next several hours. And rest would be impossible if her barbiturates had been pilfered from her medicine chest.

At that point, she now recalled a bit vaguely, she had started for the bathroom.

But, within a few steps, she was distracted by the gilt-framed photograph in the glass cabinet. Two men, one white and one black—she should have shown her guest. The young soldiers had thrown their arms around each other. They wore those foppish-looking hats. *Boonies,* her father called them—and, on the day of his return, he'd given her his sweat-faded one to wear in her sandbox. North Carolina in the summer. Hot. Humid. Bugs.

Her glazed eyes drifted to the stenciled sign on the corrugated tin roof behind them:

Welcome to Ngoc Linh
9th Special Forces Group
22nd Detachment

She focused on the black soldier's face once again. It was kindly—unlike her father's, which even back then was hard and unforgiving. The black man looked like he preferred to be surrounded by people; he needed the warmth of people. She remembered him well from Fort Bragg. He came around on Sundays and drank beer with her father. He talked to her. He listened to her. He smiled a lot.

Tears welled in her eyes—and she rushed into the bathroom and cracked open the medicine chest, only to close it again a moment later, bewildered. And how much time had elapsed since her guest had departed: three minutes, three hours, three days?

But now, all at once, she had broken free of the confusion swimming in her head. She knew why she was standing alone in her bathroom. She had come to make sure her secobarbital was still there.

And it was. On the top shelf where she'd left it. As best she could tell, not a capsule was missing.

Taking down the plastic prescription bottle, she began fidgeting with the child-proof cap. She had no children, nor could she ever have any, but the pharmacist had probably assumed her to be a young mother. She could appear to be any kind of woman she wanted to be simply by dressing and carrying herself differently. It was a knack that had paid off handsomely.

At last, the cap popped off and she shook out two capsules into her hand. Two for sleep. But then she added a third. Three for *dreamless* sleep.

Cupping her palm beneath the soughing tap, she washed down the capsules, then applied her cool, wet hands to her face. The mascara came down her cheeks in black rivulets and she quickly reached for a towel. She paused with her face buried in the soft linen—strange, but there was an aftertaste in the back of her mouth. Like almonds.

Drifting into the living room, she put a Sam Cooke disc on the stereo system—as an antidote to the sudden silence that was making her want to sob. The voice, the music swelled around her, soothed her, then seemed to draw everything in the apartment toward the throbbing speakers. Even the chemise curtains framing the balcony fluttered out from the wall.

"Oh yes . . . oh yes," she said happily, realizing once again that it was perhaps the most beautiful night in Los Angeles in years. And hard gusts of breeze, not the music, were tousling the curtains.

She ran through the open glass doors and out onto the balcony, not feeling her feet beneath her. She floated there.

The Santa Ana—a clean, dry wind born in the high desert—had swept away all the smog. There was a three-quarter moon directly overhead, but it did little to take away the brightness of the stars. To the east, she could see Mount San Antonio, pale with snow. Then she turned toward the citadel of lights that was downtown Los Angeles. And beyond the glittering skyscrapers, the twinkling carpets that were the suburbs, the ocean shone purple in the moonlight. She could even make out Catalina, the night was so unbelievably clear.

Laughing, she reached out to touch the island—but then clasped her hand to her throat. She started to gag.

But the urge to retch passed after a moment. And she was feeling too good to dwell on the burning sensation that was fanning out from her abdomen, the difficulty she felt in breathing.

It was a sky to sail across. There would never be another one like it. And if she herself could not fly, she wanted to see other things fly in her stead.

She grasped a potted poinsettia and balanced it atop the iron railing. The wind sifted her blond bangs back and forth across her eyes as she studied the blood-red plant. It was a gift from a guest. A quiet man she almost liked. However, she nudged it over the side.

Down, down it tumbled, then exploded against a car in the parking lot ten stories below, leaving a big dent in the roof.

She spun around and seized the small Christmas evergreen another guest had brought her. The pine shed its ornaments and tinsel as it fell.

There followed the satisfying crunch of a windshield disintegrating. All at once, the parking lot was scintillating with pebbles of glass. Pretty.

Then the pain found her. It seemed to violate every part of her body at once, and she felt the breath being squeezed out of her. "No!" She had no idea what it meant; she had been feeling so exquisitely good.

Yet, beyond the balcony, the evening beckoned her in the silky voice of the Santa Ana: *Come with me and escape all pain . . . come with me and I will show you how to fly above it all. . . .*

Clutching herself in her arms, she nodded. She said yes to the voice.

Then, struggling to smile through this strange excruciation, she raised one long leg and swung it over the top of the railing as gracefully as a ballerina. Poised there, she hesitated. As much as she wanted to fly, she hesitated. The warm dreaminess abandoned her eyes, replaced by a knowing sadness.

But then, before she might change her mind, she rolled outward from the balcony.

And she discovered that the voice had not lied to her: There was no pain in tonight's sky, only wind and freedom and a profusion of warm Christmas lights as apartment after apartment flickered past.

His stubble was three days past being stylish. Brushing his cheek with the heel of his hand, Martin Riggs tried to recall when he had last shaved, or bathed—or given a shit. He came to no conclusions, so he raised his arm for the bartender's attention. "Another Wild Turkey here!" He had to shout over the raucous voices in the place.

"No."

Riggs grinned in dismay. "Say what?"

"You're cut off."

"Here?"

"Where else—the Beverly Hilton?"

"That's my point, Jake. This ain't the Beverly Hilton.
It's a dump. A dive. And you keep serving people who
died of alcohol poisoning in the fifties. That's what joints
like this are for. Haven't you ever done any market
research?"

"Look, you've been here since I opened at six this
morning. It's now almost one the next day. Do you hear
what I'm telling you? Go home, Martin."

"I am home. And I want another drink."

"Okay, on one condition."

"Name it."

"Go inside the head and take a gander at yourself."

"And if I can stand what I see?"

"I'll fill her up again."

"A deal, Jake." Riggs rose from the hard wooden
bench with a wince. His buttocks had gone permanently to
sleep around noon. He started for the rest room, but
paused for a moment at the end of the bar. A television
screen, its color adjustment so lousy only drunks would fail
to notice, was floating in the cigarette smoke near the
ceiling. Channel 11. An old Pat O'Brien and Jimmy Cagney
movie. He watched the greenish screen with such complete
absorption a crone snorted from her stool, "Ain't you got
a television of your own?"

"Sure I do, Mom. And I never turn it off."

"I'm not your mom."

"Thank God for small fucking favors, huh?"

Then he shambled on toward the back, passing into a
darkened hallway in which two punks huddled around the
pay phone, probably making bomb threats to a children's
hospital.

Sidestepping them, making sure he wouldn't brush the
grips of his Beretta 9-mm automatic against their stooped

shoulders, he ducked inside the men's room and—despite three days of intoxication—was still offended by the stench.

For the moment, he carefully ignored the mirror over the sink.

A couple of butts in the urinal had stained the water to the color of tea. Sighing, he unzipped. And when he was finished, he shook himself only twice. More than twice and it's playing with yourself.

Who'd told him that a couple of light-years ago?

His training officer. Yes, that's who. Indomitable Royce Chalmers, who'd finally eaten his own gun.

At least, he'd gone like a cop—none of that pussy razor blades or pills shit. One hundred and fifty-eight grains of regulation round-nose lead drilled through the roof of the mouth. The exit wound looked like someone had taken a posthole digger to the crown of Royce's head. Like a fool, Riggs had asked to see the autopsy photographs. Maybe he'd needed to be convinced that Chalmers was really dead. Royce Chalmers was so damned good at the job he just had to be immortal, everyone had thought.

Riggs shuddered, then laughed under his breath. There was no humor in the laugh.

Zipping up, he thought to wash his hands, but then had a look at the sink. The unsettling thing was that he knew he belonged here with the stains, the stink, the damaged people whose loud voices were rumbling through the door like a freight train. This was indeed home.

At last, he braced himself and looked in the mirror.

"Oh shit!"

He left the place by the back door.

Aimlessly, Riggs drove the empty freeways, skimming thirty feet above the sleeping cities of Southern California on those concrete-capped embankments.

The lights seemed brighter than usual because of the Santa Ana. Leaving the bar, he'd been surprised to find the wind blowing like the devil. The sky was pitch black, but studded with huge stars. It had been foggy when Jake had let him through the front door yesterday morning.

Having disconnected the smog gear and thrown away the air-cleaner cover to the Plymouth, he had the fastest undercover car in narcotics. But now he was content to keep the speedometer needle on fifty.

He thought about going home but quickly dismissed the idea.

There was nobody there anymore. He had to keep reminding himself of that fact. Otherwise, false hope played tricks on his mind. He began believing in the impossible, and then the eventual letdown seemed painful enough to kill him.

So he drove.

At two o'clock, he decided he could use a sixer and left the Harbor Freeway at the Pacific Coast Highway exit. Within a block, he found a twenty-four-hour convenience market. A Stop and Rob, as the blue-suiters would call it.

He parked on the dark side of the store, but angled the Plymouth so he could keep an eye on it from inside. If not, in a neighborhood like this, he'd come out to find it stripped and propped up on orange crates.

The clerk looked Riggs over carefully, then went back to the *Los Angeles Times* he'd spread over the counter. "Morning."

"Morning." Riggs opened the cold case and tucked a six-pack of Colt .45 under his arm, then lingered a few minutes at the magazine stand. He thumbed through a copy of *Hustler* without much enthusiasm. The truth was he hadn't felt anything in that department for two months now. Maybe he never would again. And he really didn't care.

Two young Latinas—possibly hookers, possibly not— entered giggling and asked the clerk for change. One of them had a spider tattoo on her wrist, telling the initiated to this sort of thing that her man was a member of a prison gang. Riggs had his own tattoo, but it was of a globe and anchor with a rocker consisting of the words *Semper Fidelis*.

Always faithful. Perhaps the girl was saying the same thing with hers. Always faithful. After thirteen years—six in Newton division patrol, two in Wilshire vice, and five now in downtown narcotics—he could no longer make black and white distinctions between himself and the people of the streets. After even a few months out on the bricks, a cop's world turned real gray. Some couldn't stand it—the knowledge that they'd been plunked down in a fatally flawed universe. Maybe that's why Royce Chalmers had eaten his gun.

Frowning, the clerk handed one of the girls four quarters for a buck, and they went back outside to the pay phone set among the newspaper racks.

Riggs ambled up to the register. "And a pack of Winstons."

"You bet, sir." The clerk bagged the six-pack. "Fucking wets are taking over California, aren't they?"

"They weren't illegals."

"Whatever."

Outside, the wind was piling trash along the densely spray-painted cinder-block wall that separated the convenience market from a darkened McDonald's, its golden arch trembling in the wind. Riggs sat in his car and cracked open the first can of malt liquor. He could hear the young women talking on the phone, obviously to a parent or someone with a little familial authority:

"I know, I know . . . but Rudy didn't show up at the party . . . so we got no way home. Can Esther pick us up? Where's Eddy?"

Riggs leaned back and closed his eyes. He couldn't count five hours of sleep in the past week. He was exhausted but just couldn't seem to drift off. He would probably have to die to get a good night's sleep ever again.

But then he realized that he must have dozed for a few minutes, because the young women were out front on the sidewalk now, talking to some joker in his mid-thirties who was sitting in the passenger bucket seat of a fancy van conversion, his window rolled down. The conversion had a Waikiki sunset painted on the side. Aloha.

At first, Riggs thought that the girls were hustling the two occupants of the van—he could now glimpse the coal of the driver's cigarette winking on and off. But the young Chicanas looked tense, and they were inching back into the pool of light thrown by the market sign whenever they thought the passenger wasn't looking their way.

Instinctively, Riggs patted the bulge of his Beretta under his worn leather jacket.

Then one of the women said no sharply.

Enough. Riggs bailed out of the Plymouth, but had taken no more than a step when the man on the passenger side of the van burst out onto the sidewalk with a nickel-plated revolver gleaming in his hand. His partner, also armed with a cheap handgun, herded the girls through the side door and slammed it shut. Meanwhile, the first man shouted at Riggs, "Stand right there, asshole!"

Drawing his pistol, Riggs kept striding for the van, his face expressionless even when the revolver opposing him barked twice. The bullets whispered a few inches past his ear and shattered one of the huge panes fronting the store, but he didn't return fire. Not yet. He kept walking forward, his heels clipping over the grimy asphalt, the Beretta held down at his side. He could afford to send no stray rounds through the thin sheet metal of the van. Not with hostages inside.

The nickel-plated job flashed again and again. And missed each time. The shooter, obviously not intimate with handguns, was being unnerved by Riggs' emotionless advance. His tiny hand tremors were being translated into shots that were wide by a yard.

Smiling faintly, Riggs closed to within fifty feet and along a slant so he could take in most of the van's windshield. Then, seeing that the girls were being held in the back compartment, he finally raised his Beretta.

"Let's go!" the man on the sidewalk hollered with one

hand on the door latch. He was pivoting to leap inside when Riggs fired once, sprawling him half over the seat.

The van's engine rumbled to life, but Riggs aligned his open sights on the windshield and squeezed off a long burst. As expected, the first few rounds did little more than crack the shatter-resistant auto glass. But the next few blew a jagged hole in the windshield and allowed the bullets thereafter to tear gaping rents in the driver's head and upper chest. He slumped over to the side and stayed down.

The van was moving forward at idle speed, dragging along the man half out the passenger door like a gaffed fish.

Breaking into a trot, Riggs caught up with the vehicle and slid open the cargo door. The young women were huddled in the back, sobbing. "Everything's okay," he said to them. "Jump out . . . quick now."

One on the heels of the other, they flew into his arms, and he told them to hurry inside the store.

The van he let continue on its course down a vacant Pacific Coast Highway. It glided through the flashing yellow light at an intersection and eventually, some blocks distant, veered off into a parking lot where its progress was arrested by a light pole that blacked out when struck.

Back in his Plymouth, Riggs opened his glove compartment and reached for the radio microphone inside. He was on the verge of reporting the shooting incident to central communications when his thumb suddenly lifted off the transmit button.

It just doesn't fucking matter.

Instead of radioing in, he jammed the shift lever over to reverse and made a tire-screeching turn in the middle of the lot. He accelerated back toward the Harbor Freeway and was long gone before the first Harbor division black-and-whites arrived on the scene in a wail of massed sirens.

CHAPTER *2*

HE REFUSED TO sleep with a gun beneath his pillow.

So, instead, Roger Murtaugh kept a small chrome key there.

Clenching it between his teeth, he quietly opened the night-stand drawer and took out his Smith & Wesson .38 special. Last night, before retiring, he had snapped a handcuff around the frame of the gun. This kept the fully loaded cylinder from being closed, and the weapon from being fired. Deftly now, in the semi-darkness of dawn, he opened the handcuff ratchet with the key, then snapped the cylinder into place with a soft click.

His service revolver was now ready to dispense lead. Another day. Another dollar.

He preferred this safeguarding method to unloading the rounds and storing them separately from the handgun.

Finding daddy's bullets and loading them into his six-shooter was an irresistible challenge to a small child. So it didn't bother Murtaugh that it would take him a few more seconds to ready his revolver in order to deal with an intruder. It was a question of which nightmare was more probable: some loser attempting a nighttime burglary on a dwelling almost certain to be occupied when even the most addled hype in the world knew that daytime jobs were far less risky; or coming home from the movies to discover that his ten-year-old son had gotten down daddy's gun and shot himself dead.

The choice in this matter was clear to Murtaugh. There was nothing more certain to frighten him than imagining that something might happen to any of his three children. Perhaps Nam had done it to him: seeing so many children in ways he now prayed he would never see his own.

Trish said he tended to be overprotective. But Trish had not seen what he'd seen of this world since joining the army at seventeen.

Before going to bed, he had also hung today's plain-clothes and leather gear on a hook on the back of the closet door.

He now coaxed open the door so it wouldn't squeak and snugged the revolver in his basketweave shoulder holster. The handcuffs were deposited in the inner pocket of his coat until he fully dressed and could hang them on his belt along the small of his back.

Buried among the white or blue long-sleeved shirts, the herringbone and seersucker suits, was a somewhat faded blue uniform with sergeant stripes. He knew that, sooner than later, he'd have to get a fresh one tailored—if only to look presentable at department funerals. Finding a moth hole in one of the dusty epaulets, he frowned. "Shit . . ." Now it was for certain. He made a mental note to stop by the uniform store in the next week.

Carrying his clothes and his holstered revolver, he started for the bathroom but saw that Carrie's door was slightly ajar.

It was enough invitation to detour him, and he slipped inside his youngest daughter's room.

He knelt and pressed his lips to her small face, smooth and light brown like her mother's. It was unimaginable that anyone would ever want to harm such innocence, but his heart filled with fear from the truth he knew all too well.

Roger Murtaugh was a detective sergeant assigned to robbery/homicide.

He had seen babies as pretty and defenseless as his precious Carrie. . . .

With effort, he put some ugly pictures out of his mind, then kissed his seven-year-old daughter once again.

At five-thirty, with first light threatening in the east, Martin Riggs finally had to accept the fact that he had to go home and get ready for work. He'd already been absent without explanation for three days, and a fourth now would stretch the latitude given a narcotics detective to the point of breaking.

He was already on thin ice with Lieutenant Ortiz.

But, as far as his unreported shooting incident earlier this morning, he had decided to sit on it. It might be interesting to see how long it would take robbery/homicide to get on his trail. And if and when they did—so what? It was a clean shooting with hostage-witnesses. At worst, Riggs might get a month or two on the beach to consider his remarkable forgetfulness.

He told himself that he really didn't care.

He exited the Harbor Freeway one ramp beyond his usual, which happened to be the Pacific Coast Highway— where homicide might still be working at a particular convenience market. He had to backtrack a mile to the familiar two-lane road that wound up into some coastal hills. They were green with winter grass; here and there jack pumps bobbed for oil.

Veering onto a gravel lane that cut behind a sulfurous-smelling refinery, he raced down a barren canyon toward the ocean, which was choppy on this breezy dawn.

Before the road could deliver him onto the beach, it was blocked by a railroad embankment and looped back on itself. Here, on a terrace bulldozed out of the canyon slope, stood a single-wide mobile home. At the far end of the uncut lawn was a bale of straw, set upright with a pistol target attached. The X-ring had been obliterated by nearly perfect shooting.

As soon as he stepped out of the Plymouth, he could hear the television murmuring inside the trailer.

He smiled, but his eyes remained vacant, dimly sad. He used his hands to rake the empty malt liquor cans out of the car, then kicked them one by one down into the gully.

Closing one eyelid while struggling to insert the key into the lock-in-knob, he let up when the plywood porch began trembling beneath his feet. "Fucking Southern Pacific!" He turned toward the rails in exasperation, almost losing his balance. "Where's Lawrence of Arabia when a guy needs him?!"

He had to wait for ten minutes until a long train of crude-oil-splattered tanker cars was completely past. Then the rumbling died away, and he could coax the key into the lock.

Inside, his chocolate-coated Labrador ambushed him with a slobbery kiss.

"Not now, Cato!" Riggs shouted, but nevertheless hugged the rampant retriever around the neck. "Knock it off. I've got to get to work this morning. See, if I don't go in pretty soon—well, they may move and not tell me."

Cato barked twice significantly.

"What's that supposed to mean? I don't speak fucking dog. I barely speak English."

Cato underscored his point by sitting down in the middle of the kitchen. He sat on his tail so he wouldn't wag it.

Somberly, Riggs approached the portable color television on its rickety stand. He touched his palms to the warm plastic of its shell. His eyes misted. "Good morning, babe."

His stare fastened to the screen, but he seemed unaware of the program, a quiz show of some kind.

After a while, he peered over his shoulder at the vacant overstuffed chair, then at the two-month-old *TV Guide* folded open on the maple end table like a little tent.

Cato woofed, and Riggs finally nodded that he under-

stood. He took a two-pound bag of peanuts off the breakfast counter, ripped open the corrugated cellophane, and
gestured for Cato to have it. The dog rested his paws on
the phony butcher-block surface and started scarfing.

"You must hate me," he whispered, then started down
the hallway. He was nearly to the bedroom when he
shuffled to a halt and leaned over to inspect something on
the vinyl runner.

"Cato, you crapped." An angry pause. "Twice!"

But then Riggs shrugged and stepped over both piles. "I
should talk." He continued on into the bedroom, which
still held a miasma of perfume that he hadn't been able to
mask with the half-dozen air fresheners he'd tried.

Sinking into the double bed, he reached for the princess
phone and dialed.

A bored female voice answered, "Narcotics, Parker
Center."

"Riggs here. Messages or detail for today, please."

"Riggs . . . Riggs . . ."

He could visualize her bony, tobacco-stained finger gliding down the long list of names.

"Got a note here for you to see Lieutenant Ortiz ASAP
this date. No excuses, no exceptions."

Briefly, Riggs wondered if they were already on to last
night's little caper, but then decided that it wasn't possible. "Thanks." He hung up and lay back across the bed.
His half-closed eyes drifted to the wedding photograph on
the bureau.

She had looked a bit frail even on that day, her most
beautiful. But maybe that's what had drawn him to her—
that delicacy, the need to be protected. After Nam, he had
ached to protect something tangible, someone who would
clearly benefit from his strength. And after Royce Chalmers killed himself, Riggs had needed a living crutch to
fend off his own worst fears—someone loving who would
murmur from time to time: *There, there, everything's
going to be all right, Marty.*

He heaved himself to his feet, then wondered if he had any clean clothes.

He didn't, so he started sorting through the musty hamper in the utility room.

Murtaugh floated contentedly in the liquid warmth.

It was one ritual of many he had adopted to make his days seem less harried: He took a long bath each morning, unless rousted out of bed early for a homicide.

His slow rise to detective sergeant had not been without its stresses.

After his excellent showing on the promotional exams, the brass had tried to entice him into internal affairs, which in those days had no minority investigators.

The IA unit had always been a fast track to top rank, but anyone assigned there was immediately branded a fink, an ass-kisser who loved nothing more than wallowing in the dirty linen of their fellow officers. Needless to say, IA investigators partied alone. And Murtaugh had already had enough of the *Blue Chill* as one of the handful of black officers serving in the San Fernando Valley division—and more than enough of the shit-kicking music played in the West Valley station, the endless Charlie Pride jokes he had to suffer with a tight grin.

When he refused the IA offer, the brass tried to shunt him into the communications division, which in some quarters was considered little better than a disciplinary tour.

But Murtaugh stood firm.

He had known from the first day he donned his blues that he wanted to wind up in robbery/homicide, although— when push came to shove with the big boys—he damned near had to threaten an equal-opportunities lawsuit to pull down one of the coveted detective slots.

Two years later, he had made sergeant, only to be dumped back into patrol—southeast division, its decayed turf better known to the world as Watts. But finally, three years ago, he'd made it home to robbery/homicide at

Parker Center, and now planned to retire out of the division even if it meant passing up a lieutenancy.

As in the army, he'd forged a place for himself by always doing more than he was asked to do, and he was proud of what he'd achieved with his life—a gorgeous college librarian for a wife, three decent kids, and a two-hundred-thousand-dollar house in Glendale. Not shabby for a skinny kid who'd pitched pennies on the backstreets of New Orleans.

The bathroom door flew open and the light clicked off.

For an instant, Murtaugh didn't know which to go for—the washcloth or his revolver hanging in its holster on the back of the door.

But as soon as he saw the birthday cake ablaze with what he immediately knew to be fifty candles, he covered himself with the sopping cloth.

"Surprise!"

"Yeah, yeah, yeah," he muttered, grinning self-consciously as he rested his hand atop the crater of the old shrapnel wound in his right pectoral muscle. "You all get a gold star for timing."

"Are you happy, Daddy?" Carrie cried.

"I was till you reminded me how old I am." When her face dropped, he quickly added, "Yeah, baby, I couldn't be more happy."

"Mama's only thirty-eight."

"Well, that's one of the reasons I'm so happy."

In the unexpected ambiance of candlelight, magnified by the angled dressing mirrors, Trish looked strikingly pretty, even sans makeup. Hell, she looked *radiant*, he reminded himself and reached his dripping hand out for hers.

Nick, as always, was leering like everything was an enormous surprise to him. His school grades indicated that he was reasonably bright, but he acted so goofy at home. Murtaugh wondered if it was only intended to infuriate him, and hoped that somehow Nick would emerge from puberty a reasonably competent human being.

Halfway out in the hall, standing on her toes to peer over her brother's head, was Rianne, seventeen and perilously beautiful—given her affinity for loser beaus who grunted their replies in monosyllables and had no ambitions other than doomed stabs at musical careers. The current one, Mark, was typical of them all, although he was *white*—something Murtaugh assiduously failed to bring up when discussing him. He realized that any objections he voiced about marvelous Mark would only make him that much more enticing in Rianne's eyes. Frankly, he couldn't stomach the thought of being forever linked by matrimony to Mark's parents, who at first meeting had asked the Murtaughs if they wished to be called Negroes, blacks, or Afro-Americans. Trish saved the evening by breezily explaining that they wanted to be called the Murtaughs, although Murtaugh himself had been on the brink of saying that *darkies* would do fine, thank you.

But now, Rianne defused all his worries about her by sweetly saying, "Make a wish, Daddy . . . please."

He closed his eyes. He didn't tell them, but it was the same wish he'd made for each of his past fifteen birthdays: He wished that nothing horrible would ever break the circle of their safety.

Then he blew as hard as he could, casting the bathroom into sudden darkness.

A rumble vibrated in the tub.

"Oh gross, Mom!" Nick giggled. "Dad farted in the water!"

One summer's night, with the sound of the breakers coming over the railroad embankment, she had asked him what his work was really like.

Riggs was silent for a long while, but she was patient with his silences and sat waiting in her overstuffed chair, just a hint of the ominous blue shining through her lips that night.

He thought about telling her about his squeezes, the pathetic, egoless creatures who sold their souls for nickel bags; about the recent undercover drug transaction during which he'd had the muzzle of a submachine gun pressed against his back; about the constant bullshit with Lieutenant Ortiz, who'd been a ball-buster of a street cop in his day but now suffered from some strange form of amnesia he'd caught from all the paperwork a lieutenant does.

But no—like Nam, these things were truly understandable only if a person had experienced them. So Riggs had tried to tell her in another way that night. "It's kind of like being Michelangelo doing that fucking church over in Italy."

"The Sistine Chapel?"

"Yeah, that's the one. See, babe, you spend months, sometimes even years, putting together that ceiling in the chapel. You go half blind from paint dropping in your eyes. You get arthritis from the cold, from laying on your goddamned back in cramped places. But finally, one night, you finish. You come down the scaffolding and look up. 'Jesus,' you say to yourself, 'I don't know how, but I brought the big picture together. I made it all work.' Then, exhausted, you go home." The smoke of his Winston curled back on him, making him squint. "The next morning you race back to the chapel. You know, to see what the Pope thinks. And you find out he changed his mind. He had the ceiling Gunited while you were sleeping. . . ."

She was silent for a long while before she asked, "Then *why*, Marty?"

"Because I still need to get up each morning and paint ceilings. I don't really know why, babe."

Rousing himself back into the present, Riggs realized that he was tailgating the school bus in his lane. Backing off, he rolled down his window for some air.

He was taking the long way to work, hoping it would give him time to come up with a line of bullshit for Ortiz. The Michelangelo story he'd shared with his wife probably wouldn't do.

He was brainstorming when a call came over the Motorola concealed in his glove compartment: "Eight-Adam-six, an anonymous report of shots fired in the vicinity of Washington and Navy. Adam-six, take the back.''

The two Pacific division patrol units calmly acknowledged the call, and Riggs thought nothing more about it until the dispatcher came back on a minute or so later with a heightened timbre to her voice: ''All Pacific in the vicinity of Washington and Navy, a shooting in progress with victims down. Numerous reporting parties now. Be advised the location is a private school.''

''Adam-six copies, control.'' Adam-six's mike picked up the throaty roar of his patrol car in acceleration.

Sirens began yelping all over West Los Angeles.

Disregarding the traffic signal at Washington Boulevard, Martin slapped his metallic emergency light atop the roof of his Plymouth and punched in a four-wheel drift through the intersection—car horns braying at him from four directions—and joined the blitz of all available units converging on the shooting scene.

''A moth to his flame,'' he chuckled to himself, reaching under the front seat for an extra magazine of 9-mm ammunition.

The rangemaster was handing Roger Murtaugh his monthly qualification rounds when he suddenly lowered the tray of cartridges. ''You doing okay, Sarge?'' he asked, sounding genuinely concerned.

Murtaugh shrugged meaningfully, giving him a helpless grin at the same time. ''Kids.''

''Don't I know it,'' the man blurted. ''My sixteen-year-old's gone again. Last time it was for six months. And God only knows what she was doing. Probably banging half of San Francisco. . . .''

Still grinning, Murtaugh began backing off toward the firing lanes. The rangemaster's sympathy had been a trap, and the detective sergeant didn't want to spend the rest of the morning hearing out this endless tale of woe.

''. . . so we put her in the drug rehabilitation program like the court says and—''

Murtaugh was rescued by the appearance of another shooter in need of ammunition. He ducked around the end of an earthen revetment and onto the first range, tapping the benchrests with his knuckles as he quickly marched toward his favorite firing station, the one down at the far end where his concentration was least likely to be disturbed. He took range qualification seriously: He intended to survive this job.

"Kids," he muttered again.

It was Rianne who had caused an otherwise joyful morning to end on a sour note.

Murtaugh had been riffling through the Rolodex next to the kitchen phone for the range number—he'd wanted to make sure the academy classes were tying up the facility—when he came across the note in Rianne's flippant scrawl: *Phone Michael Hunsaker*. The number she'd taken down had a Pacific Palisades prefix.

The name itself had been good for an unpleasant moment of *déjà vu*. "Rianne!" he hollered throughout the house. "Who gave you this message?"

"What message?" she asked in a disinterested voice from upstairs.

"About Mike Hunsaker."

"The department, I think."

Murtaugh took the stairs at a run. "*When,* goddamn it?"

For the first time, she seemed to have an inkling that it might be important. "Day before yesterday."

"How many times have I begged you to put all phone messages on my desk in the study?"

"I'm sorry, Daddy. Is it important?"

Trish had come upstairs and was hovering at the door protectively. "What is it, Rog?"

In that brief moment, he had found himself feeling thankful that Trish had Christmas vacation off and was home; otherwise, he was sure he would have spanked Rianne for the first time in at least a decade. But then he looked both of them in the eye and started downstairs, his face abruptly expressionless. "Nothing . . . forget it."

Now, shucking off his coat and loosening his tie, he tried to forget about Michael Hunsaker. Shooting required absolute concentration; otherwise, the effort was wasted.

He opened the cylinder and pressed the star-ejector, dumping the factory ammunition loads into his palm before transferring them to his front pants pocket.

Next, without looking—for the time might come when he might have to reload in darkness—he fed six of the rangemaster's reloads into the slotted wheel. Then he closed the cylinder with a resounding click and put the weapon on the grimy carpet covering the benchrest.

At this point, in a ritual that never varied, he donned his ear protectors, which blocked out the chanting of the cadets on the nearby athletic field, a sound he'd not noticed until it was suddenly gone.

He took a deep breath, which carried with it the medicinal smell of the surrounding eucalyptus stands. He picked up his revolver. With respect. With affection even. He tested its heft in his hand.

The webbing between the thumb and forefinger of his right hand was high on the back strap. His index finger bent slightly at the first knuckle around the trigger. And then the union of his weapon and his right hand acquired even more stability as he cupped the butt of the grips in his left palm.

The man silhouette waited at the far end of the lane, wiggling a little from the Santa Ana gusts spilling over the top of the revetment. At any moment in this job, it could be a real man, not a paper one, looming down there. Murtaugh reminded himself of this.

Relying on his dominant right eye, but not closing his left, which would only distort his sight picture, he began applying steady and measured pressure to the trigger.

The hammer was almost fully cocked when he let the firing pin ease forward again, slowly as not to set off the primer. He lowered the revolver to his side. And stared at the target as if he couldn't believe his eyes.

For an instant, the silhouette had become Michael Hunsaker in his boonie hat and jungle fatigues, shouting happily as he fingered some kind of crude necklace he was wearing, "Hey, lookit, Rog—ears! I got fucking ears!"

CHAPTER 3

RIGGS SKIDDED HIS Plymouth to a sideways halt behind the logjam of black-and-whites in the intersection of Washington and Navy. He took his red magnetic light off of the roof so it wouldn't be stolen, then sauntered toward the thickest clot of blue uniforms.

At the corner, he ducked out of the wind into a telephone booth to light a smoke and make a little reconnaissance. He surveyed the scene through the smudged glass: Maybe fifteen patrolmen hunkered down behind their cars, revolvers in hand as they gaped up at a three-story Moorish-style beach-front apartment building.

One blue-suiter was urging an old woman with blue-dyed hair to come the rest of the way down the fire escape into his waiting arms. She finally refused and went back inside the second story.

Around the edge of the apartment, through a four-foot chain-link fence, Riggs could glimpse a swing set—the playground of the adjoining day-care center that wrapped halfway around the apartment on its ocean side.

Not bothering to crouch as he strolled forward, although everyone else who ventured from cover to cover was moving like Quasimodo, he approached one of the Pacific division units, behind which were squatting two teenage-looking patrolmen.

"Morning," Riggs said, still standing. From this vantage point, he could peer down the western face of the building but couldn't see into any of the windows. The playground was half concealed by the chock-a-block array of hastily parked police cruisers.

"Get down," one of the patrolmen hissed. "There's a fucking sniper up there!"

"No shit?" Riggs turned and regarded the building more carefully. "I've never seen a sniper fornicate. They're usually too busy shooting."

"Who the hell *are* you?"

Riggs parted his leather jacket, revealing the shield he'd remembered to clip to his belt for once. "Which window is he firing from?"

"How the fuck should we know?" The young patrolman jerked his thumb toward the rear window of the unit parked behind them. There was a hole in it from which crazing radiated; the design was kind of pretty, Riggs thought. "We've been a little busy."

"What's he using?"

"A fucking gun."

"Oh, a *gun*." Riggs nodded thoughtfully. It was a barometer of a cop's tension level, how often he peppered his sentence fragments with the word "fuck." And if a cop graduated from tense to panicky, he dispensed with the sentence fragments and just made do with the "fucks."

Sitting on the warm hood of the car, Riggs made himself comfortable. "I suppose you guys know the difference between the report of, say, a handgun and a shotgun."

They just glared at him. "Look, buddy—why don't you get down here with us?"

Riggs shrugged, picking a tobacco flake off the tip of his tongue. "Why?"

"So this fucking car can stop the fucking bullet that's coming any second for you!"

"Sorry."

"What the fuck do you mean—*sorry?*" The patrolman was grinning with exasperation now. Perhaps it was his first brush with the narcotics division.

"Where you guys are hiding," Riggs patiently explained, "this car won't do crap for you. Motor City don't build 'em like it used to. And anything but a marble fired by a slingshot is going to stitch right through that trunk and knock you into taps. Come on down here behind the engine block, and keep your ankles behind the front tire. Bullets don't angle like billiard balls. They travel along hard surfaces."

They looked at each other, then duck-walked in tandem down the front of the unit. The leather of their Sam Browne belts was so new it creaked as they waddled.

The radio blared to life over their public-address speaker: "Any unit at Washington and Navy, Robert-ten-David is inquiring if the scene is contained. Has communication been established with the suspect?"

Smiling, Riggs shook his head. "Hey, guys, how about one of you crawling inside your chariot and turning off the PA?" It always happened at these Chinese fire drills: As a patrolman bailed out to do battle with the forces of evil, he flicked his radio onto his outside speaker so he could keep abreast of developments—never realizing that he was also keeping the sniper nicely informed of how the police department intended to deal with him.

Shame-faced, one of the blue-suiters squirmed across the front seat and snapped down the offending toggle switch on the radio.

Having decided that he had learned all he ever would from these crime fighters, Riggs ambled forward to the next echelon of patrol cars, smoking thoughtfully, ignoring the windows above, which from this angle now had an unobstructed view of him.

Sitting cross-legged, holding his Ithaca shotgun in his hands like a peace pipe, a two-striper glanced up at Riggs as if he'd just been interrupted in the midst of meditation.

"You heard anything on D platoon's ETA?" the senior patrolman asked a bit guiltily.

He wanted to know when SWAT would be showing up, and was going to stand pat until they did. No dummy, he probably knew exactly how many days he had until retirement.

"Well, let's see," Riggs mused aloud, jumping up on another cosy hood and presenting his back to the windows. "They're coming from central police facility on Georgia Street, right?"

"Right."

"So that means they've got to get across maybe ten miles of city at rush hour in a blue bakery truck that corners like the *Queen Mary*." Riggs pursed his lips. "I'd look for them in a week or so, say Christmas morning. Hey, maybe that's why they're late—they're gift-wrapping their van."

"Funny."

"Anybody think to try a little gas?"

"Sure, the crazy son of a bitch is wearing a gas mask."

"Then you saw him?"

"Yeah—twice, when he fired."

Suddenly, Rigg's voice turned insistent. "Which window?"

"Top floor, third opening from the left."

Riggs craned his neck and checked. "The one with the shade halfway down?"

"*And* the marine steel plate to hide behind. This guy must've been a Boy Scout—he believes in being prepared."

"What's he toting?"

"Looked like an M-1 carbine to me."

"Scoped?"

"Nah, open sights."

Riggs quickly processed this information: Not exactly the Cadillac of sniper weapons, this World War II relic was nonetheless light and reasonably accurate. Its .30-caliber short-rifle cartridge had less punch than more modern rounds but could still penetrate most everything the cops at the scene were taking cover behind. Open sights were good news, unless the scumbag was a decent marksman. "Was he taking aimed shots?" Riggs asked the two-striper.

"Nope. He emptied a magazine each time he opened up."

Riggs scanned the playground. "Where are the casualties?"

"See that chrome pipe? We saw one kid hit and crawl inside. But she must be dead by now. He fired a whole fucking clip right through the pipe."

The cigarette tumbled out of Riggs's fingers. *"What?"*

"You heard me," the two-striper said quietly.

Rigg's eyes went cold with anger. "And nobody went to check?"

"Some hero ran out and dragged in another kid, but she was already dead." The two-striper inclined his head toward a small lump in a body bag out behind a sergeant's unit. "And a couple who were wounded badly have already been transported."

Riggs started for the chain-link fence.

"Hey, where the fuck are you going?"

Riggs bent down the top of the fence and stepped over it.

"Hey, idiot! SWAT is on the way!"

During those first strides across the sandy playground, Riggs considered two things that would affect the sniper's accuracy: sight picture distortion because of the gas mask and this morning's brisk wind.

But then he found himself not really caring if the sniper was accurate or not. It seemed strangely superfluous. This entire event seemed superfluous, although intensely sad.

He didn't look up at the top-story window, although for an instant he thought he could feel eyes on him. He continued toward the pipe, a plaything through which children had crawled on their hands and knees this morning, their giggles jiggling in their throats from their rapid movements. Then the sky had been torn by thunder, and it had started to rain insanity.

Riggs no longer asked himself why these things hap-

pened. It was enough, at the moment, to realize that no
.30-caliber short-rifle projectiles were kicking up the sand
around him.

"Hey, dipshit!" someone shouted on a bullhorn from
the thicket of patrol cars. "Get back here—now!"

Riggs tossed a friendly wave without looking back.

"Is that you, Riggs? Is that Marty Riggs from narcotics?"

Again, he gave an insouciant wave, then knelt in the
mouth of the chrome pipe.

All the air left his lungs in a groan, but he couldn't
bring himself to touch the dead child. She didn't look like
she was sleeping. She was gray and twisted with death.

"Oh, babe . . ." He clenched his teeth and squeezed
his eyes shut for a few seconds.

There were jagged little rosettes where the bullets had
sliced through the sheet metal before slamming into her
body.

But then something stirred in the gloaming behind her
lifeless form.

Another child. A little Oriental boy who was whimpering.

"It's okay, babe. Everything's going to be okay. I'm a
police officer. A detective. Like *Miami Vice* or something.
This here is my badge." Smiling, although he felt nothing
like smiling, Riggs motioned for the boy to crawl over the
dead girl. There was no other way to extricate him, and
Riggs was glad when he finally did so, rushing into the
detective's arms, clinging to him. "It was very loud in
there, wasn't it?"

The boy nodded.

For the first time, Riggs peered up at the window.
Nothing. He suspected that the sniper thought the crazy
plainclothesman in the leather jacket had been sent into the
playground to entice the rifleman into exposing himself.
Riggs knew that if he were barricaded up there, he wouldn't
show himself if some psycho diddy-bopped into his field
of fire. Anything that seemed too good to be true *always*
was. It was one of Riggs's maxims.

"I'm going to hide you somewhere safe now," he

whispered into the boy's ear. "And when my business is done, some policemen in blue suits are going to take you home to your mom and dad. All right?"

Again, a timorous nod.

Riggs carried him five meters to the merry-go-round, then instructed him to wriggle under the platform of the one-inch steel plate. Just to be safe, he gave the thing a shove, knowing that the spin would further help deflect rounds from above. He knew that car tires were hard as hell to shoot out simply because they were spinning so fast.

Then he stepped away from the merry-go-round and whistled softly. "Hello?"

The Santa Ana breeze rattled the fronds of some nearby palms and made the swing chains ring against the supports.

"Mr. Sniper, sir, can we talk?"

Silence on high. No movement even in the shadows beyond the open window.

"See, there's a terrible mistake—and I'm here to apologize and tell you that, yes, you did indeed win the lottery—"

A muzzle swung over the steel plate and fired three reckless rounds that sizzled at least ten feet over Riggs's head.

The sniper had fired blindly—just a protest against not being taken seriously. And that's what Riggs wanted of him—a bit of indignation, a brief and lethal flaring of temper. An accompanying tactical mistake.

"Now that's no way to ask for your check." Slowly, Riggs reached inside his leather jacket for his pack of Winstons, shook a cigarette out, and clamped it in the corner of his mouth. "And I'm going to have to see some I.D., of course."

And he was returning the pack to his pocket when the opportunity came. His hand darted to his shoulder holster and came out with his Beretta 9-mm.

Riggs grinned as he felt the trigger cave back under the pressure of his forefinger.

The first round caught the sniper in the upper chest,

making him drop his carbine, which tumbled out the window end over end before shattering into splinters and scraps of tooled iron on the sidewalk. It had not yet struck the concrete when Riggs's next two rounds found the sniper's head: One grazed the temple, unfurling a flap of skin like a torn page, but the other slug entered the mask, took out the eye and exited the rear of the cranium with a chunk of skull in tow.

He slumped over the steel plate. It rained blood on the sidewalk for a few seconds until his heart decided it was useless to keep pumping with half the brain gone.

Riggs holstered his gun.

Standing between Detective Sergeant Murtaugh and Detective Burke was a porcelain tray. It was cross-ribbed with little gullies to carry body fluids down to the drain at its lower end. And on this tray was the corpse of what twenty-four hours ago had been a beautiful young woman. There was always a sense of waste when a stunner was mangled this badly, even though an investigator reminded himself that a body is a body is a body.

"Okay, Burke, give me the *Reader's Digest* version. I've got a shooting-investigation team out at Pacific station—and my message spike looks thick enough to be a phone book."

The detective glanced up from his report. "What happened at Pacific?"

"Sniper in Venice." Murtaugh motioned for him to get on with the briefing.

The white-smocked pathologist waved his scalpel for both of them to get out of his way so he could start the main incision. In the corner of the brightly lit room, his assistant was changing blades on the saw that would be used to open the top of the skull.

"Okay, okay," Burke began, "she jumped at approximately 2345 hours last night—"

"How many stories?"

"Ten—Westmont Towers. Landed on a Porsche. This'll

get you—it was her own. Hit it so fucking hard all four of the hubcaps popped onto the pavement.''

"Okay, it got me. Any witnesses? Patrol fill out some field interrogation cards for us?"

"One reluctant witness—patrol got there pretty fast and scarfed her up. Remember Dixie, the hooker we thought for a while clipped Tyrone the Bone?"

"Oh yeah." Murtaugh looked up with a hint of a grimace. He'd been staring at the bloodless gash the pathologist had just slit from pubis to throat. "Dixie Monroe. Avalon is her turf. What was she doing up in Perrier country?"

"Maybe she's moving up in the world." Burke's long pale face was without expression.

Murtaugh wondered if the remark had been racially motivated, but then decided to ignore it. He nodded at the tray. "What was her story?"

"Call girl."

Murtaugh hiked an eyebrow. The undamaged side of her face was that of a debutante. "Priors?"

"Only one—class act."

"Who posted bail for her?"

Burke shrugged, which—as always—irritated Murtaugh. His son, Nick, commented on everything with a shrug like that.

"Well, get humping on it. I want to know whose stable she worked for." Murtaugh snapped his fingers on a thought. "Try this angle—see if somebody bought that Porsche for her. Dig for her sugar daddy."

"Right."

"Did she use an A.K.A. on that prior?"

All at once, Burke looked sheepish. "I forgot to tell you, the name on my initial report turned out to be an alias."

"Amanda Boudreau?"

"Yeah, fingerprints came back to an Amanda Hunsaker."

Murtaugh's fingers tugged at his underlip for a moment, then suddenly fell away from his face. "Sweet Jesus."

"What's wrong, Sarge?"

"Is her place of birth Tennessee?"

Burke turned back to the face page of the thick report. "Uh . . . yeah."

Murtaugh's restless fingers began tapping out a calculation on his thumb. "Date of birth ought to be 1964. May or June."

Burke began chuckling. "Shit, let's take this act to Vegas. Mind readers make a fucking fortune."

But Murtaugh didn't laugh. "Give me her apartment number."

"Ten-sixty-five."

"I'll meet you later back at the barn. Meanwhile, find out who shared her receipts."

As Murtaugh hurried out, the pathologist fired up his bone saw.

As always, the buzzing sound gave Murtaugh chills from head to toe.

She had played out this frustrating little scene so many times before she knew precisely what Lieutenant Ortiz would say before he said it. So it took her aback when he suddenly uttered from the office window, "It's over."

She hoped that Ortiz was referring to Martin Riggs's bloody career. "What's over, Lieutenant?" she asked, trying to control her excitement.

"The Santa Ana." His Spanish pronunciation was impeccable. "It's stopped blowing. Getting misty out there. Somebody told me it's supposed to rain tonight."

"Oh," she muttered, crestfallen, looking back down at her plump file on Riggs. They were all nut cases in her book, even this meteorologically inclined middle manager. "About Riggs, Lieutenant—"

"What about him?" He was still gazing outside, his eyes dreamy. Ortiz was probably the next candidate for a stress disability. In the last year, his teenaged son, an honors student and football star, had committed suicide. *Peer pressure* was all the man would say about it.

But Detective Sergeant Martin Riggs, not poor depressed and repressed Ortiz, was the basket case of the hour. "Lieutenant, I want Riggs pulled from duty."

"You don't have that authority, Doctor."

"Granted, but *you* do."

The lieutenant turned back to his cluttered desk and frowned. "On what grounds? The shooting today?"

"If we can agree that it's the straw that breaks the camel's back, yes. He wantonly exposed himself to fire."

"According to the shooting-investigation team, he distracted an armed suspect long enough to effect the rescue of a small child. I should probably recommend him for the Medal of Valor."

"But you're not, are you? Because you *know*. Correct me if I'm wrong, Lieutenant."

Ortiz didn't answer.

She sighed loudly, then bit her lip before she might say something that would earn her one more mortal enemy in the department. It made her want to shriek and pull her hair. The code of silence these cops kept was every bit as stringent as the Mafia's *omerta*—*Thou shalt not accuse a fellow officer of being so unmacho as to require psychological help*.

She composed herself before saying, "Lieutenant, for just a few minutes, I'd like to talk about Martin Riggs the human being, not the cop."

Ortiz's face softened. "All right."

"His wife of eleven years died unexpectedly two months ago. Simply looking at that—ignoring the cumulative stress of this job, of his four other *justifiable* shootings—you cannot expect him to keep functioning as he did in the past. You cannot keep subjecting him to potentially lethal situations. Not without the vase cracking."

"And you think the vase is cracked?"

"Beyond repair. It's my judgment that his condition is permanent and stationary. He'll never be fit to be a police officer again. But his career is a minor concern compared to his self-destructive tendencies. I am asking you to help me save Martin Riggs's life.''

Ortiz stared at her for a long while, then he smirked faintly. "Riggs is a tough kid. A fighter. He'll make out okay."

With a copy of the evidence inventory in hand, Murtaugh drifted through Amanda Hunsaker's silent apartment.

He tried to keep his mind on the job, but the personal past kept intruding on his concentration. And he realized, sadly, that he was not terribly surprised that the pretty blond terror, who'd had the run of NCO housing at Fort Bragg, had wound up in digs like these—and then had died the way she had.

Her mother had been one of those quasi-Southern belles, so delicate and helpless and confused she just didn't know what *I'm going to do with that child, Roger, deah.*

Blistering Amanda's hide would've been a good beginning.

But her mother had to share the blame—Mike Hunsaker had gotten a kick out of his daughter's high spirits.

Murtaugh's first investigators on the scene had emptied the medicine chest of its prescription bottles and bagged the contents for analysis. The entire apartment had been lousy with coke and barbiturates and other junk the criminalistics lab would have to identify.

"Sweet Jesus," Murtaugh whispered to himself, experiencing a stab of fear for Rianne. How seriously had his own daughter experimented with drugs? With marijuana, he could almost be sure. But anything beyond that? And was she still a virgin? He didn't expect the impossible of a normal girl with normal desires, but he wanted *it* to be with a boy who would love and care for her. And he wasn't sure Mark was that person.

Then he turned his thoughts back to work.

There were still black smears of volcanic powder where the identification officer had dusted the medicine chest mirror for latent fingerprints. Like any other "apparent suicide," this one would be treated as a potential homicide until the possibility of foul play was ruled out beyond a reasonable doubt. And Murtaugh's progress in a case was often characterized more by the elimination of doubt than the acquisition of facts. He groped toward what had happened by determining what had not happened. It was a clumsy way of doing business, but it was the only way that worked in the real world. Dazzling epiphanies were usually the province of television.

He moved from the bathroom into the living room, stuffing the unread evidence list into his coat pocket. He'd been ignoring it so far, but finally regarded the framed photograph in the glass case.

It surprised him that none of his detectives, none of the identification people, with whom he'd shared this grisly work for years, had recognized a younger Roger Murtaugh in jungle fatigues and a boonie hat.

Murtaugh had to smile: He remembered the day. One of the few good ones. Michael Hunsaker and he had just returned from some playtime in Saigon, and they were still buzzed on Johnny Walker Red and San Miguel chasers when Callahan, the team's inveterate shutterbug, had asked them to pose on the steps of the headquarters building. They were all DFRs, Dumb Fucking Rookies, at that point. Innocents looking to fulfill JFK's invocation that the oppressed might go free.

Callahan died screaming on a hot landing zone a month later.

Murtaugh now wished that it had been Michael Hunsaker. Had Hunsaker gone that early in the game, he would at least have died with a soul.

Well, what's past is past.

Shaking off the reverie, Murtaugh continued on his rounds through the apartment. Sam Cooke on the turntable. He nodded his approval.

Rianne's note was burning a hole in his wallet. He had to phone Hunsaker, especially now. But, for a variety of reasons he didn't care to dwell on, it would be the most difficult death notification of his career. And why had

Mike attempted to contact him after all these years—and on the virtual eve of his daughter's death?

After twenty more minutes of methodically going from room to room, Murtaugh slid open the glass door and went out onto the balcony. He looked over the railing, and—in his vivid imagination, the imagination of a man who must constantly come up with reasons for bizarre human behavior—he visualized Amanda's plunge of ten stories to the parking lot below.

He stepped back from the precipice, gasping. He really didn't understand the world; he just knew how it operated.

Looking westward, he saw that dark clouds were rolling in above the ocean.

"It's going to rain," Lieutenant Ortiz said, his shoes up on the typing shelf he'd pulled out of a slot in his desk.

In the long silence that followed this observation, Riggs lit up a smoke.

The lieutenant was staring at him as he shook out the match. "What the fuck were you doing over in Venice this morning? You were supposed to see me ASAP. That means 0700 hours, Martin."

"I overslept, Lieut. I'm finally getting some decent sleep again."

"You didn't answer my question."

It was a mistake to lie to Ortiz. He'd bronze your balls for lying to him and put them on display in the trophy case inside the detectives' headquarters lounge. But tell him the truth, no matter how sordid, and he'd probably just give you three days on the beach—unless your fuck-up involved the death of a nun or a major government official.

So Riggs heaved a sigh and came out with it: "I was taking the long way in this morning. . . ."

"That's a start. Why?"

"I needed time to come up with a line of shit for you."

Ortiz's eyes were smiling a little. "And did you?"

Martin shook his head no.

The humor left the lieutenant's eyes. "I have one major

requirement of my people—that they produce. And you're not producing, Martin.''

''It's a slump. Even all-stars go cold now and again.''

''All-stars don't fail to show for three games in a row. Where have you been for the last three days, man? It better make the French connection look like a nickel-bag bust.''

''I don't know. Prioritizing. Getting my case load in perspective.''

''You mean fucking off, Martin?''

Riggs gave a tiny shrug. He knew the moment had arrived for *Welcome to Maclovio Ortiz's World*. He tried not to look bored.

''There are 239 investigators in this division, Martin. But if only one of them is out fucking the dog, we all feel the pinch. Your load falls on somebody else's shoulders. Somebody who is already staggering under his own load. I'm tired of fielding gripes from your own friends in the bullpen. Tired of reminding them that you've had some personal misfortune and need a little time to come around. You've had a little time, Martin.'' A tic, which had sprouted the week after his son's death, tugged at Ortiz's cheek muscle. ''We've all had our misfortunes. But we put them behind us and go on with the job.''

''Look, Lieut—I'm sorry about the shooting today. It was a case of being in the wrong place at the wrong—''

''I'm not talking about what happened this morning in Venice,'' Ortiz interrupted. ''I've got no problems with that.'' He paused and shook his head. ''You just don't give a crap anymore. *That's* my problem, Martin. I can't use any deadwood. And you're so dead you're petrified.''

Riggs just slumped in his chair, staring distantly at his cigarette. He could hear Ortiz riffling through some paperwork.

''All right,'' the lieutenant finally went on, ''you know the routine. Four days on the beach, or until such time as the shooting-investigation team renders its review. Between us, I have it from the SIT dicks that this one will be just a four-dayer. They think you did one hell of a job—in an eccentric kind of way." Ortiz stood to shake hands with Latino civility, ass-chewing or not. "See you in four, Martin, 0700 sharp."

"What the fuck am I going to do for"—Riggs's eyes rolled upward as he did a quick multiplication—"for ninety-six hours?" He chuckled, but it was shrill with desperation. The prospect of having that much time on his hands made him dizzy.

"You might start by bathing and shaving. I don't recall loaning you to the decoy section."

Riggs shuffled to the door but hesitated there with his hand clenching the knob. "And then what, Lieut?"

"Pardon?"

"You wanted me in here this morning so you could drop the hammer. But it's my guess that, because of the shooting, you don't want to overload me with bad news right now." Riggs tried to grin. "I can take it."

Ortiz frowned, then motioned for Riggs to sit again. "I'm going to detach you to a task force."

"South L.A. anti-drug?" he asked hopefully. This unit was hitting rock houses, fortified crack stores. It was like Dodge City with firefights ensuing on a good number of the raids. Just what Riggs felt he needed to jolt him out of the doldrums.

"No, not South L.A."

"What then?"

"Pressure's on above for greater cooperation between narcotics and robbery/homicide at the supervisorial and mid-managerial level—"

"Oh, Lieut, not that!" Riggs groaned. "That's going to be a shit detail!"

"Yes, Martin," Ortiz said evenly. "That's going to be a shit detail."

CHAPTER **4**

THE TWILIGHT ON Avalon Boulevard was blue with rain.

Slowing and taking the right lane as soon as he crossed the storm-swamped intersection with Firestone, Roger Murtaugh kept a watchful eye on both sides of the street. Leaning over the steering wheel, he craned his neck to check the recesses between the rib shacks and the shops with boarded-up fronts.

He knew that, despite the drenching storm, he would find Dixie Monroe on the boulevard. The half-black, half-Italian prostitute gravitated to one hard master after another: face-thumpers, cigarette-butt-torturers . . . lovely guys.

Her first had been an illiterate scumbag with the street moniker of Tyrone the Bone. His treatment of Dixie had been so vicious, homicide detectives immediately suspected her when Tyrone was discovered slumped over in his parked Maserati with more holes in his five-hundred-dollar suit than he had buttons.

Yet, as in many cases, the first suspect was not the one to wind up in court. Information was eventually developed that Tyrone had ventured out of his league by dealing with some fast-lane heroin traffickers of the Caucasian persuasion—all with heavy Nam service records. Mercenary types, rumor had it.

The narcotics division had never bullied or twisted its way inside this operation: One of its lackeys had willingly taken the second-degree murder rap on old Tyrone. Although the district attorney dangled an ice cream cone or two in front of his obstinate eyes, the Special Forces veteran went off to Chino for seven years without revealing a thing about his associates. He was interested in no deals, and that in itself was pretty unusual for a man in his circumstances.

But the big puzzler about the case was: How had the merc gotten close enough to Tyrone to clip him? Tyrone the Bone moved around with heavier security than Yasser Arafat.

Suddenly, Murtaugh chuckled to himself in satisfaction as his headlights swept over the shiny asphalt. He flipped a U-turn and started up the west side of Avalon. He had just glimpsed a wraith in satiny black tights and a cheap plastic raincoat standing under a marquee:

REV. J. J. FONTAINE
"The Hustle for Happiness"

The slightly bowlegged figure had darted down a covered walkway crowded with winos. It connected in the back to an alley.

Murtaugh took the next right turn at forty miles per hour, his front bumper throwing up a roostertail out of the flooded gutter, and cut back down the alley, catching in his lights the figure who was now madly clip-clopping along in her high heels.

He pulled alongside and rolled down his window. "Hello, there."

"I don't know you." She gave him nothing more than the profile of her face.

"The hell you don't, Dixie."

"Get lost, Murtaugh, I got no time for this shit."

"Looks like you got nothing but time tonight."

"Tell that to my man."

"Get in."

"No way, I just got my face nice again. Everybody knows you down here, Murtaugh—'specially my man." She looked genuinely frightened as she continued walking. "I can't be seen with you."

"Tell him it was a car nob."

She humphed. "The gash ain't gash without the cash. I can say I done Ron Reagan with Nancy watching, eating popcorn, and it don't mean shit to my man without the cash."

"Yeah, yeah, yeah." Sighing, Murtaugh took a twenty from his wallet and laid it on the dashboard. Then he stopped driving, and she came around the grill, shivering as she clutched herself in her arms.

"Turn on that fucking heater, Murtaugh, and keep off Avalon. My man's at the table inside the front window at Trafficante's Pool Palace." She smelled of wet clothes, but at least the cold rain had diluted her perfume. Her raincoat crackled as she shed it and tossed it on the back seat. The prettiness of her golden, fine-boned face was ruined by a habitual sneer.

Murtaugh realized that, sometime during these moments, his twenty spot had vanished from the dash. He took the Imperial Highway toward the airport. "What the hell were you doing up north last night?"

"Appointment," she said matter-of-factly, punching in the cigarette lighter with her trembling fingers.

Murtaugh chuckled. "Say *what?*"

"Yeah, some corporate type."

"What's his name?"

She smiled as she puffed her cigarette to life. "Lee Iacocca."

He knew it was useless to press on this one; he had no intention of taking her downtown for a long chat. His birthday party was slated to start at home in forty minutes.

Trish would have his balls on next year's cake if he missed yet another party. "Run your shit past me again, Dixie."

She exhaled. "Okay, I'm walking past that big round high-rise—"

"Is that where your trick lives?"

She ignored the question. "—and I hear this wreck. Except there ain't no fucking wreck on the street. Then I notice this white chick laying on the roof of her Porsche. 'Bout then, a car pulls up and two of your ofay associates ask me what I seen."

"How'd you know it was the woman's Porsche?"

Dixie's irises reflected the red of the massed taillights ahead. The traffic had come to a standstill. "One of the cops rips the registration off the visor. He be laughing about her hitting her own car. *Laughing*." She grimaced. "Motherfucker."

Murtaugh glanced at his wrist watch: He should have started for Glendale ten minutes ago. And he really didn't know what, if anything, new he'd expected to learn by personally interviewing Dixie. But he wanted to gather as many facts as possible before phoning Michael Hunsaker from home tonight.

Of course, Dixie was lying about her appointment yesterday in the vicinity of Amanda's apartment. But Murtaugh saw nothing extraordinary in this: Most people—white or black, rich or poor—lie to the cops, even when they really have no reason to. Lying to the cops was as American as apple pie.

He decided to make one more stab at the truth. "Bullshit, Dixie," he said angrily, as if he were on the verge of striking her, although in fifteen years he'd never used physical force during an interrogation. "What the fuck were you doing up there in Century City, girl?"

Snarling, she bounced out of the car and slammed the door. Her eyes shone with the Mediterranean fury inherited from her mother. And then she was gone down a side street before the traffic in Murtaugh's lane started inching forward again.

She had left her raincoat in the back seat. It gave him a peculiar feeling. Rianne had done the same thing a few weeks earlier when he'd dropped her off at high school.

"*Ciao*, Dixie, see you around."

Riggs paused in the doorway of his mobile home, even though the rain was coming down hard and cold through the night. Over its rattling on the aluminum roof, the pounding of the distant surf, he could hear the reassuring murmur of the television set inside.

Cato didn't greet him at the door.

"All right, asshole, what'd you do now?"

The runner in the hallway was clear of turds, so Riggs began to widen his search.

Cato himself was cowering in the utility room. Balefully, he looked up from the pile of dirty clothes.

"Fess up, you son of a bitch."

Cato glanced away with his shifty, unblinking canine eyes.

"Get your ass outside." Riggs cracked the back door, and the Labrador slithered out as low to the floor as a snake.

Riggs left the door open to the rain noises.

The damage was in the bedroom, the night-stand lamp knocked over, having come to rest on the solitary pillow.

'What do you do on this bed while I'm gone? Invite some bitch in and party?"

Riggs righted the lamp again, thinking that he really should give the animal away. It was unfair to keep Cato cooped up, but his wife and he had already lost two retrievers to the railroad tracks, despite a five-foot fence surrounding the back yard. If moving automobiles were fun to spirited dogs, freight trains were irresistible.

He wrestled out of his wet leather coat, then inspected his beard in the bathroom mirror. It was filling in. Nicely, he thought. But it would have to go before he reported back to work in four days.

Turning off the bathroom light, he wandered back into the kitchen.

Pfft!

He drained his first Budweiser right at the refrigerator, then grabbed two more cans for the living room, where he settled into the overstuffed chair uneasily, as if it were not really his chair.

He began staring at the tube.

Once, his eyes grew anxious and darted to the small green channel number. They quickly relaxed again: it was still tuned to channel 11. Humphrey Bogart was giving Elisha Cook, Jr. a ration of shit in *The Maltese Falcon*.

Cato padded back inside, leaving little roundels of mud on the linoleum that was supposed to look like genuine Italian tile but didn't. It didn't even look like genuine linoleum.

"Go away," Riggs growled. "I don't love your rotten ass anymore."

The dog turned completely around before lying down, but then sprang up when the floor began to tremble.

The rumble from outside grew in intensity.

Rigg's eyes faded on Bogie's face and instead began visualizing himself, slope-shouldered in his leather jacket, trudging up the railroad embankment.

He halted to listen to the gravelled waters of the seasonal creek rattle through the tin culvert. He started up the slope again, his chupka boots slipping every other step on the ooze. Then, reaching the top, he flinched at the blast from the locomotive's air horn. But still, he straddled the rails and faced squarely into the blinding, gyrating light as it bore down on him with a roar and the clacking of iron wheels . . .

Riggs bolted out of the chair, his eyes wild with fear.

Then he laughed. He reached for his beer but didn't sit again. "I can't stay inside here for four fucking days straight, Cato. You behave yourself until tomorrow morning. I'm going to do a grand prix. Then maybe I can sleep."

• • •

"There's been a mistake," Murtaugh said to the on-duty criminalist. On his way home, he'd decided to swing by the crime lab for the substance analysis reports, saving himself the trouble in the morning. "I wanted the return on the Amanda Hunsaker case. You just handed me a potassium cyanide death."

"Yeah," the technician said between a bite into his submarine sandwich, "right."

"Well, where's the Hunsaker report?"

"You're holding it, Sergeant."

"Explain."

"This afternoon I got a call from the pathologist, who'd just wrapped up the organ dissection of his postmortem—"

"Wait, wait—we're not communicating here." Murtaugh closed his eyes and pinched the bridge of his nose between his fingers. "The victim in this case died of a ten-story fall, not poisoning."

"Right. But the doc said the DB smelled like almonds when he cut it all the way open. Seemed to him she'd ingested cyanide or some like toxic crystalline salt in addition to enough coke to stun an elephant. So I ran all the substances your people collected at the scene. Surprise, surprise—the barbiturate capsules had been mickeyed with potassium cyanide. A fairly slow release with that kind of gelatin capsule, but definitely a fatal dose in each one."

"Sweet Jesus."

"I guess you got a homicide then—thanks to the wonders of modern science."

Murtaugh looked up out of his racing thoughts. "Pardon?"

"I said, you probably won't be able to kiss this one off, right?"

Riggs inched his Plymouth around the street corner so he had a better view of the two Newton division patrolmen. They were seated at a yellow plastic table under the awning of an all-night donut hut.

The beefier one, who wore on his winter long sleeves

two stripes plus a rocker, had been in Riggs's academy class.

He was known to all of LAPD as Rainbird. Of course, in his academy days, he'd a normal name: Sandusky or something like that. But an armed-robbery call at a Spring Street bank had forever erased that prosaic name and given him a new one more befitting his accomplishment: Rainbird had fired over fifty .38-caliber special rounds in the course of the gunfight and sprayed three of the four perpetrators full of lethal holes. Normally, a blue-suiter carried a total of eighteen rounds on his person—six chambered and twelve in the speed-loaders on his Sam Browne belt.

Rainbird had somehow intuited that one day, eighteen would not be enough.

Now Riggs waited until Rainbird had hoisted his paper cup of coffee to his lips before he stomped on the Plymouth's accelerator and rounded the corner with tires chipping. He gave the astonished patrolmen the bird as he roared past the donut hut at sixty miles per hour.

As hoped, Rainbird and his partner tossed away their cups and galloped for their patrol car. Red lights and siren came on right away.

Riggs let them chase him for a half mile, then abruptly pulled over on a dark side street.

Through the light mist, Rainbird bounded up to the Plymouth on Riggs's side, and his partner approached on the sidewalk, his hand resting on the grips of his revolver.

"Hello, Rainbird," Riggs cooed out his open window.

"Oh, fuck me." Rainbird flashed four fingers at his partner—code four, everything was all right. "What're you doing back down here, Riggs?"

"In rooting-tooting-shooting Newton, where the real cops work?"

"At least you still got that straight. So what's up?"

"I don't know, 'Bird. I just don't know." Riggs got out and leaned against his rain-beaded car. "I was kind of thinking of throwing down the gauntlet tonight."

Rainbird licked his lips. "Grand prix?"

"Oh no—no fucking way!" the partner wailed from the sidewalk. "I need this job!"

"What you need is a little more libido," Riggs said. "Besides, I'll pop for your gas."

"Hey, Rainbird, if Riggs gets red-lighted, that's no sweat off our balls. But what happens if the CHP stops *us*?"

"Tell them you're running some rare blood to Las Vegas Memorial. It's always worked before." Riggs then turned to the senior patrolman. "What do you say, 'Bird?"

He slowly grinned. "Why not? It's not every day you get to grand prix against Marty Riggs."

"Shit, shit, shit," his partner hissed, but Riggs knew by the defeat in his voice that he'd go along for the ride.

Walking toward his car, Rainbird said over his shoulder, "I've got to arrange beat coverage first." He intended to put out a special code, one unknown to the brass. In this secretive way, he'd ask the other Newton units to handle his calls for him using his radio call sign in the five or six hours he'd be absent from his beat.

"Control, check for wants or warrants on one," he could be heard transmitting, having reached through his open side window for the mike.

"Go ahead with your subject, thirteen-Adam-ninety-seven."

"Last name, Palacio—" Rainbird held up a hand to hush his partner, who was still arguing, while he spelled out the name for dispatch. "First of Cesar. Address of 711 Las Vegas Street."

"Adam-ninety-seven, stand by for wants on Cesar Palacio." And a few moments later: "Negative on your subject."

A flurry of clicks came over the radio like crickets— Newton patrolmen thumbing their mike buttons, acknowledging the code.

Rainbird tapped his horn for Riggs to start.

"And this little piggy is off, ladies and gentlemen,"

Riggs chortled to himself, "on the annual Los Angeles to Las Vegas Grand Prix. . . ."

Both cars were doing 110 miles per hour by the time they passed through Pomona on the rain-blackened San Bernardino Freeway.

As instructed, Mendez rapped on the metal service door. Waiting for someone to answer, he glanced back down the darkened alley, which was pooled with rainwater. No one was in sight. Around the corner on Hollywood Boulevard, his own people were waiting in the Mercedes, concealing their Ingram submachine guns, disgruntled that they had been barred from accompanying Mendez to the meeting.

But the general was a gentleman—a West Point graduate, for chrissake—and had requested that Mendez appear with neither his *pachuco* bodyguards nor a weapon concealed on his person. Although his retinue was composed of East Los Angeles street gang graduates, Mendez had somewhat resented the racial overtones of the remark.

Still, this connection was much too big to allow personal feelings to interfere.

There was an electric whine, and the wide door rolled up. A Korean, dressed in soiled whites like a navy mess boy, stood before him, looking confused and a little frightened.

"Who the fuck are you?" Mendez demanded.

The Korean answered in his native tongue, which made Mendez shake his head. "Great, doesn't even speak English. The general send a gook to welcome me."

But then, suddenly, the Korean was shoved aside and three armed men rushed out onto the loading dock. Their automatic weapons, which they brandished at him, made Mendez take a step backwards. He wished now that he had brought his men along.

A big *goldie*, as he would be called on the streets, strolled out onto the dock. His pale blond hair was almost white, and his eyelids were tinged with red like an albino's. Hell, maybe he was an albino. He displayed no firearms, but his hands seemed large and hard enough to be weapons. "Mr. Mendez, how nice of you to come."

"What's this shit all about?"

"Kindly step inside. You're getting wet."

Mendez knew he had no choice. He clenched his lower lip between his teeth as he watched the door slowly roll down and lock against the concrete floor. It was dim inside the power plant room, and the albino had to almost shout to be heard over the whirring of fans and other machinery: "I'm sure you're familiar with what I will now ask, Mr. Mendez, from your cruising days."

Mendez sensed that he was being watched from above. He glanced up: A man on a catwalk was training an Uzi submachine gun on him. "What are you talking about?"

"Kindly put your hands behind your head. Interlace your fingers. . . ."

Sighing, Mendez complied.

"Thank you. Now drop to your knees and cross one foreleg over the other."

"You're shitting me!"

"Indeed I am not, Mr. Mendez."

The albino's tone of voice persuaded Mendez to sink to the gritty floor.

"Thank you, Mr. Mendez."

"What's going on? Two weeks ago I was eating caviar and sipping champagne with your boss and his fancy bagman in some fucking bank in Pacific Palisades. Now this—"

"You may take this as a sign that negotiations are progressing nicely. After a thorough background investigation, you have qualified for the next round of discussions."

The albino then began frisking him more thoroughly than any cop had ever done to Mendez.

"I've got no gun, man."

"I know. I just wanted to touch your body."

Reflexively, Mendez recoiled. "Hey, you fucking queer—!"

But the albino had Mendez's fingers firmly in his grasp

and now twisted them viciously, making the man freeze and hold his breath as he prayed for the agony to stop.

"Just kidding," the albino chuckled. "I just wanted to mess with your machismo a little. A practical joke. Don't you think my joke was funny?"

The pressure on Mendez's fingers increased immeasurably. He'd never imagined that they were so laced with nerves. He forced out a ghastly laugh. "Yeah, funny— come on, man. You'll break them . . . you'll break my fucking fingers."

"Not even close," the albino whispered. "And it hurts so bad only because you *believe* I'm breaking them. Concentrate, Mr. Mendez. Block out the nerve impulses. Tell yourself that this is nothing. A cool breeze far over your head, Mr. Mendez."

"*Please*, man," he hissed, close to vomiting now.

"Shit." The albino finally let go. "You just don't have it inside. That's okay—so very few do. Please come with me."

Clenching his throbbing hand in his armpit, Mendez staggered after him, down a corridor with three more armed thugs at its far end. Athletic-looking bastards with Ivy League haircuts. "Who are you?" he asked the albino.

"You may call me Mr. Joshua."

Music could be heard swelling through a pair of swinging doors. Mediocre music that'd be booed and bottled off the stage in East L.A.

Mendez followed Mr. Joshua through the doors, and they emerged onto the main floor of a nightclub. Another Korean, this one in a red steward's outfit, was polishing shot glasses behind the mahogany bar, an automatic pistol within easy reach atop the cash register.

An all-Korean band was rehearsing on stage. The general stood watching them from the dance floor—posture erect, as always—a finger curled under his chin as he listened intently. He wore a turtleneck sweater and a woolen coat with kidskin patches on the elbows. All at once, he waved off the music and turned to a club manager type, who came to attention like an aide-de-camp. "No, no, Kwak, tell these yokels this isn't Seoul!"

Before the manager could translate, the lead guitarist piped up, "No, General, not *soul*. Rock and roll. Do you want rhythm and blues? We do R and B as well."

"I give up. Kwak, hold the front doors for a few more minutes." The general turned and noticed Mendez in escorted approach. "Ah, Joaquin, how are you?" He shook Mendez's damaged hand warmly.

"I don't know," Mendez answered carefully—but, inwardly, he had begun to seethe at his humiliating treatment.

"What do you mean?"

Mendez watched in silence as yet another bodyguard emerged from the shadows and took his place two steps behind the general. The man wore sunglasses, although the interior of the club was as dim as starlight. Finally, Mendez could contain his anger no longer. "I like this joker's sunglasses. Very Hollywood."

The general failed to laugh. "Mr. March lost an eye to a rocket-propelled grenade. For anonymity's sake, he chooses to forego wearing a patch."

Mendez shook his head. He was now beyond controlling himself. "Fucking mercenaries. You're using mercs—tell me I'm wrong."

"No, you're quite right."

"Then you don't understand the scene here in Southern California."

"In what way, Mr. Mendez?" The general now looked amused. "I'm all ears."

"Bring in mercs and you change the complexion of all our operations."

"*Our* operations?"

"Wholesalers like myself. The blue-collar sons of bitches who can get your product out on the streets. We understand the need for enforcement—but this is overkill. In time, we'll ask ourselves—why does this supplier need a goddamned army to do business with us? What does he have in mind that he trusts us so little?"

"Precisely," the general said.

And with that, Mendez clenched his sweaty fists. He now knew why he had been treated so badly after being wined and dined and cajoled at their previous meeting. The general was doing something no one had tried in a long time: asserting control over the middlemen. It amounted to extortion and price-fixing, which would be answered with total war. "Do you know what you're saying, man?"

"Precisely," the general repeated.

Mendez still couldn't believe his ears. Although an independent himself, he still tithed to the organized-crime movers and shakers in the local trade, and the bosses would be outraged at this affront to a status quo they had so carefully constructed. "Well, General, your fucking mercs better be damned good."

"They are." He inclined his head toward a slender young man who had drifted in from the wings of the stage and was seated on the apron, a Thompson submachine gun resting in his lap. "Take Liam there—a Provo on loan to us from Belfast. Don't let the altar boy's face fool you. He killed four of the five members of the Special Air Service team—that's the elite British counter-terrorist group—who were so foolish as to try to arrest him. Maggie Thatcher was a bit too ashamed to release that one to the world press."

"Afternoon to you, Mr. Mendez," the man said with a lilt to his voice. "Be seeing you in Sunday mass, I'm sure."

"Not me, man. We go to different parishes."

The bright voice turned surly. "Ah, yes. Then it must be your *rosary* I was thinking of, Mr. Mendez."

"Damn you!" Mendez exploded at the general. "You've got no idea what you're starting! And don't feel safe. The bosses will buy off these whores the minute you turn your back!"

Infuriatingly, the general laughed, then motioned for Joshua to approach.

"Sir?"

"Joshua, my boy, are you up to a demonstration?"

"Always, sir. *Airborne*, sir!"

The general smiled again at Mendez. "Do you smoke?"

"Yeah, sure—why?"

"You shouldn't. Abominable habit. But please give me your lighter."

Mendez handed it over, then watched in confusion as the general adjusted the flame to its maximum height.

Joshua extended his forearm, the hand curled but not fisted. With his right hand, he rolled back the sleeve of his crisp white shirt, then waited impassively.

The general passed the flame along the underside of Joshua's arm. The man's pallid face remained so stony that Mendez was left wondering if he'd only imagined the pinkish eyes to distend slightly for an instant. "All right," he said and tried to interrupt the meaningless exhibition, "so your man digs pain."

"Oh, Mr. Mendez, you miss the point entirely. Watch again, more closely now." The general held the flame to the heel of Joshua's hand. *Five seconds.* A jaw muscle twitched. *Ten.* The sweet stench of burning flesh began assaulting Mendez's nostrils. *Fifteen.* The skin was now blackened.

"Jesus!" Mendez cried. "Stop this shit!"

The flame sputtered and died. "Do you now appreciate my point?"

"Yeah, sure," Mendez said hoarsely, "these psychos adore you."

"*Sir.*" Joshua was glaring at him pinkly. "From this point on, you shall always address the general as *sir.*"

Mendez nodded, then looked away.

"Now, I would consider it a favor if you will advise the other middlemen that new market conditions have developed unexpectedly. My overhead for this shipment—through no fault of my own—has increased dramatically. A few of my growers in Laos believed that their heroin was worth more than the figure we first agreed upon. I then had to bear the additional expenses of making an example of those recalcitrants. So, what goes around comes around. And we must now insist on a higher price per unit from you . . . and those allied to you. Can we still do business as the gentlemen we are?''

Mendez said nothing for a long moment. Then he dipped his head once. ''But I can only speak for myself.''

''I understand completely. Your associates, no doubt, will need a demonstration as well.''

CHAPTER 5

TEN DESERT MILES east of Barstow, the California Highway Patrol caught up with Martin Riggs.

And the patrolman, bundled up in his black Tuffy jacket and winter cap against the icy rain, did not look pleased when Riggs flashed his LAPD shield. However, he quit clutching the grips of his Colt .357 Magnum.

This was the second time in the same night a brother cop had unsnapped his holster while approaching Riggs, which made him wonder if his appearance might be scruffier than he thought—so much so that his *copness* was now hopelessly buried beneath several layers of neglect.

He vowed solemnly to shave the day after tomorrow.

"Are you on the job?" the patrolman asked, not bothering to disguise his suspicion.

"Yes." Riggs sounded displeased at being delayed.

At that moment, Rainbird and his partner roared past in their glistening black-and-white, its yellow-amber light winking to the rear. The amber was referred to as the "bitch" light, switched on to convince the public that the unit was carrying out some urgent task, even if it wasn't. Especially if it wasn't.

"Christ, what outfit was that?" the patrolman cried, spinning around. "Is he in pursuit?"

"No, he's my escort in case I break down."

"Why?"

Riggs tapped his six-pack-sized cooler case meaningfully. "We're transporting a donor heart from Martin Luther King Hospital to Las Vegas Memorial."

"Christ, why didn't you say that in the first place?" But then doubt narrowed his eyes. "Wait, why didn't they fly this heart to Vegas?"

"Look, I'd love to explain, but there's a small child waiting on an operating table for what I've got in this case."

"You hang tight. I'm going to have my dispatcher make a call—"

"All right, all right. I'll explain. They didn't fly it because it's a baboon's heart—"

"A fucking *what?*"

"You heard me. A monkey's heart. And they go completely anaerobic at altitude. I didn't want to get into all this, but if you *insist* on knowing."

There was no sound but the rain popping against the patrolman's vinyl Tuffy. Then he nodded gravely. "Need another escort?"

"No, but get on the horn to your buddies ahead. Nevada Highway Patrol, too. Tell them we're coming through, and that kid in Vegas can't afford another delay."

"You got it!" The patrolman jogged back for his mike.

Riggs's foot jammed the accelerator to the floorboard, and rain began sizzling loudly against the windshield again. The wipers could barely keep up with it, but once in a while he had a fleeting glimpse of the Newton unit's yellow flasher.

A mileage sign sailed past like a green kite:

Las Vegas   139 miles

Riggs had been married in Vegas on a night like tonight.

In December of 1975, he had finally put aside his doubts about his fitness as a husband and asked the delicate-looking clerk at municipal court to share his shoddy little existence. And then she'd frightened the crap out of him by growing serious as all hell and saying, "There's something we should discuss, Marty, before we talk about marriage."

He was scared to death she was in love with somebody else, for he knew of at least a half-dozen vultures in blue who'd been scoping on her angelic face.

But then she said, "I had rheumatic fever as a child. It weakened my heart. A lot, Marty. So much so I should never have babies."

"Is that all?" Riggs finally started breathing again. "I thought you were going to tell me you'd been a hooker or something."

She laughed in surprise. "Really! Can you see me as a hooker?"

"Sure, and I know a novelty shop on Sunset where I can buy the getup for you. What a party idea!"

Now, slumped behind the wheel, Riggs found himself smiling. He was listening to her laughter once again.

Then, two years after they'd married, she had gotten pneumonia, and when it had run its course she was too weak to return to work. At times, a bluish tint came to her lips, which she tried to hide with lipstick as soon as it appeared.

He knew damned well she couldn't take stress, and it was terrible for her to be alone while he worked nights, the television her only company. She stopped watching modern cop shows and usually kept the dial on channel 11, which mostly played old B-movies. And she probably waited for the visitation all cops' wives waited for—the deputy chief showing up with a face as long as a horse's, her husband's buddies rattling around in her kitchen, trying to make coffee because they didn't know what to say.

Whenever he considered quitting and finding a quieter occupation, Riggs lied to himself that he couldn't because of the department's great medical insurance. But deep down he knew he could never quit.

He needed the job as much as he needed her.

It was an impasse he felt helpless to resolve. All marriages, even good ones, have at least one, and this just happened to be theirs.

Roaring past the flyspeck of Baker, which looked good only for a tank of gas and a case of ptomaine, Riggs saw Rainbird's black-and-white shining in the neon of a service station awning. He laid on his horn in triumph, and Rainbird let go of the nozzle long enough to flip him off with both fingers.

The freeway started up a grade into some mountains. Big wet flakes began spinning down out of the black sky. They crashed against the windshield and turned to slush that piled up beneath the stroke of the wipers. But Riggs was unaware of the snow.

He was trooping up the porch steps to his mobile home once again, after a frustrating and exhausting night in which a buy-bust caper had gone sour. Lieutenant Ortiz had blamed Riggs's informant, but Martin had argued in vain that his squeeze could be trusted as far as any squeeze could be. It was just one of those shitty things.

But never mind now—he was home. He could hear the television going. She was still up, which was good. He didn't want to be alone in the trailer, drinking until first light.

Cato, more hyperactive than usual, pawed him at the door. And from this alone Riggs got a sudden sinking feeling.

He rounded the partition into the living room. "Babe?"

And then he told himself that she was just sleeping in the overstuffed chair, that any moment she'd stir and put down the *TV Guide* she was still clutching in her marblelike fingers.

But he knew that this was not possible.

He knelt at her feet. He hugged her cold legs. "Oh, babe . . . not this . . . not this."

By the time the deputy coroners arrived to take her away, he had composed himself and dried his eyes. In a calm voice, he told them about her medical history, gave the name and phone number of her doctor. He nodded agreement to their preliminary opinion of congestive heart failure.

Yet, when one of them reached around to find the off button to the television, Riggs cried, "No—stop!" He startled both of them by the sheer ferocity in his voice: "Leave it on!"

And in the two months since that night, Riggs had not turned off his television even for a second. Nor had he tuned it to a station other than the one she'd been watching. It was admittedly crazy, but he couldn't bear the thought of breaking this last connection with her. If the screen faded to darkness, so would his strange certainty that she was only temporarily gone on a trip she'd failed to tell him about. He would come home any night now and she'd be sitting there, smiling up at him sleepily.

"Oh, babe . . . "

Then he nearly jumped through the roof of his Plymouth as Rainbird, running without lights, hit his yelp siren two feet from Riggs's rear bumper, then sped around—flashers scintillating, turning the falling snow to red, blue, and yellow confetti.

"Kiss my root, Riggs!" Rainbird shouted over his public address. "See you on my way back from Vegas!"

Wiping away his tears with the sleeve of his leather jacket, Riggs laughed. "That's what you think."

But he didn't attempt to keep pace with the patrol car, whose brash lights were soon swallowed up by the storm. Instead, Riggs took the next exit, which delivered him onto an abandoned two-lane highway announced by a birdshot-riddled sign that said the road was not maintained and the driver used it at his own risk.

He continued at freeway speeds, although he spun out twice on tight curves. And then the asphalt was whited over with snow. Still, he did not let up on the accelerator.

His gaze seemed to penetrate no farther than the windshield.

Murtaugh's birthday table, crowned by the cake whose candles he had already blown out this morning, was untouched as if everyone had gone to bed expecting him home at any minute.

He glanced at his wrist watch: twelve-fifteen. "Fuck."

In his experience, women had three ways of manifesting anger: vehemence, which he secretly preferred; silence, which he detested with a passion; and leg-crossing, which he detested with even more passion. Trish, as the gods would have it, was born and raised a leg-crosser, and he now felt a twinge in his groin, a harbinger of the deprivation to come.

"Fuck."

He cracked open the refrigerator door, saw nothing appealing inside, then shuffled across the floor to the pantry. He took the bottle of Canadian Mist from the top shelf and began searching for a clean glass. He had to settle for a Road Runner–motif cup, whose plastic ruined the smoky aroma of the whiskey.

"Fuck."

He had fully intended to head home at full steam after picking up the lab report on Amanda Hunsaker. But the evidence of poisoning had so unsettled him, he had returned to his office to mull over everything he'd learned thus far. After an hour of staring out his window at the clouds, which were grayly underlit by the city lights, he decided to phone Michael Hunsaker.

Yet, with warning bells beginning to go off in his head about this case, he decided not to reveal *everything* to his former brother in arms. He felt that he had a good reason for withholding on Hunsaker.

The Pacific Palisades number was picked up on the first ring. "Hunsaker here." He sounded tired and older than Murtaugh had expected. And the Tennessee drawl was more subdued than twenty years before, or maybe it was just the tension in the voice.

"Mike?"

"Who's speaking?"

"Roger Murtaugh."

"Rog, where have you been?"

"You mean since Nam?"

"No . . . I'm sorry. It's just that I've been trying so hard to get in touch with you."

"Yeah, well, your message got mislaid. I apologize."

"Look, I hate to bother you at all. But I've got a personal problem. I can't discuss it over the phone."

Murtaugh realized that Hunsaker didn't know yet about his daughter's death, but the detective sergeant wanted to find out how much the man did know. "Does this concern Amanda?"

Only the sound of Hunsaker's shallow breathing came through the receiver. "It might, if things get out of hand. God, I don't know." Then he sensed the bad news. "Why do you ask about her, Rog?"

"Are you alone in the house?"

"Well, no, my housekeeper's here—" Then Hunsaker gasped as if he'd been punched in the chest. He had realized. "Oh, God—*when?*"

"Last night. She jumped from the balcony of her apartment."

"Oh, God . . . God. Why wasn't I told until now?"

"That was my decision, Mike. I wanted to find out as much as possible before breaking the news to you."

"Yeah . . . okay."

"Is Clare home with you?"

"No, Rog, she died five years ago."

"I'm sorry."

"Well, we were divorced at the time." Hunsaker took a swift, deep breath. "Look, I don't want to talk right now. I've got things to do. So many things."

"I understand, Mike. But I'd like to get together in the next few days."

"Why?" Hunsaker now sounded frightened again.

"To go over everything with you."

"I see. I guess." He gave Murtaugh his work number, then said, "You know, back then . . ." His voice trailed off.

"You mean Nam?"

"Right. Had you known what lay ahead for you—-would you have come back?"

"Yes, Mike, I'd have been even more desperate to make it home in one piece."

"You're a lucky man, Rog. Good-bye."

Murtaugh sat alone in the kitchen for another hour. Through half the bottle of Canadian Mist, he lived it all once again.

How Michael Hunsaker had become enamored with the killing. How he had begun exceeding his sanctions and started snuffing whomever he pleased, whenever he pleased. He became his own law; the war became his own crusade, to conduct however he deemed fit.

For Murtaugh, the last straw had come at some nameless village on the lush fringe of the highlands.

Hunsaker had gone in with a couple of his favorite Montagnards, who had been ostracized by their own people for being virtual brigands, and shot up everything that moved. Hunsaker came out of the one-sided firefight with the expression of a man who has just enjoyed very good sex. And Murtaugh, shaking with rage, told him outright that this massacre would be reported to the inspector general. The party was over.

"Do what you have to do, Rog," Hunsaker said with a faint smile, then turned on his heels.

But, in the nastiest turn of fate in Murtaugh's life, the team was mortared by NVA regulars on their race back to the landing zone. Roger took a piece of shrapnel through the pectoral muscle and into the lung. It was hard enough to breathe, let alone even think of walking.

Hunsaker stared back down the whisper of a trail at him,

oblivious to the rounds that were still warbling down through the triple-canopy jungle. "Problem, Rog?"

Knowing that the best he could hope for—*if* he survived his wound—was a POW camp, Murtaugh still could not find the words to beg. Frothy blood had begun to seep out of the corner of his mouth, yet he gnashed his teeth together.

At last, his camouflage-painted face exultant, Hunsaker strode back down the path and hoisted Murtaugh onto his shoulders. "You owe me, Murtaugh. For as long as you fucking breathe, you owe Mike Hunsaker. Airborne!"

"We got him! We got Marty Riggs!" Rainbird skidded the Newton division patrol car to a halt under the glittering porte-cochere of Caesar's Palace. "Give me some cash quick!"

"I only got a twenty left, 'Bird."

"Give it to me, dammit!" Ripping the bill out of his partner's hand, Rainbird bailed out, screaming for the bewildered parking valet to stand aside. He'd taken about ten running strides for the battery of front glass doors when he turned and bellowed, "Get the fucking Polaroid out of the trunk, dipshit!" Then the pure joy of the moment made him fist his hands and tell a band of Japanese tourists, "I got Marty Riggs by the short hairs!"

They bowed, and one of their number popped a flashcube at the gleeful senior patrolman.

Racing down the labyrinthine aisles of slot machines, Rainbird kept hopping up on his toes, looking for a keno girl.

Finally, he was able to grab one near the crap tables. He pressed the twenty into her hand. "Come out front with me, baby!"

"But—"

"It's just for a picture. I need you and the name of this dump in the snapshot to prove I beat fucking Marty Riggs to the halfway point! Nobody's ever beat even him this far!"

She tried to speak again, but Rainbird nearly snapped her neck as he yanked her by the arm toward the front.

Flying outside, he cried to his partner, "Here we come! Polaroid ready?"

"Yo!"

He halted on the steps and, tucking the keno girl under his arm, chortled. "Riggs isn't going to believe this."

"But that's what I'm trying to tell you . . . about Riggs."

His grin dissolving, he slowly looked down at the scantily clad woman. "*What* did you just say?"

"A guy calling himself Riggs asked me to give you this—" She dug a Polaroid shot out of her sheaf of keno tickets.

"No, no, no," Rainbird moaned as he took hold of the still sticky print.

Riggs was leering at him—the middle finger of his right hand erect.

"There's a message on the back," she said, beginning to smile.

Rainbird flipped it over:

> *Why aren't you cocksuckers on your beat?*
> *M. Riggs, Deputy Chief*

CHAPTER 6

MURTAUGH SAT RAMROD straight behind his desk, half fuming about the order that had just rolled downhill from his lieutenant, half listening to Detective Burke ramble on about the Amanda Hunsaker investigation.

"So, Sarge, another check with the apartment residents on her floor resulted in zip."

"What about the people one floor below?"

"Zip."

"And above?"

"Zip."

"Hmm." Murtaugh's eyes glazed over once again. Detective headquarters had just seen fit to promote better relations between narcotics and robbery/homicide. Some kind of supervisory liaison program—he'd already forgotten the fucking acronym and what it stood for. There were no substantial problems between the two elite divisions. Just a personal feud between Lieutenant Ortiz and Murtaugh's own lieutenant, arising from a few insults traded during a budget hearing so long ago there'd probably been an outstanding warrant for Zorro at the time. As if Murtaugh didn't have enough to do in the coming weeks without babysitting a narc sergeant.

And now, by virtue of his personnel selection, Ortiz was letting robbery/homicide know what he really thought of burying the hatchet with his counterpart.

He was loaning Detective Sergeant Martin Riggs to the pilot program.

Murtaugh had never met Riggs. He had no idea what he looked like. But the man was infamous for his shooting incidents. He'd had more firefights than some medium-sized European armies. All justified, of course. But Murtaugh couldn't help but think that where there's smoke, there's fire. And Riggs, by reputation alone, was a smoldering fire.

Murtaugh had no intention of getting burned—not if he intended on retiring out of this division instead of some bullshit post like communications or police commission investigations.

Although the shooting-investigation team had minced words about Riggs's latest turkey shoot, it was clear to Murtaugh that the man would not be around for many more shooting incidents if he continued handling them in this lunatic manner.

Still, all in all, Riggs had gotten the job done, and nobody—even the gun-shy brass—liked to argue with success, especially when the public perceived it to be heroic. Already, there was talk of a Medal of Valor.

"Sarge?"

Murtaugh glanced up out of these thoughts into Burke's doughy face. "Yeah?"

"I asked, what do you think?"

"About what?"

"The bed."

Murtaugh took a loud slurp of acrid coffee. "Fill me in again, man. I've got a thousand things on my mind this morning."

"I noticed. I said, I didn't put it my report, but it seemed to me that Amanda Hunsaker's bed was super rumpled. Used. Know what I mean, *consensually?*"

"Yeah, well, her line of work is hell on sheets. I've

only seen the blood panel results on her. I'm still waiting for the pathologist's full report. I made sure to ask for a vaginal swab, an anal swab, a stomach—''

"Oh, shit."

"Oh, shit what?"

"I forgot to tell you—I picked up the postmortem report yesterday afternoon. Slipped my mind that I was holding it until now."

"*Oh, shit* is right! Get it in here, now! I've been waiting on pins and needles for that damn thing!"

Burke rushed out the door, leaving it open.

Murtaugh stared out through it into the main office. His nostrils suddenly widened with distaste.

In the midst of the typing pool, slouching on the corner of a desk like he owned the thing, was a variety of subhuman that instantly evoked a litany of descriptions in Murtaugh's mind: worm, maggot, mope, puke, sleazebag, hairbag, scumbag. The man's oily brown hair fell around the flaking shoulders of his leather jacket; and his chukka boots should have been quarantined for mange, then incinerated.

Puffing on a cigarette, the stranger slowly turned his bristly face and regarded Murtaugh with vacuous blue eyes. In Special Forces jargon, it was called the thousand-yard stare.

He had no badge clipped in plain sight to his jacket. No visitor's badge. Nor was he handcuffed and being attended by one of the detectives as all arrestees were supposed to be who were not immediately transported to county detention.

Yet, this scumbag seemed perfectly at home in the inner sanctum of LAPD robbery/homicide.

That insouciance made Murtaugh see red.

A memo on station security had just come down from above: Any violation in robbery/homicide that came to the deputy chief's attention would cost Murtaugh—as the on-duty supervisor—a pound of flesh. And then some.

Recently, some loony had strolled unchallenged—nobody

knew how—into Devonshire station and proceeded to shoot the houseplants and telephones off a half-dozen desks before being subdued by a captain, who then suffered a mild heart attack because of the excitement and the exertion. Captains were not used to excitement and exertion.

So the specter of another in-house shooting was on everyone's mind.

Murtaugh rose from his swivel chair and started for the stranger. "Who are you?"

The filthy man also lumbered to his feet, but as he twisted around to face Murtaugh his jacket front bulged open, revealing an automatic in a basketweave shoulder holster.

This was definitely indicative of a cop, but Murtaugh still wasn't certain, given the stranger's rough appearance.

"Is that a gun there?" he asked, still rushing forward, realizing that his question had been inane. Of course it was a pistol. He quickly amended: "What are you doing with a gun there?"

The stranger seemed confused by the questions. He tapped his own chest with a finger as if to inquire, *you mean me?*

"Hell yes—you," Murtaugh said. "You with the goddamned gun under your arm!"

"Gun!" Someone in the detective bullpen took up the cry.

"What? We got a man with a gun?" Another voice hollered, "Where?"

The stranger responded to these shouts by rubbernecking around the large room as if in search of someone with a weapon. Suddenly, he drew his pistol and held it at the ready, muzzle pointed toward the ceiling.

"Shit!" Murtaugh bellowed as he lunged desperately for the handgun. He'd left his own piece in the top drawer of his desk. Yet, his groping hands never connected with the automatic, for—with surprising grace, given his shabby-looking condition—the stranger flipped him over the desk.

Murtaugh landed hard on a stapler and yowled in pain.

The chiming of the overturned phone slowly dwindled to silence.

One of the stenographers screamed that Sergeant Murtaugh had been killed, and another woman could be heard bursting into tears.

"You all right?" The stranger peered down at him, his eyes still wide with bewilderment. Burke was looking over the man's shoulder, his expression sheepish. "Sarge, you okay?"

Murtaugh stabbed a finger at the stranger. "*Who* in the name of sweet Jesus are *you?*"

"Oh, shit, oh, holy shit," Burke murmured. "I forgot to tell you, Sarge. This is Riggs from narcotics. He was waiting to see you."

Murtaugh lowered his head to the floor and closed his eyes. "Someone rip the Bostich off me. I think it's stapled to my ass."

As they passed within a few miles of Century City on the Santa Monica Freeway, Riggs tried to break the silence that had gone stale since Murtaugh had pulled out of the underground parking lot. "Which was it?"

Murtaugh had to clear his throat to speak. "Pardon?"

"Which one did this Hunsaker broad jump from?"

Murtaugh squinted through the cloak of smog. "Uh, the cylindrical job there. And I knew her. When she was a little girl."

"Oh."

"Her father and I served together."

"Sorry."

"That's okay," Murtaugh said. "You didn't know."

"And that's where you're headed now? To break the news to him?"

"I already phoned. This is just a follow-up."

"See how he's taking it?"

"Right."

"Sure."

A tractor-trailer rumbled past on Murtaugh's side of the

car, and the two men used its passing as an excuse to fall silent again.

Murtaugh turned up the volume knob on his Motorola, which has been dead for the last several minutes. A disconcerting lull in the existential stream of consciousness that murmurs over a police radio network.

Riggs reached inside his jacket for a Winston, hesitated briefly as he wondered if Murtaugh might object, but then lit up anyway. The silence had begun to get on his nerves again. He wondered if Murtaugh didn't like white people, but then decided no. Murtaugh didn't like *him*. That made Riggs feel a little better. At least he wasn't stuck with a bigot. "What branch?"

"Pardon?"

"What branch of the service?"

"Oh . . . army."

Riggs had privately thought so. "Nam?"

"Right."

"Whereabouts?"

Murtaugh named off a province and a half-dozen *villes*— all in the highlands. From this, Riggs guessed that Murtaugh had worn the Green Beret, but still asked, "Special Forces?"

"Yeah. And you?"

"Recon marine. Two tours. How about you—how long in-country?"

"Two months." When another silence followed, Murtaugh added, "Two months, then a chest wound and nine months in the thoracic ward at Tripler." Murtaugh smiled a bit uneasily. "Four days ago, your caper in Venice. Was that the Marine way?"

Riggs didn't smile back. "No, my way."

"You sure like milking that automatic of yours, don't you?"

"Something against autos?"

"I didn't say that."

"You still carry a wheel gun?"

Murtaugh nodded serenely.

"Yeah, well, most of the old-timers do," Riggs said.

Murtaugh's eyes darted to Riggs's smirk, then back to the freeway. "I value quality over quantity."

"Whatever." Riggs yawned and stretched. "Any idea what we're supposed to do until downtown figures out what we both already know?"

"What do we both know?"

"That this is some bullshit to make your lieutenant and my lieutenant kiss and make up and never bad-mouth each other ever again."

Murtaugh shrugged. "The memorandum said for us to *establish lines of inter-divisional communication and inculcate the resultant symbiosis with a new operational awareness.*"

"Yeah, but are we supposed to do any fucking work?"

For the first time, Murtaugh laughed. "Hell if I know. But let me suggest this, Riggs—" His eyes sobered again. "Whatever we do or don't do, let's go about it so a minimum of attention comes down on our butts. The sooner this project is forgotten, the sooner it'll be declared a big success and dismantled."

"What do you mean by a minimum of attention?"

Murtaugh gave a meaningful glance to the lump under Riggs's leather jacket.

Chuckling, Riggs slid open the ashtray. It was stuffed with gum wrappers, so he cracked the window wing and tossed the butt outside. "You don't want to work with me, do you?"

"No," Murtaugh said coolly. "I don't."

"What's your reason?"

"I think you're a lightning rod."

One corner of Riggs's smile turned down, and his eyes softened, almost to the point of moistening. "You're right. I sure seem to draw the shit. Even on a cloudless day like today. But I've stopped worrying about it."

"That's obvious."

Nothing more was said until Murtaugh turned off the Pacific Coast Highway into a parking lot studded with Greek sculpture and little junipers growing out of amphoralike pots. Riggs was surprised to see that the mock Roman villa building was a bank. "I'll say one thing . . ."

"What's that?"

"You homicide folks sure move in better circles than us dope cops. I suppose you want me to stay in the car."

Murtaugh seemed a little embarrassed. "Well, it's up to you."

"No, it's up to you."

"Well, ain't nothing really."

"Yes, it is." Riggs felt like digging him a little for the lightning-rod comment. The truth in it had smarted: Riggs often did feel like a Jonah. "But hey, Roger, I understand. You'd have to explain to your buddy why your partner looks like a dirtbag. And that could take a week. No problem."

"It isn't that," Murtaugh went on, with one nicely polished oxford on the pavement and the warning buzzer tattling that the key was still in the ignition. "This is kind of personal."

"Sure."

"More personal than job, I mean."

"Understood."

Murtaugh started for the front door, then stopped and came back to Riggs's window. "In my briefcase there's the pathologist's report on Amanda Hunsaker. The toxicological stuff, too. And the bulk of the narratives. You might as well start familiarizing yourself with the case."

"Good idea."

"I won't be long."

"Take your time. This is the first day of the rest of my life." Then Riggs waited until Murtaugh was inside the bank before he whispered to himself, "Fucking cream puff."

Naturally, Michael Hunsaker looked older. But Murtaugh had not expected him to look fifteen years older than himself. Hunsaker's face had leaned out, leaving deep gullies around his mouth and crow's feet at his watery eyes.

When Murtaugh glanced away momentarily, if only to have some relief from the man's hunted-looking stare, he thought he saw the necklace of ears strung across the front of the man's tasteful and expensive suit. Only a chimera, Murtaugh reminded himself. But his mind's eye would always see those shriveled ears.

"First, let me say how sorry I am about Amanda, Mike."

Surprisingly, Hunsaker gave Murtaugh's arm an affectionate squeeze. "Sit down, Rog, please." When Hunsaker sank into his own leather wing chair, he sighed heavily, but smiled. "Surprised I found you?"

"Kind of. Last time I saw you I was flat on my back on a Huey deck with a sucking chest wound."

"You were fortunate you got out when you did. A new brigadier took command. I don't think you two would've meshed—philosophically." Hunsaker took a sip of brandy, although Murtaugh had refused the offer of something to drink from the wet bar in the corner of the Greco-Roman office. "Several months ago, I saw you interviewed on the tube—the Southside Slayer case. Looks like you've found a good place for yourself."

"I have. And you, Mike? Vice president, I'm sure, in charge of what here?"

"Venture capital."

When Hunsaker suddenly fell silent, Murtaugh knew it was time to set off his bombshell. "Mike, we're treating Amanda's death as a homicide."

Hunsaker's face remained expressionless. "You mean, someone may have pushed her?"

"No, I don't think so."

"Then what?"

"Her barbiturates has been doctored with potassium cyanide. Even if she hadn't jumped, the dosage would have been fatal."

During his career, Murtaugh had broken death news to over a hundred parents. And he could now predict the changes that Hunsaker would undergo: the abrupt shifts from shock to disbelief to outrage that anybody could do this to his loved one. But the last thing Murtaugh had expected to see in Hunsaker's eyes was panic.

"Do you have any idea who did this?"

"We're working on it, Mike."

"You've got to find the bastards."

"We'll try."

"No, that's not good enough. You've got to get them!"

Murtaugh changed the subject before the man started shouting. "Mike, last week—before Amanda's death—why were you trying to get in touch with me?"

"Shit, does it matter anymore?"

"It might."

Hunsaker hesitated a moment, then went to his marble-topped desk and unlocked one of the file drawers. He removed a video cassette and brought it to Murtaugh. "I wanted you to find her. To take her out."

"Of what?"

"Movies. The same kind we used to watch in the back room of the NCO club, Rog. Except back then, I never imagined that those girls might have parents. . . ." Hunsaker stopped to fight back tears.

But Murtaugh sensed that the tears were for himself. "You sure you want me to see this?"

"If it'll help track down the motherfuckers."

Murtaugh quickly tucked it in his coat pocket. "How'd you get hold of it?"

"Came in the mail one day."

"Any note?"

Hunsaker shook his head no, then went to the bar and refilled his snifter. "You know, I have another daughter."

"Yeah?"

"By my second wife." He smiled lamely. "That marriage didn't work out either."

"How old's your girl?"

"Seventeen."

"Same as my Rianne."

Hunsaker seemed not to have heard Murtaugh. He drained

the snifter. "Beth and Amanda were pretty close for half sisters. She'll take this hard—the murder part. But, thank God, I can tell her that you'll find the people who did this to her sister. That you'll make the sons of bitches suffer for what they did."

"I'm a cop, Mike, not an executioner."

Then Hunsaker held his eyes with a vengeance. "You owe me, Rog, which means you're anything I say you are."

CHAPTER 7

"HAVE A BEER?" Riggs asked Murtaugh as he got back inside the car. "I've got plenty."

Murtaugh shook his head at the four remaining cans of the six-pack on the carpeted hump over the drive shaft. The two empties had been crushed and chucked over the seat. Reflexively, he checked the parking lot to make sure no one had seen Riggs chug-a-lugging. Even though the unit was unmarked, it still had government-exempted plates and a city motor pool number. "Man, are you nuts? Where'd you get that shit?"

"They have establishments in this realm that dispense it. All you can carry off. There's one right around the corner."

"We're on the job."

"Right."

"I mean, I don't drink on the job unless the assignment calls for it."

"Well, you're safe then. This assignment definitely calls for it."

"Dump it, man."

Riggs looked genuinely taken aback. "You're serious."

"Hell yes, I'm serious. I'm not working with some

joker who stumbles through his eight hours with a buzz on.''

"All right." Whistling "Getting to Know You" between his teeth, Riggs rolled down his window and hurled the remaining cans out into the parking lot. One sprang a leak and threw a garland of foam back across the windshield.

Murtaugh hit the wipers, which only left two arched smears on the glass, then pulled out into traffic. "Thank you.''

"Don't mention it. How'd it go in there?"

Murtaugh's eyes turned thoughtful. "No picnic."

"Never is. He took it pretty hard then?"

"I'm not quite sure how he took it." All at once, Murtaugh looked like he didn't want to discuss his former buddy. Riggs made a mental note of it. "When not hoofing it to the liquor store, did you get a chance to go through those reports?"

"Yes, indeed, Roger."

"What'd you think?"

"I was reading, not thinking."

Murtaugh pressed his lips together. "Man, I am bending over backwards to get along with one of the biggest flakes in this department! But in about two seconds the back of my head is going to touch ground and—"

"I apologize."

Murtaugh slowly closed his mouth. Then he eyed Riggs carefully.

"I'm sincere, Roger. Some people just don't know how to take me at first. You just must be one of them."

Murtaugh grunted.

"Now, as far as the reports, it seems to me your people are fumbling around for something."

Murtaugh took a calming breath. "For what, if I might ask?"

"For the somebody who was in Amanda Hunsaker's apartment immediately prior to her death."

"Okay . . . any ideas?"

"Right off the top of my head, one of her clients. But

you could find more semen in a convent than what showed up on that pathologist's swabs.''

"It's a bitch. I just didn't expect that finding.''

"That's because you're thinking like a cop, not like a whore.''

"And *you* can think like one?''

"I worked Wilshire vice before narcotics. I can even dream like a whore.''

"What's the point, man?''

"Well, Burke told me that Amanda's sheets looked like she'd been playing with somebody that evening.''

"Right, but one thing about a john, he pays to *come*. Even if we found no traces in Amanda, we should have found some stains on the sheets, maybe some tissues in a trash can.''

"Look, if you'd straddled and blown and jerked off ten thousand guys in your short life, would you be interested in man love, if you were given the choice?''

Murtaugh's eyes widened a little.

"Hell no, Roger. You'd go after some woman love on your own time. And it'd probably be with a sister hooker—''

Murtaugh suddenly hit the brakes hard, nearly throwing Riggs onto the dash. "Fuck me, mama!''

"Shit, Roger, when you think like a whore, you really get into it.''

"Her appointment book was empty for that evening. She *was* on R and R. Had to be!'' Murtaugh drummed the steering wheel with his palms. "Yeah! And I've been hovering that far away from it these past four days.'' He held his fingers about an inch apart. "Oh, it's thin. But it's something. Lord, it could really shine up for us—Dixie Monroe, right?''

"I wish I had a cigar for you. I really do.''

"I don't think my mobile phone will reach downtown from out here. Public booth, Riggs, fast! I'll bet a six-pack that one of those latent prints we lifted in Amanda's apartment will match up with Dixie's. I've got to phone ID. Have them pull Dixie's cards. Hell, she's been busted more than a secondhand piñata. You see a booth yet, Riggs?''

''Chevron station on the corner.''

''Got it.'' Murtaugh chuckled again. ''Yes, sir, I'll bet a sixer.''

''Good, I seem to have mislaid my last one.''

While Murtaugh was in the booth making his call, Riggs began humming to himself, then whispered as if someone were in the car with him, ''I don't ever want to get off work again. When it's good, it's really good. So good I don't need a past . . . a future. I just have the job, and it has me. And the time. It goes by in a blur. And I need that now, babe. I need it now that you're away.''

Murtaugh peaked his shoulders as if he thought Riggs was trying to say something to him.

Riggs waved off the man's questioning look.

At that moment, the alert tone over the radio, followed by a dispatcher's voice: ''All units and seven-Adam-twelve, a jumper at 99556 Whilshire. Adam-twelve, handle code two.''

''Copy, no siren,'' the patrol unit responded.

Riggs slid over behind the steering wheel and laid on the horn.

Murtaugh folded back the glass door. ''What?''

'' 'Tis the season—a jumper up on Wilshire.''

The Wilshire address turned out to be a Mercedes-Benz dealership, and the manager met Murtaugh and Riggs at ground level. ''What a shitty way to end a Christmas party, what?'' He gestured at the figure perched on the roof parapet—four stories above the glass-fronted show room. ''Who needs fruitcake for the occasion? I got MacCleary.''

''What's his first name?'' Murtaugh asked.

''Leonard. One of the lesser lights of my sales staff. I had to give him notice this morning.''

''Right before *fucking* Christmas?''

The manager looked at Riggs's clothes before meeting

his eyes. "You bet, pal. Unfortunately, this happens to be our busiest quarter. People who can afford our product aren't exactly strapped this time of the year. Come to think of it, they're never strapped. God bless us, everyone."

Murtaugh glanced up again. "Why'd you fire him?"

"Maybe I shouldn't say this, but he's got a bit of a nose problem. What he inhales on his own time is his business. But, Jesus, he's started arguing with customers. I mean it—really testy with them. Treats them like they're idiots. Which they are, but it's not his place to remind them. Leave that to their creditors. So lately, he couldn't a sell the last gold SEL 450 on earth to a Saudi prince on amphetamines. I mean it—his production really sucks. I can't afford him, especially now, when every sugar daddy in town is buying a Christmas toy for his poon."

Murtaugh waved for a female blue-suiter to approach. "Homicide, officer—where's the psychologist?"

"Stuck bumper-to-bumper on the San Diego Freeway."

"Swell."

"I can handle it," Riggs said.

Murtaugh hoisted an eyebrow. "You qualified to talk to jumpers?"

"I can relate to them."

"How's that?"

"As a kid, I always wanted to fly."

A patrolman blocked the final flight of stairs to the roof. "Who are you?"

Riggs flashed his shield and bumped past the man, rushing up the concrete steps into the lead-colored sky. It was a lousy afternoon to die: Both mountains and sea were obscured by smog, and the sweet stench of car exhaust hung in the breezeless air.

Riggs could see the back of a head on the other side of the parapet, the man's pale face was inclined downward. He wondered if he might be able to sneak up on him, but then the man heard Riggs's footfalls in approach and spun around angrily, almost losing his balance. "Go away!"

Riggs halted and splayed his arms to his sides as if to say that he intended no harm. "Name is Riggs. Martin Riggs. Your friends down there told me your name is Len."

"Fuck off, I've got no friends."

"Well, I didn't want to argue with them . . . it being Christmas and all." Riggs advanced a few more steps, then paused, letting the man grow accustomed to his presence. "They seemed worried enough about you." After a moment, he took three more steps forward.

"I said get out of here!"

"I can't do that. And I'm not sure you really want me to do that, Len."

Leonard wiped a sweaty lock of hair off his forehead. He looked all around anxiously, as if thinking that Riggs had not come alone. "Look, I know all the psychology bullshit. It won't work."

"I'm not a psychologist."

"Yeah? What are you?"

Given poor Leonard's addiction, Riggs didn't want to admit that he was with narcotics. "Cop. Homicide."

"You're early. But hang on a couple of minutes."

Riggs laughed.

Leonard's expression turned fierce. "Is something funny about this to you?"

"I'm sorry. Your remark—it was kind of funny. But maybe you have to be in the mood." Riggs patted his jacket pockets. He found a ball-point pen, but had to make do with a matchbook cover. "Listen, this is going to require some paperwork. And you can save me a few days of legwork by just answering a few questions here and now. Okay?"

Leonard said nothing for a moment, then: "I guess."

"Spelling of last name?"

"Christ, buddy, my driver's license will be in my wallet. You can take it off my body."

"Good thinking." Gingerly, Riggs sat on the guano-splattered parapet. "Then how about motive or other reason for the offense?"

"Is this a offense?"

"Not quite. At least not yet."

Grimly, Leonard surveyed the scene below, then pointed out the manager with an accusatory finger. "See the Armenian prick? Last year I sold more 300 CDs than the rest of those suck-asses combined. For him. For his million-dollar English Tudor in Toluca Lake and his wetback mistress. I sold more than anybody else in the whole western region."

"What happened this year?"

"None of your goddamned business."

"Fair enough. Listen, Len, I'm coming out on the ledge now."

"Don't come near me!"

"Sssh. Easy. I just can't hear you over the noise of the generator."

Leonard's gaze threshed wildly across the growing crowd, the traffic jam of emergency vehicles blocking two lanes of Wilshire. "What's a generator going for?"

"See the firemen there? They're inflating a big air bag right below us."

Leonard smiled contemptuously at the scurrying figures in yellow turnout coats. "Big deal. I'll just move around the building."

"Can't. Patrolmen hiding on the roof. Waiting for you with butterfly nets."

"Then I'll just jump to miss their fucking bag. Bounce off the edge onto the cement."

"I knew you'd come up with something. Do you smoke?"

The bag was billowing up into its plump shape, but altogether too slowly to suit Murtaugh. He could see that Riggs was now perilously close to the jumper on the parapet, close enough for the man to snatch the detective by the jacket sleeves and yank him down to a mutual death.

Murtaugh turned to the battalion chief standing with one boot on the running board of the lime-colored engine. "How much longer before she's fully inflated?"

"Two minutes, Sarge."

"Shit." Shading his eyes against the declining sun, Murtaugh peered up again, then laughed softly in disbelief.

Perhaps it had been the distance involved, or the hazy sunlight or even his own tension, but he thought he'd seen Riggs and the jumper joined together by a pair of handcuffs.

"You know, you don't have the patent on this," Riggs said, looking down between his piebald chukkas at the parking lot. The manager was shouting at his salesmen to start backing a line of anthracite and champagne and silver-gray Mercedes out of the way—in case Leonard did indeed miss the bag. "Been thinking about it myself lately."

"Sure."

"No really, Len. See, my wife died two months ago. I came home from work one night . . . and she was like asleep. Except she wasn't asleep. She was *gone*."

"You're breaking my heart."

Riggs nodded sadly, then began inching the seat of his Levi's across the top of the parapet.

But Leonard recoiled from his furtive approach. "Stop! Don't touch me! I'm not doing anything wrong!"

Leonard's lips were slightly blue, which made Riggs turn his face. "I know that. Not like you're murdering anyone."

"Right. The only one hurt is going to be me."

"I know you said you don't smoke. But would you like one now, considering the occasion?"

"Yeah, maybe."

Rigg's fingers were trembling as he pried two cigarettes out of a fresh pack. Leonard noticed. "Are you scared?"

"Yes and no," Riggs answered with a hint of a smile. "I don't know how to describe it."

"Me neither."

"Jump!" a beefy woman in a turquoise muumuu shouted from the boulevard below. "Get it over with!"

Riggs cupped his hands around his mouth. "Only if you give me a target—lie down and spread your legs!" Then below his breath: "Fat chance, cunt."

A rumble came from Leonard's throat that Riggs only dimly recognized to be a laugh. "You're bonkers—for a cop, I mean."

"Well, before you get to feeling superior, just ask yourself why they picked me to come up here and talk to you. Here you go."

When Leonard reached out for the cigarette, there followed a loud click, and before he could jerk back his arm he realized that he was now wearing a handcuff around his wrist. "Hey!"

Riggs snapped the other cuff around his own wrist.

"Hey, you rotten fuck!"

"We're in this together, Len. Till death do us part. You can go if you want. But you'll be taking me with you. *Now* we're talking murder."

"The key! Give me the key!"

"Oh, thanks for reminding me." Riggs fished the small chrome key from the change pocket of his Levi's, and then watched it fall away. "One-one thousand . . . two-one thousand . . ."

"Nice try." A calmness had come into Leonard's face, which had gone from looking agonized to strangely tender. "But I still have to jump."

The key tinkled against the pavement below.

Riggs fixed his eyes on Leonard. They shone with anger, but his voice was low: "Then let's get it over with."

And with that, Riggs dived out into the smog, which was now redly lucent from the sunset, and Leonard came tumbling after him.

Screaming all the way down.

•   •   •

"In here, crazy fucker!" Into the Mercedes show room, lustrous with the latest models, Murtaugh dragged Riggs by the handcuff chain that had just been severed by a fireman's pair of bolt cutters.

A salesman saw the look in the homicide sergeant's eyes and rushed for a back office, leaving the two cops alone.

Murtaugh started to speak, but found himself too confused and enraged, and even frightened for Riggs, to string words together. Instead, he seized the man by the front of his leather jacket, which was still splattered with the jumper's vomit.

Riggs stiffened in his clutch, but said quietly, "Please, let go of me."

"What the fuck did you just *do?*"

"You've got eyes. Trust them."

"Answer me, man!"

"If you let go of me." An ominous light came into Riggs's eyes. "Don't let go of me, and I'll have to bury your dick in the carpet."

Murtaugh's lips parted at the corner, revealing clenched teeth. But he released Riggs, pushing him back slightly as he did so. "What was that stunt?"

"I controlled the jump. You wanted him down. He's down."

"And screaming about a lawsuit!"

Riggs shrugged. "At least he's alive to sue. Dead men don't sue."

A yowl escaped from Murtaugh's throat, and he spun around to begin pacing in the space between two SELs. "Okay, okay, okay," he chanted to gain control of himself. Then he stopped and faced Riggs again. "Martin, give it to me straight—do you want to kill yourself?"

"Oh, for chrissake, Roger—"

"Shut up. Direct question. Yes or no?"

"I got the job done here, didn't I?"

"That is not the answer I asked for!"

Suddenly, Riggs advanced on him, and Murtaugh's immediate thought was to go for the man's eyes and kill this nut case before he himself was killed.

But then Riggs halted short and did nothing more threatening than gesture with the blade of his hand. "What do you want to hear, man? Sure, it's crossed my mind, like it has to everybody else in this godforsaken line of work."

"Then why don't you do it?"

Riggs's eyes misted, and he glanced away. "The job . . . that's the reason. I've still got the job to do."

"But you ain't going to step aside if death makes a grab for you, right?"

Riggs looked back again. He grinned defiantly. "I'm not afraid."

"Well, here, baby . . ." Murtaugh's voice was singsong with sarcasm as he pulled out his revolver and offered it to Riggs. "Some guys are sentimental about using their own pieces. Take mine. In the mouth. Forty-five-degree angle to maximize tissue damage. Not the temple. We've both been out on some poor asshole who just knocked himself silly by deflecting a round off his temple."

Riggs seized Murtaugh's gun hand at the wrist and brought the muzzle tight under his chin. Then his index finger overlaid Murtaugh's on the trigger and began to apply pressure.

The hammer crept back, then went still, amazingly still, before it started to fall forward.

Their gazes met and held fast as the hammer continued to fall forward.

"Jesus!" Murtaugh jammed the webbing of his hand in front of the firing pin and prevented it from striking the cartridge primer.

Laughing, Riggs let go of Murtaugh. "Give me your handcuff key."

Then Murtaugh also gave a laugh, but his was less strident, more thoughtful than Riggs's. "Wait, wait, wait. I've got it. I've finally got a handle on it. You're bucking for a stress disability pension, right?"

Riggs said nothing.

"Yeah, baby, fifty percent of your pay. Tax free, too. Plus a big workmen's compensation settlement." Still laughing, Murtaugh patted Riggs's shoulder. "One of my men pulled it off a couple of years ago. Sat at his desk clicking ball bearings between his fingers. Told the psychologist he could get hard just thinking about ammunition. Said he couldn't make it with his girl unless there was a war movie on the tube. He's got a pizza joint in Encino now. Is that what you want, Riggs? A pizza joint in Encino?"

Riggs smiled. "I'd blow my brains out first." Rubbing the cuff that was still attached to his bruised wrist, he started for the door, but then shuffled to a halt and turned, his face serious. "Roger?"

"What?"

"Is there something *wrong* about getting hard when you think about ammunition?"

CHAPTER 8

OVER A LONG, sleepless night, Murtaugh came to the conclusion that there was only one way to proceed in the matter of Martin Riggs.

If he came right out and bitched the narcotics sergeant, detective headquarters would construe the grievance to be the old inter-divisional animosity rearing its ugly head—and the deputy chief would make sure Murtaugh would have Riggs stuck to him like a barnacle until his retirement in the year 2001.

No, the Riggs problem required more subtlety than that.

And the solution hinged on a telephone call Murtaugh found difficult to make on the morning after this restless night.

For one thing, Riggs went everywhere he did, and Murtaugh didn't want to arouse the man's razor-sharp paranoia by asking him to step out of the office while he handled some "private matters."

But also, Murtaugh felt more than a little guilty about what he had to do. He wanted to make the career-busting call in complete privacy.

Burke, after some legwork that led to the dealership where Amanda Hunsaker had purchased her Porsche, had gotten a line on her sugar daddy. It was only an address, but that was a start. And, as Murtaugh and Riggs drove out to Bel Air to have a chat with this philanthropist, Roger suddenly snapped his fingers. "Damn."

"What is it?" Riggs asked from behind the wheel.

"I forgot to make a call."

"Want me to find a booth?"

"Yeah, pull off the freeway."

As soon as they were on Crenshaw Boulevard, Murtaugh said, "Wait, we're close enough to downtown for me to use my mobile radio phone. Pull over in that vacant lot there so I can get it out of the trunk."

"Sure." Riggs popped the trunk latch from a lever under the dashboard.

Just to make it look good, Murtaugh tried several times to dial the portable unit before saying irritably, "Shit, I've got to transmit out in the open. Can't make the connection from here."

"Be my guest," Riggs tucked a Winston in the corner of his mouth, lit it, then closed his eyes as the smoke curled up around his nose and into his hair.

Murtaugh cut across the litter-strewn lot, frowning at the dust that clung to his oxfords, then strode out onto the Crenshaw overpass on the Santa Monica Freeway.

Below, the mid-morning traffic was whispering past as he hastily dialed the number he had memorized from a department bulletin on job-related stress.

"Personnel support," a receptionist chirped.

"Psychologist, please."

"One moment, please."

Then the doctor answered. "Good morning."

"Yeah, uh, this is Sergeant Murtaugh, robberty/homicide, ma'am . . ." His voice trailed off as he drew a blank on what to say next.

"Yes, Sergeant, how are you this morning?"

"Fine, ma'am, thank you. Listen, I'm phoning about an associate of mine . . ."

"Yes?"

All at once, Murtaugh knew exactly what it would have felt like had he sold out and gone to internal affairs years before. Glancing back at the car and Riggs's drowsy face, he almost choked on the fink words he was about to utter. "And this associate of mine really needs help. Bad. Otherwise I wouldn't be doing this."

"I see. Well, how about telling me something about *him*, Sergeant. Is he a cop like you?"

"Yeah, same grade, years in. Everything—almost."

"Is he drinking heavily? Increasingly moody? Exhibiting symptoms of social withdrawal?"

"All of the above. And then some."

Then the psychologist chuckled. It was friendly and supportive and utterly professional, but Murtaugh still didn't like it.

"Sergeant," she went on, brightly, "why don't we drop the pretense and just make an appointment? Everybody begins by talking about some *associate*—just as you are." She could be heard leafing through some pages. "Now . . . how does next Tuesday at nine-thirty jibe with your commitments?"

"No!"

Her sigh gusted in the receiver. "Sergeant, there's no shame in having a little talk with me."

"I mean it *really* isn't me."

"Are you serious?"

"Sweet Jesus, yes. My elevator still goes all the way to the top floor. At least, I think it does." He laughed a bit too loudly, then winced when she didn't join him. "But honestly, I'm talking about somebody else. Somebody with a fuse lit to blow the works."

"In what way?"

"He's going to kill himself. I mean it. He had a squirrelly shooting last week. And now, last evening, he takes a swan dive off—"

"Martin Riggs."

For an instant, Murtaugh thought she might be a mind reader, but then he dismissed the notion as being absurd.

Just mention the words "squirrelly" and "shooting"—and the entire free world knew you were talking about Riggs. "Yeah . . . him."

"Thank God, you've called," she said gratefully.

"How's that, ma'am?"

"At last, somebody has the courage and good sense to break the blue barrier. Thank you, Sergeant."

"Then I guess you're on to him?"

"*And then some*—to borrow your own words."

"Well, in your expert opinion, is he nutso?"

"Nutso?" She chuckled, but then hesitated to go on. "Well, I suppose I can trust you with this . . . seeing how you're willing to help him."

"Please do."

"I first saw Martin Riggs four years ago, after another one of his famous shooting incidents. Then I would've said that he's a depressive neurotic."

"Is that bad?"

"In stressful occupations—yes, according to the book. But fifty percent of the people in this department are depressive neurotics. It's the unfortunate truth: Pre-morbid obsessive-compulsives are drawn to cop work like flies to sugar."

Murtaugh considered asking her about the behaviors typical of this personality type, but then decided against it. Trish had already reminded him that there were periods when he drank a little too much. And he often wondered what the question meant on the psychological test he'd taken for sergeant: *Do you enjoy a sporting event more if you bet on it?* Shit, he'd just lost fifty bucks to an bunco-forgery detective on last Sunday's Rams game. And he had a C-note riding on the play-offs. "But what about now? Is Riggs over the edge?"

"Has there been psychotic decompensation? Maybe. But it could also be an excessive grief reaction. As you know, he just lost his wife—"

"No . . ." Murtaugh gazed back in amazement at the car. "I *didn't* know, Doctor."

"You mean you're working with him, and he didn't tell you?"

"Not a word."

"Christ."

"What happened to her?"

"Heart failure. Thirty-four years old. With no children, his parents both deceased, the woman comprised his entire support system. In layman's terms, he adored her."

"Shit," Murtaugh whispered. "He's *really* a funny guy, isn't he?"

"To say the least."

"Well, Doctor, what do I do from here? Drop him by your office?"

"You mean, promise him the circus and ice cream after—while I wait here with the straight jacket? No, I'm afraid it's not that simple. Not with patient's rights. The peace officer bill of rights. The stonewalling administration of this department. And Riggs himself. He's a brilliant obstructionist, you know."

"Then what do I do?"

"Sergeant, you know the provisions of section 5150 of the welfare and institutions code. We can hospitalize him for a seventy-two-hour evaluation—only if certain conditions are met. Is he gravely disabled, say, by delusions or hallucinations?"

"Uh, he told me he wanted to fly. But he also said that was when he was a kid."

"Sorry, a common enough anal-retentive fantasy. Has he declared an intention to harm himself?"

"Not outright. He's awful cagey that way. Says he's thought about it, but the job keeps him from carrying through. What do I do?"

"Are you friends with him?"

"Not really."

"Well, try to win his trust. Get him to reveal his innermost feelings. And when he declares that he intends to commit suicide, slap a 5150 hold on him and phone me immediately."

Murtaugh exhaled. "Okay, Doctor, if that's the only way to go."

"It is. And again, thank you, Sergeant Murtaugh. It's people like you who restore my faith in the criminal-justice system."

"Yeah, sure." Murtaugh slowly returned the receiver to its cradle, then turned and bumped squarely into Martin Riggs's chest. "Shit!"

"Sorry," Riggs said evenly.

"Don't you ever do that again, man!" Murtaugh started marching toward the car. "Why're you sneaking up on me like that?"

"I got bored. What took you so long? Are you sick or something?"

"What do you mean?"

"You said *doctor* on the phone."

Murtaugh paused, his eyes darting back and forth for a moment. "Yeah, well, don't put it out, but my prostate's been killing me. You mind?"

"No, sorry I asked. I figured I was the only pain in the ass you had right now."

"Funny."

Riggs lowered his voice. "You know, there's no excuse for anyone to sneak up on you unless you're beside running water or the wind's hard in your face. It's amazing you didn't wind up in a POW camp."

"Well, I've been out of the jungle for damn near twenty years, Riggs. How about you? You out of the jungle yet?" But then, grumbling under his breath, Murtaugh halted and shook the anger out of his hands. He turned and tried to apologize with a smile. "I didn't mean that, Martin. I don't know what I meant."

"No problem, Roger."

"Yeah . . . no problem."

As Riggs sped farther and farther up the palmetto-lined street, ever higher into Beverly Hills toward Bel Air, the yards became broader and more expensively landscaped.

The houses began sprouting second stories, gables, and genuine slate roofs. The gin probably became drier and the cocaine purer, too, he thought to himself, taking the sylvan curves at sixty miles per hour. "You got anything on this joker we're supposed to roust?"

"Slow down. And no, he's clean except for a DUI six years ago."

"Does he know we're coming?"

"Do I look stupid or something?"

Riggs didn't answer. "What about ID—do they have a match on Dixie Monroe's prints?"

"Not yet."

"Why not?"

"Sweet Jesus, Riggs, they had to take elimination prints from the neighbors, the building maintenance crew, and a dozen customers Amanda was stupid enough to note in her book by full name. And the quality of what they were able to lift off the bathroom mirror, the coffee table, the two wine glasses on the night stand—fucking mud. Smears and smudges. They'll be lucky to come up with any kind of comparison."

"I know, I know. Just kidding. You'll just have to get used to me."

Now it was Murtaugh's turn to fall silent.

Riggs drove past the Bel Air address twice, and still Murtaugh was not entirely convinced that Burke had come up with the right residence.

"Maybe it was the one down the lane."

"That was a half *mile* down the lane," Riggs said. "This is it unless your detective is dumber than he looks." He pointed at the brass numbers bolted to the granite wall. This ten-foot-high barrier was breached only by a massive wooden gate that looked like it belonged over a moat. In a planter of English ivy was a blue Westinghouse security system sign with a warning that the arrival of an armed patrol was imminent. "What do you want to do, Roger?"

"Drive up around a minute. I expected rich but not

royal rich. Six years ago, he had an address in lowly Eagle Rock.''

"You afraid he'll beef us to the deputy chief, or maybe even the chief?''

"No. Let's just get some idea what we're walking into. It's called caution. It's why some cops retire to Lake Arrowhead after thirty years and others retire to taps.''

"You really should be teaching at the academy.''

The sycamore-shaded lane meandered up onto a bluff. Riggs parked on a curve that overlooked the estate and asked Murtaugh if he had binoculars.

"Careful, they're mine, not the department's.'' Murtaugh handed him a pair of Bushnells from under the front seat. Then after a moment he asked, "What do you see?''

"*Nada*—this joint has more trees than Nam. I'll be back in minute.''

"Whoa.'' Murtaugh had snagged him by the sleeve of his leather jacket. "We're going to have a little talk first.''

"Talk?''

"Yes, an understanding. I want some assurances from you.''

"About what?''

"Your behavior in there.''

"You want to climb over instead?'' Riggs gestured at the wrought-iron spikes that bristled blackly over the entire length of the wall, then at Murtaugh's crisp-looking suit. "What do threads like that cost? Five, six hundred?'' Then he indicated his own clothing. "Last year's leather clearance at K-Mart. 'Bye.''

Murtaugh held fast to Riggs's sleeve. "Listen, man, don't kill anybody. I don't care what happens—no killing. Ix-nay on the illing-kay. And I want you back here in ten minutes, preferably with nobody having seen you.''

"You mean, no prisoners?''

"No prisoners.''

Murtaugh knew that it was asinine.

But as soon as Riggs was over the wall—having scaled

it with that grace which seemed all the more surprising because of his appearance—Murtaugh was filled with a powerful urge.

He tried to think of something else. Anything else. He even reminded himself that he'd erred mightily by letting the maniac off his leash. God only knew what Riggs would do without supervision.

"Shit."

But then Murtaugh could resist it no longer.

He slid the ashtray out of the dash and, first looking up and down the lane for cars, flung the contents out into the chaparral.

There must have been three or four thousand stinking butts in there.

Then and only then did he feel free to worry about what Martin Riggs might do on his own.

Shifting the binoculars from the baronial house to the first terrace below the solarium, Riggs suddenly smiled. Through a breezeway he had a peek at the swimming pool, and circling around it was a young woman on a red scooter. He could barely hear the engine at this distance.

Upon completing each lap around the pool, she laughed and waved at someone Riggs couldn't see from his vantage in an avocado tree. And when she waved, her breasts jiggled in her halter top.

"Oh yes . . . oh yes . . . hello."

He couldn't follow her progress all the way around the pool: The roof of a pool house blocked part of the deck.

Then she failed to appear from behind the obstruction on schedule.

"What gives, babe?"

But about thirty seconds later, she putted back into view, one hand on the throttle and the other cupped around her nose. Then her thumb stemmed a nostril while she inhaled deeply.

"Naughty, naughty." Riggs hoped that her companion would show himself. Somehow, he had no doubt that it was a man—perhaps from her laugh, which seemed a bit too eager to please.

And, from his exhaustive experience with the species, he felt he could describe the man sight unseen: white shoes, white slacks, and a triangle of gray hair showing in the "V" of his yellow silk shirt. Gold chains, unless he'd heard that they were no longer in vogue. At this point—in the first heady flush of his instant cocaine wealth—he would have no outstanding warrants, unless they were for traffic violations or nonsupport of his first brood. And he was so full of his own candy, his sense of mega-power, his invincible cleverness—he would probably be crazy enough to fight and run if badged. And why not? He was such a mover and a shaker he could abandon these digs this afternoon and buy better in the morning. Of course, if he were really smart he'd take the rap and go downtown with a smile on his puss and a four-star attorney at his side. The judge was probably into recreational use himself. Suspended sentence. Maybe a fine the loser could pay out of pocket money.

Yet, Riggs found himself praying that this one wasn't very smart. The law became meaningful only when the judge got by-passed. Sad but true.

"Okay . . . where's your security?" So far, Riggs had spotted no armed weightlifters in three-piece suits. If this guy had had anything to do with Amanda Hunsaker's death, he would have some heat on the premises: You couldn't kill without thinking about getting killed yourself; the association was inevitable.

He scanned the pool again, and realized that his opening had arrived, one big enough to let both Murtaugh and himself slip through and perhaps make a tidy little bust as well.

The woman on the bike had just waved farewell to the unseen man and was coming down the long drive toward the front gate.

Riggs dropped out of the tree and hit the ground running, his chukka boots crashing through the thick mat of dry leaves.

"Where've you been?" Murtaugh asked a bit drowsily. "I said ten minutes, not a half hour."

Riggs sprang the door hinges in his haste to get behind the wheel and fire up the engine. "Get down."

"Why?" Murtaugh's eyes narrowed. "Hey, what'd you do in there?"

"Nothing. Lie across the seat—quick!"

"If you did nothing, why are you so happy?"

"God just showed me the way to cut the small talk with this joker and get right to the squeeze play."

Murtaugh was still sitting erect. When he spoke, his voice was very calm: "Are you saying *God* just spoke to you, Martin "

"Yeah." Riggs turned up the private drive and braked hard in front of the formidable wooden gate.

"And what did he say to you, Martin?"

"He said: 'Tell Roger to get his mug and Brooks Brothers suit out of sight so we got half a chance not to be made out as cops in this fucking government-plated rig.' " He forced Murtaugh down by the neck.

"Is somebody coming out?"

"You're getting smarter every minute you spend with me."

Murtaugh, his head between his knees and the muscles in the small of his neck bearing the strain of the awkward position, heard an electric whine and then the rumble of the gate sliding open. "Who is it?"

"Shut up."

Now a two-stroke engine, perhaps to an ATV or a motorbike, could be heard over Riggs's sudden laughter. "Is it still on?" he called out to someone as if he knew the person.

"Oh yeah, sure," answered a female voice. Pure valley girl. He was glad he'd broken Rianne of the inane dialect.

"Who are you?" she asked, giggling a little.

"John's friend." Riggs didn't miss a beat; even Murtaugh believed him. He'd heard that, despite his excessive extracurricular gunplay, he was a gifted dope cop.

"Oh yeah, sure. I remember you."

Riggs started driving forward. "You coming back later, babe?"

Her answer was lost in the rapid acceleration of the car up the serpentine driveway. "It's clear, Rog."

At the far end of this tunnel formed by red eucalyptus trees, Murtaugh could see the front entry of the house, an oaken door that belonged up at the Hearst Castle. He took his revolver out of his belt holster and, from nervous habit, cracked open the cylinder to make sure it was fully loaded.

It was a cop's most repetitive nightmare: pulling the trigger in a deadly moment and nothing happening. Trish claimed she could hear it coming just in the way Murtaugh's breathing would suddenly change. "What's the plan, Martin?"

"I think our boy's on the pool deck. And he's as dirty as spring snow."

"Any weapons?"

"That's a big unknown."

"Security?"

"Ditto."

"You're absolutely sure he's dirty?"

"No. Maybe we should phone first." Sighing, Riggs skidded the car to a stop next to a fountain of pissing cupids. "This is it."

They bailed out, and Murtaugh followed Riggs down a breezeway between the solarium and a four-doored garage. At its far end a swimming pool could be seen, covered with clear vinyl until the weather warmed up again.

"Bingo!" Riggs was staring through the panes of the solarium like he couldn't believe his luck. "Oh, thank you, God."

Inside, two young women in bikinis were standing at a patio table that was heaped with more snow than Murtaugh had ever seen outside the department's evidence storage room. They gazed at the two cops uncomprehendingly, the demitasse cups they'd been using to measure the stuff into baggies poised delicately in their hands as if they'd been interrupted at high tea.

Then Riggs, grinning broadly, buzzed them with his shield and gestured with his automatic for them to remain where they stood.

But, debutantes that they were, the pair bolted toward a door that connected to the living room of the mansion.

"Take 'em down, Martin! I'll check the pool!"

"Right."

As he trotted down the breezeway, Murtaugh heard the sound of breaking glass: Riggs smashing the obviously locked door to the solarium. "Go, Martin, go." He had one thought as he rounded the end of the shadowy passageway and broke out onto the sunlit pool deck, clutching his revolver in both hands before him—a bust of this magnitude would give him some real leverage on Amanda Hunsaker's sugar daddy. He'd thought Riggs had been talking about a line or two of coke. But this—

Murtaugh suddenly cringed, his left hand instinctively flying up to protect his eyes.

He felt the pellets swarm past his face before he heard the throaty bark of the shotgun.

"Jesus!" Murtaugh dived behind a lava waterfall, the liquid noises unsettling him until he took stock of his body and saw that he hadn't been hit.

Using a chunk of lava for a benchrest, he then squeezed off two rounds.

The figure across the pool—little more than a silhouette in the amazing brevity of the moment—dropped to the cement, the shotgun clattering beside him.

"Stay where you are! Move and I shoot again!" Keeping his revolver trained on the prostrate man, Murtaugh cautiously sidestepped around the pool. His heart was beating like it wanted out of his chest, but he was also experiencing an intense gratification that he was still alive. It was such an overwhelming feeling, he knew that standing on the gold-medal tier at the Olympics would pale in comparison.

Riggs came flying out of the breezeway, his automatic held at the ready.

"Easy, Martin, I already dinged him."

They closed in on the man at the same time, and Riggs kicked the shotgun out onto the lush dichondra.

"Keep your hands away from your waistband," Murtaugh demanded. "Do you understand me?"

Squinting up at them, he nodded yes. His face was sweaty with pain. He was clutching a bloody shoulder, but there was no muscle deformation or visible bone splintering—so he'd been lucky. Murtaugh took pride in this. "See that, Martin? A nonfatal shooting incident. Far preferable to a fatal one."

"Why?"

"We now have a prisoner with whom we might communicate, correct?"

"I thought you said no prisoners."

"We *always* try to take prisoners, Martin."

"I must've been sick the day they covered this at the academy."

"Undoubtedly." Murtaugh had just holstered his revolver and was reaching for his handcuffs, which were folded over his belt along his back, when the instant slowed to a fraction of ordinary speed.

And from this illusion of slow motion he knew that he'd made a mistake.

On an agonized groan, his eyes pinched shut, the man had curled into a fetal crouch. But only when his hand hiked up the cuff of his trousers did the ankle holster become visible. Slowly but inexorably, a nickel-plated snub-nosed gun was pulled out of that holster, and Murtaugh found himself with nothing more lethal than a pair of handcuffs in his right hand to answer this unexpected threat.

Even worse, Riggs was to his back, and Murtaugh was afraid the lunatic would open fire right through him.

The muzzle of the nickel-plated gun was now swinging around, and the man was baring his teeth viciously, as he raised himself up on an elbow and began applying pressure to the trigger. Murtaugh could only wonder how badly it would hurt. His shrapnel wound in Nam had not immediately caused him pain, although it had been frightening not to be able to breathe. He would prefer pain to that hell of slow suffocation.

Then, in this excruciating moment of slow motion, Murtaugh felt himself being hurled aside as Riggs's ratty chukka boot glided past his face and connected with the gun, sending it spinning and glittering against the reddish sun and then far out onto the lawn. Riggs's pivot kick did not stop there: His boot slammed against the man's flank to the unmistakable crack of shattered ribs. Like a rag doll, the screaming man bent at the middle and rolled into the pool.

For a split second, he was suspended on the vinyl cover like a water beetle on the surface tension of a pond. But then, he slowly sank into the material, ripping it free from its moorings on the sides of the pool. Despite his thrashing, it clung to him, then completely enveloped him, suspending him a foot below the surface in a translucent cocoon that quickly conformed to the shape of his body.

Murtaugh and Riggs looked at each other.

"Shit," Riggs muttered.

"I don't believe it. Well, let's get the son of a bitch."

They shed their shoes, tossed their guns and wallets onto the dichondra behind them, then dived in.

The water was shockingly cold and tinted green with algae. All this money, Murtaugh thought as he breaststroked down, and the loser still can't maintain a decent pool.

He grabbed a handful of vinyl and started pulling, but it felt like trying to tow the *Queen Mary*. The cover itself probably weighed two hundred pounds dry. He tugged again with everything he had.

Riggs was doing the same thing when he suddenly let go and raised his palms in a gesture of futility.

The cocoon slowly sank to the deepest part of the pool.

Murtaugh took a quick breath, then went down after the body once again. He grasped and turned the dying face toward him, and the sight of it made bubbles rush out of his mouth. Behind the vinyl mask, the eyes were uncaring, the material had bulged inside the gaping lips, probably blocking the airway.

He was gone.

Murtaugh broke the surface, gasping for air.

Riggs was clinging to the side of the pool, his wet hair covering his eyes. ''Ooops,'' he said.

CHAPTER 9

WHEN MURTAUGH PARKED in front of his Glendale colonial but didn't immediately get out, Riggs knew what he was about to say.

"Martin . . ."

"Yeah?" Riggs hid his smile behind his cigarette.

"Look, I'm sorry about all that shit I said back there in Bel Air." He gazed down the twilit suburban street as if searching for something that might rescue him from the words that were about to tumble from his lips. "You saved my life. Thanks."

Riggs remained deadpan and silent.

"Well, let's get inside."

Riggs waited until Murtaugh was half out of the car. "I'll bet that hurt to say."

"You have no idea," Murtaugh said without turning around.

Detouring around a skateboard, which Murtaugh gave a kick as an afterthought, they trudged up the walkway in their khaki LAPD jumpsuits, their wet street clothes tucked in bundles under their arms.

A little girl was sitting on the stoop, ministering to a black Cabbage Patch doll. She was pretty, as Riggs had known she would be. And Murtaugh's wife would be very pretty because Murtaugh was a handsome, although somewhat stuffy-looking, man. It was one of Rigg's observable axioms: A person tended to marry a person of approximately equivalent looks, good or bad. Unless money or power was involved; then even a frog could wind up with a princess.

"Hi, Daddy." Giggling, the little girl squirmed rather than have Murtaugh tousle her doll's hair, which she had been setting with tiny bobby pins. Then she eyed Riggs. "Is he a crook?"

Murtaugh started to say something, but then changed his mind. "No, honey, this is Martin, my partner." He scooped his daughter up and hugged her.

Riggs watched them for a moment, then looked away.

"Tell Martin what you think of crooks."

"They're butt heads."

She giggled again, and the sound brought goosebumps to the back of Riggs's neck. He had no idea why. "Kid's no dummy," he said at last.

"Come on, I can hear ice clicking in a couple of glasses."

Murtaugh threw back the front door, the kind with a slender pane of bumpy amber glass, and the smells of a living house hit Riggs like a slap. The aura of the place was so instantly pleasant and comforting that he really didn't want to go inside—only because he would then have to leave again.

"Go ahead, man," Murtaugh said. "Don't worry, after that little dip, you smell better than you have all week."

The axiom held true: Mrs. Murtaugh was a beautiful woman with warm, slightly sad eyes, which now registered the fact that her husband and Riggs were in jumpsuits. Something had happened; but she would wait to ask. She smiled. "Hi."

"Honey, this is my new partner, Martin Riggs. Martin—Trish."

"Pleasure."

"Is roast okay with you, Martin?"

"Fine, thanks."

Meanwhile, Murtaugh had crouched at the oven and opened the door a few inches to the splattering sounds of meat juices. "No," he said gravely, then more anxiously. "Sweet Jesus, no!" With that, he slammed the oven shut and bolted out of the kitchen, his eyes feverish. "Burbank!" he cried from the other room.

Trish ignored him. "Have you been in robbery/homicide long, Martin?"

"No, I'm actually assigned to narcotics. Roger and I are teamed up temporarily. Headquarters project."

Her eyes dimmed at the shoptalk, until a more interesting question occurred to her. "Are you married?"

"No." Riggs coughed, although he had no reason to. "Well, sort of."

Her smile revealed nothing, although he suspected she thought that he was separated.

"Oh mercy!" Murtaugh burst back into the kitchen, clutching a bored-looking tabby cat to his chest. "I thought you was a goner, Burbank!"

Trish swatted him around the head and shoulders with a potholder. "You insult my cooking one more time, you conceited Creole and—!"

"Sugar, sugar, please!"

It was obviously a ritual. And, watching them laugh, Riggs suffered an envy so strong it felt like hatred. He tried to grin for their sake, but realized that it was more of a grimace because the Murtaughs quit playing and seemed somewhat embarrassed.

Roger started fixing the drinks. "Canadian Mist all right, Martin?"

"Great." He tried not to sound too eager, but he was dying for a stiff shot. He reached down to pet the cat, but it scampered through his legs and hid under the table.

"Mom—" A girl of perhaps seventeen stood in the entryway, a deeper color coming to her light brown face when she noticed Riggs leaning against the refrigerator.

She was better looking than either of her parents, which Riggs wouldn't have guessed. "Oh hi, Daddy."

"Rianne, this is Mr. Riggs, my partner."

"Name's Martin," he told her, not missing the point behind Murtaugh's *Mr. Riggs* business. "And nice to meet you."

She gave him a look that was all eyelashes. "Hi."

"Notice the shoes," Trish stage-whispered to Murtaugh.

He handed a highball glass to Riggs, then inspected his daughter's feet as if for trench foot. "Nice shoes, honey. How much were they?"

"One seventy-five."

Murtaugh finally blinked. "Dollars?"

Rianne nodded innocently.

"Dollars?"

Trish put a hand on his forearm. "They were the only ones like it. Handmade in Milan."

"Shit, I don't care if those are the shoes that got Dorothy back from Oz—they ain't worth one hundred and—"

"Watch your mouth, Rog."

"It's my wallet I got to watch around here!"

Riggs slipped through a swinging door into the family room, which was illuminated only by a color television. A boy—ten, maybe eleven—glanced away from the screen, realized that Riggs was neither a threat nor even vaguely interesting, and went back to the scene in which The Dirty Dozen killed off most of the German high command.

Having successfully broken the news about her Italian shoes, Rianne swept out of the kitchen, coming close to brushing against Riggs as she made her way upstairs. She was wearing pink Danskin tights, which he hadn't been able to scrutinize with Murtaugh watching him like a hawk. Now the unrestricted view of her high buttocks and long haunches made him wince.

Then it came to him with a sense of shame: This was the first inkling of a sexual urge he'd had in two months.

It felt like cheating.

But it had to be a good sign—the desire to make love again. Didn't it?

Filling his mouth to the roof with Canadian Mist, Riggs finally decided not to put too fine a point on the matter.

Murtaugh and Trish were down to whispering with the tap running to cover their voices, except that Riggs could hear every word drifting out of the kitchen.

"Okay, what's going on, Rog?"

"What do you mean?"

"What do you mean, *what do I mean?* You come home with a man who looks positively depressed. Both of you with wet clothes. And you ask?"

"Yeah, yeah, yeah, keep your voice down." Murtaugh paused. "We were involved in a shooting this afternoon."

"Down at the beach?"

"No, a swimming pool in Bel Air."

"What were you doing with guns in a swimming pool?"

"We weren't in the goddamned pool with our guns."

"Then how'd you get wet?"

"I mean, we jumped in the pool after I shot this loser."

"Oh, Rog," she said somberly. "That doesn't sound good . . . it doesn't sound good at all."

"What?"

"Shooting a swimmer. Was it his pool?"

"Let's discuss it later."

"Are you off work for a couple of days?"

"Just tomorrow, while the shooting-investigation team wraps up. I plan to catch up on my paperwork here."

"Did you have to do it, baby?"

"Yeah, I did. Everything's okay with the department, honest."

"Are *you* okay?"

"Yeah. Just tired."

"I love you."

"I love you, baby."

After dinner, Murtaugh freshened their drinks and asked Riggs if he wanted the grand tour.

"Sure."

Cops adore their homes, love to repair and improve them even when there's no reason. As the perception becomes stronger and stronger and finally overwhelming that the world outside is forever lost to violence and greed and vice, home improvement becomes an obsession; Riggs was secretly gratified to see that Murtaugh was busting out a dining room wall for a breakfast nook. Roger was infected. Sheets of dry wall were neatly propped in a corner; nails waited in a coffee can. Order in the midst of chaos— the impossible but persistent human dream.

"Trish is on my ass to finish this. Then we're going to build a redwood deck out back for a Jacuzzi."

"Hmmm."

"You look like you'd be pretty handy with tools, Martin."

"No—all thumbs." He'd been suckered with that line before.

Eventually, after inspecting eight rooms and the gun collection in Murtaugh's study, they wound up in the triple garage, which harbored a trailered bass boat and a yellow Ford station wagon with room to spare.

Murtaugh climbed up the stern ladder like Admiral Halsey being piped aboard his flagship, then waved for Riggs to come on deck, too.

They each took a swivel chair, and unconsciously sighed as if they were out on Lake Perris.

"Thoughts?" Murtaugh asked.

Riggs immediately knew what he meant. "Why would this joker kill Amanda Hunsaker?"

Murtaugh nodded. "Jealousy?"

"Won't do. He had more gorgeous pussy on his trap line than he knew what to do with. No, that lounge lizard wasn't the kind to suffer a broken heart over an angel-faced hooker."

Murtaugh took a long, thoughtful sip. "There's always blackmail."

"You need a reputation before you can be blackmailed."

"Then how about a double cross, strictly business? Amanda decided to set up shop on her own? So he clipped her wings the old-fashioned way—he *burned* her."

"Sounds promising. I've seen it a thousand times before. But then that blows our idea about Dixie Monroe right out the window. She doesn't exactly mesh with this guy's scene. The broads we rounded up at the estate weren't professionals. Coke whores, maybe, but definitely not street types. I mean, was there a solicitation prior in the whole bunch?"

Murtaugh slowly shook his head no. "Damn."

"What about your pal, Michael Hunsaker?"

Murtaugh's eyes flashed at him. "What do you mean?"

"Any chance he offed his own daughter?"

"Jesus . . . no."

"Just a thought."

Murtaugh looked lost in his thoughts for a few moments—and from this silence Riggs realized that the man was withholding information from him. But he had learned long ago that saving a man's life will not necessarily make him trust you.

Murtaugh finally looked up. "Ready for another, Martin?"

"No thanks, I've got to get going."

"Why rush off?"

"Who's rushing? I'm just going."

"That's one of the problems of this profession. Rushing at all hours of the day and night. It gets where a man doesn't know if he's coming or going. They say you can become severely depressed just by having your biological rhythm messed with. They say it can even lead to suicide."

"Yeah, right. Mind giving me a lift back downtown to the lot?"

Murtaugh was silent for a moment, then shrugged. "Just take my unit. I'm going to sit out the shooting investigation here at home. The lieutenant promised no more than a one-dayer. Then we can get moving again. Pick me up Thursday morning at eight."

"You got it."

"And Martin . . . thanks again."

"Forget it."

"I mean, I really can't tell Trish every last thing that happened today. Not out of shame. You pulled my oysters out of the fire, and that's the long and short of it. I told the SIT crew that verbatim. It's just that she'd worry if I told her about the close calls. And I don't want her sitting here worried to death every time I go out the door. Know what I mean?"

"Yeah." Riggs's eyes softened. "I do."

Murtaugh hoisted the garage door and Riggs went out without saying good-bye to Trish and the children.

The house was silent, sleeping.

Murtaugh sat on the couch in the family room, greenly lit by the digital time readout on the video cassette recorder. Twenty minutes to three. Still, he wasn't ready to punch the play button on the remote control clenched in his left hand. He knew too much about the slave world behind skin flicks to take any pleasure in viewing them.

But there was another reason at the heart of his reluctance to now run the tape Michael Hunsaker had given him.

Riggs had sensed it: Hunsaker was not blameless in the death of his eldest daughter.

But how was he involved? Incest? Rage at her line of work?

Murtaugh couldn't quite make the cerebral connection that seemed so close. And the harder he strained, the more it seemed to elude him.

Why had Mike Hunsaker really tried to get in touch with him last week? Certainly not the bullshit reason of trying to locate Amanda. He knew damned well where she lived. What had compelled him to make that call, knowing full well that Murtaugh despised him, everything he stood for? Why had he attempted to call in the most valuable marker he had?

The ice in his drink had melted to tiny pills, and Murtaugh swallowed them down with the last of the Canadian Mist. "Fuck."

Sitting on the boat in the garage, he'd wanted to share everything he knew—or thought he knew—with Riggs. But he just hadn't been able. Maybe because of what Riggs had said while looking over Murtaugh's firearms collection. Hefting the Weatherby .460 Magnum sporting rifle, he said, altogether too wistfully, "Killing people. Only thing I was every really good at. In Laos, on a long-range recon, I had to take out a dink forward observer on a knob of rock above us. He was directing mortar fire that was chewing our team to pieces. The guys were capping at him with their sixteens, but I told them to knock it off. It was only making him keep his head down more."

"What range?"

"Thousand meters."

Murtaugh whistled. "And a crosswind?"

Riggs smiled. "And a crosswind. With him never showing anything more than his NVA helmet . . ." He paused.

"Well, did you get him?"

"Roger, Roger," Riggs had said with that unnerving smile, "I was *born* to get him."

And now, if Murtaugh gave voice to his suspicions, would Riggs decide that he had been born to get Michael Hunsaker, too? The simple fact of the matter was that he could not control Riggs. Letting him out of his cage was one thing, but getting him back inside was entirely another.

And Murtaugh could deny it all he wanted, but the truth remained a running sore on his memory: His career, his marriage, his family—all had come into being only because Hunsaker had picked him up off that jungle trail and carried him, under fire, back to the landing zone.

He owed the man. He owed a man who was hiding something terrible.

At last, Murtaugh hit the play button.

• • •

Unnoticed, the clouds crept in from the ocean, concealed by the dense layer of smog, and suddenly it was raining in Los Angeles. Hard.

Like wrapped meat, the hookers on Sunset Boulevard were all wearing clear plastic raincoats. Riggs passed up several of them before deciding on one. At least she wasn't wearing cadaverous makeup like the others.

He rolled down the passenger-side window.

"No way, baby," she said before he got a word out.

"Say what?"

"I see the E-plates on Santa's sled. Is Santa getting short on cold-plated sleds down at vice?"

Riggs chuckled. "You honestly think I'm a cop?"

"I *know* you're a cop."

Riggs found this somewhat reassuring: At least someone wasn't mistaking him for a loser, even if she was a whore. "Okay, I'm a cop."

She laughed, but covered her mouth with a hand. Crooked teeth. "Your honesty is refreshing, Officer . . . ?"

"Ah, *Sergeant* . . . Sergeant Forno Cate. Look, this is not what you think—"

"It's exactly what I think: entrapment. A new twist on it. But it's still entrapment." She'd been around.

Riggs ran a thumbnail over his underlip as he considered this. "Okay, here's the way to convince you." He took a hundred-dollar bill from his wallet and laid it on the seat, then reached in the glove compartment for the small dictation recorder every conscientious detective stored there. Murtaugh proved no different. "Testing— one, two, three . . ." He played it back, nodded in satisfaction at his own voice, then began recording again: "This is Detective Sergeant Martin Riggs of the Los Angeles Police Department offering you . . ." He motioned for her to give her name.

"Daphne."

". . . offering Daphne one hundred dollars in United States currency to come home with me and do something unusual. Daphne may hold this cassette in her possession as insurance against arrest on the grounds that I, not she, engendered the solicitation in this carnal transaction and thereby nullified by entrapment any chance of prosecution for violation of section 647(b) of the California penal code or any other sections which become applicable as the night progresses. Of course, she will return this cassette evidence to me at the conclusion of this transaction.''

He ejected the tape and offered it to her wrapped inside the C-note.

"I've got to do this if only to tell the girls.'' Daphne took off her raincoat and shook it before getting in.

Ten minutes was all Murtaugh could take of *Les Nymphettes*.

He turned it off and sat in the near darkness, feeling nothing that even resembled arousal. He held his breath for a moment to listen outside. It was raining—he could hear it on the window awnings.

He made a mental note to ask vice to try to ID Amanda's sister nymphettes in the group shower scene, but he didn't really anticipate a promising lead out of this.

"Dear God,'' he muttered to himself, "what's with this fucking world?''

Then he finished his lukewarm drink with a grimace, got up, and set the glass on the drain board. This was followed by a quick rattle of all the door locks—front, back, garage access—and a check of the ground-level windows. Only then did he pad upstairs in his slippers.

He now regretted having viewed Hunsaker's tape in his home. Somehow, it violated the atmosphere of sanctuary he so prized about this island in Glendale. He'd grown up in a strict Southern Baptist household, and this was not the kind of thing you brought home.

But, had he tried to view it at work, his entire unit would have crowded into the squad room and gone into instantaneous heat. Before the day was done, Burke would have been hawking pirated copies of *Les Nymphettes* up and down the corridors of Parker Center.

Rianna's door was ajar.

Murtaugh looked in and smiled.

Her face, in sleep, looked very young. A faint, tinny strain of music came from her bed: She'd left her Walkman radio on.

Gently, he slipped the headphones off, recognizing the song to be "Girls Just Want to Have Fun."

He kissed her cheek, and she stirred. "Mark . . . Mark . . ."

Murtaugh frowned and withdrew.

Sliding into bed beside Trish, he found himself thinking about two things.

Why had Michael Hunsaker given him the damned tape in the first place? As a red herring—to divert Murtaugh's attention from the real question in this case: What was frightening the hell out of Hunsaker, who was a hard man to frighten?

And the other thing on Murtaugh's mind was Rianna's Mark once again. He was a nice enough Caucasian boy, but he had no ambition other than to play his electric guitar and drop by for dinner as often as possible. It was his utter lack of ambition that bothered Murtaugh. Why couldn't she . . . ?

Then he gave up and said to hell with the world. Drowsiness quickly followed.

"You left your TV on while you were out."

"I know." Riggs petted Cato and let him out the back door. "Beer?"

"Sure. Okay if I turn the channel?"

"Please don't."

Shrugging, she sat in the overstuffed chair and paged through the *TV Guide* before it dawned on her that it was two months out of date. She glanced to Riggs for an answer, but quickly decided to let it drop.

"Let's sit on the floor," he suggested, although he remained in the small kitchen, loading kernels into an electric popcorn popper.

"Why don't you want me sitting here?"

"I just like it on the floor."

"Whatever works for you."

"Do you care for television?"

"Kind of."

"I love it, especially the old movies. Like this one . . ."
He squinted at the screen. "*Mutiny on the Bounty.*
Both Clark Gable and Charles Laughton are dead more
than twenty years. But don't you believe it."

She drew her skirt halfway up her thighs, then slowly
cocked a leg so he might glimpse the crotch of her black
panties. "What do you mean?"

"Well, look at them—breathing and walking and arguing. *Mistuh Christian!*"

"I still don't get it."

"They're still alive, for chrissake! TV isn't just TV. It's
a window on another dimension. There's *life* on the far
side of that picture tube!"

"Oh." She didn't say anything more until he sat down
beside her with a bowl of buttered popcorn and two
Budweisers. "Is this going to be *it* tonight?"

His pat on her shoulder seemed brotherly, not sugges-
tive. "Babe, it don't get any better than this. Popcorn?"

"Sure."

And she smiled genuinely for the first time.

CHAPTER 10

MURTAUGH OPENED HIS eyes into a bloodshot pair that were opposing his from only six inches away.

"Good morning, Roger. Your mission, should you decide to accept it, is to—"

Bellowing with shock, Murtaugh pushed the stranger back and was fumbling for his revolver in the night-stand drawer when he realized that it was Martin Riggs, who was now convulsed with laughter at the foot of the bed.

"You stupid, stupid son of a bitch!" he shouted at Riggs. "You can get shot pulling that kind of shit!"

"I checked with Trish first. She told me you do the handcuff through the frame thing." Then he went on laughing.

"What's so fucking funny, loser?"

Riggs pointed upward.

Murtaugh craned back his head: Nick had crawled up onto the oaken headboard and was perched there with a glass in hand, which he slowly upended.

"My own son," Murtaugh said desolately, cringing under the splash of cold water. "You've gone and turned my own son against me."

• • •

"Traitor," Murtaugh said to Trish as she served him his eggs.

She winked at Riggs. "More eggs, Martin?"

"No thanks, six'll do it."

"*Six?*" Murtaugh looked at Trish, who confirmed it with a nod. "Jesus, Riggs, I hope you don't come around regularly."

"We won't mind if he does," Trish said. "He was kind enough to drive Rianna to school this morning while you were oversleeping."

A muscle rippled the skin along Murtaugh's jawline, but he said nothing.

"Aren't you going to ask me what I did on my administrative day off, Roger?"

"No."

"Well, I thought about making a little haul to Vegas, thank you. But I've been to Vegas lately. So, instead, I tripped on down to ID and goosed a buddy of mine to get going on the Hunsaker latents."

"Oh?" Murtaugh arched his eyebrows hopefully. "You got an eight-point comparison on Dixie?"

"No."

"Damn." There would have to exist eight matching characteristics between the latent fingerprints—better described as *finger smudges*—lifted with adhesive tape from Amanda Hunsaker's apartment and Dixie Monroe's on-file arrest card in order for the comparison to fly in court. "There goes our hooker brainstorm."

"What's a hooker, Daddy?" Carrie asked.

"Quiet."

"Don't get down in the mouth yet, Roger. My buddy came up with six comparison points."

"This ain't horseshoes or hand grenades—close don't count."

"Okay, not good enough for Hoyle, but good enough to call on old Dixie and see how well she does on the hot seat. Right?"

Murtaugh finally said, "Worth a try, I guess."

"Know. where she lives?"

Murtaugh nodded yes, but then said no before Trish could turn around from the stove. "I'll check with some informants." He coaxed some ketchup out of a fresh bottle onto his hash browns. "But before we do anything, I want to drop by one of the ranges. Maybe Central's—it's on the way."

"Good idea," Riggs said, smiling. "Get right back up on the bicycle. That's my philosophy."

Murtaugh kept his eyes on his plate.

He was on the verge of squeezing off his first round at the silhouette target at the far end of the underground range when a sudden thought made him lower the revolver and nudge the protector off his right ear. "You know, Martin," Murtaugh had to raise his voice over the booming issuing from the other firing lanes, "there's another way to go ahead with this Dixie idea."

The slide to Riggs's Beretta had extended back: He'd gone through a fifteen-round magazine in the time it had taken Murtaugh to load his practice rounds. "How's that?"

"Well, ID vacuumed Amanda's sheets."

"Hairs?"

"Yeah."

"Hair can't be used to prove the identity of an individual."

"I know, but we sure as hell can use it to shore up our case against her, especially since she has a nap that's kind of chestnut colored. Not many of the sisters have that color, and I think it's natural."

"Fine, but I'm not going to write the affidavit asking the judge to let us mow some grass on Dixie's lower forty."

Murtaugh shook his head and his lips curled. "You're a filthy-minded man, Martin."

"You noticed."

"Just one thing bothers me about Dixie as our suspect—"

"What?"

"If she was the one to plant the mickeyed barbs in

Amanda's medicine cabinet, why'd she admit to witnessing the jump? That's the last thing she'd want to do if she were dirty—link herself with Amanda in any way. Why didn't she just say: *I saw nothing, no how?''*

"No choice. She already knew she was under suspicion for just being there." Riggs tapped another magazine into his pistol. "Visualize this: After taking a little time to spruce up the place, especially wipe off the wine glass she used, Dixie went down the elevator and out into the parking lot. Maybe a car was waiting for her on Olympic Boulevard, whatever. She thought she was free and clear at that point until Amanda came tumbling down. Next thing, a patrol unit was on the scene lickety-split. Dixie knew damned well she didn't fit the neighborhood and had to account for her presence fast. She decided to bluff her way through and say she was coming away from a client when she heard this white chick squash her Porsche. That sounded a lot more convincing than *I don't know nothing, no how.* Especially to West L.A. patrol. Those guys frisk their wives before getting it on. They bring home the bomb dog to sniff their Christmas packages.''

Murtaugh lofted his revolver to eye level once again. "I don't know—it's all so thin.''

"Hey, the closer to the bone, the sweeter the meat.''

"Lord help me," Murtaugh muttered to himself. "His shit is beginning to make sense to me.'' He fired twice, then grinned askance to Riggs. There were now two eye holes on the previously blank face of the silhouette.

Riggs suddenly ripped through his entire clip. It almost sounded like fully automatic fire.

When he was finished, there were two nostrils and a smiling mouth below the two eyes Murtaugh's bullets had created.

"Have a nice day, Roger.''

"Keep to your own silhouette, dammit.''

In the 1920s, the house would have been referred to as a "California bungalow,'' but now Riggs felt hard pressed to call it a shack. The paint on the clapboards was blistered, and the lawn gone to knee-high wild mustard. "You want me to go around the back of this . . . this place?"

"Hang on a minute," Murtaugh said. "Let me ask this kid if Dixie's home first."

"He's not going to tell you shit."

"Not to you, maybe." Smiling, Murtaugh approached the small black boy who was apparently letting a Darth Vader toy hump a Luke Skywalker toy. "What's happening?"

Silence.

Riggs sniggered from the curb.

"My name's Roger. What's yours?"

The boy scooped up his toys and adjourned to the next yard over, where three other children were chalking pictures on the sidewalk. Murtaugh started after him, but then halted with a deep frown.

"The whole world can smell a cop, Roger. Accept it. If you wanted to be loved, you should've become a fireman."

"Come on," Murtaugh said, striding across the street toward Dixie's house on the corner.

Riggs fell in beside him. "No car—pimp doesn't trust her with one?"

"That's be my guess."

"Does she use?"

"Chips now and again. Never seen her on the nod."

"Will she fold under pressure?"

"I think so. But let me handle that end. I've dealt with her before. I've got a bit of rapport developed."

Riggs gave a meaningful look back toward the little boy. "Right, Roger." He was going to laugh as well, but then it seemed that he was riding an ocean wave on his back, staring up into sky that in a split second went from washed-out blue to a startling reddish-orange to a dusty brown color. In the same instant, his spine thudded painfully against the raggedy lawn of mustard. He saw a big spray of broken glass and splintered wood pass over him. A two-by-four came down out of nowhere and impaled itself in the rain-softened ground beside Murtaugh, who was hollering something Riggs couldn't make out.

Then South Los Angeles went dead quiet for Riggs, except for the ringing in his ears.

It came to him while he lay there stunned: Murtaugh had screamed, "Incoming!"

Riggs sat up and braced his reddened hands on his knees. He squinted against the heat at the house. "Well, Dixie, we'll always have Paris . . ."

"What'd you say?" Murtaugh was trying to unstop his ears with his fingertips.

"Never mind."

"What?"

"Never mind!"

Dixie Monroe's California bungalow was raucous with crackling and popping noises. It had also been reduced to a three-foot-high pile of rubble that was burning briskly. A porch pillar collapsed into its midst, sending up a shower of sparks that attempted to set the dead fronds on a nearby date palm afire.

Slowly, Riggs came to his feet.

Murtaugh started pummeling him on the back. "Martin!"

"What?"

"You're on fire!"

"Bullshit."

Then the flames nipped at the back of his neck. Lowering his head, Riggs squirmed out of his leather jacket, stomped on it several times with his boots before giving up. It was ruined. He could also smell singed hair—his own. "Crap."

Then he laughed.

The firemen pulled the charred section of roof off the bedspring, and Riggs knew at last that Dixie Monroe had been caught at home this morning.

Of course, what remained of her was no larger than a child's body: The heat had shrunk her to that surprisingly small size, plus contracted her muscles so that she'd curled up into what was called the pugilistic attitude. Her lips had shrunk away from her teeth, which looked to be in good enough shape to get a dental comparison. *If* she had ever been to a dentist. Pimps didn't care much for overhead.

"Whew," one of the firemen said, grimacing at her corpse. He wouldn't be lighting the old barbecue on the patio for a few weeks.

As difficult as it was, given the condition of the body, Riggs looked for any bullet or stab wounds. The explosion could have been used as a cover for a murder by more prosaic means.

Nothing on the corpse, as far as he could tell.

Then he began searching for the cause of the explosion— before the arson investigator arrived and told him to mind his own business. And then Riggs would have to smack him.

Murtaugh sat on the rear platform of the fire truck while a paramedic salved the second-degree burns on the backs of his hands.

"How'd you get this, Sarge?"

"I was jacking off and my balls blew up." Murtaugh jutted his chin at the still smoldering house. "How the hell do you think I got this?"

"Sorry."

The paramedic finished up in time for Murtaugh to flag down a Southeast division patrolman, who'd been running around the scene like he owned it. "You canvassed the neighbors yet?"

"In progress, Sergeant. Oh, I got something interesting from that little kid over there." He pointed at the boy who had switched front yards rather than spill anything to Murtaugh.

"Him? You're kidding. He wouldn't say squat an hour ago."

"Well, I kind of got a rapport developed with the people down here," the blue-suiter said modestly. "The kid wouldn't shut up."

Murtaugh frowned. "What's his name?"

"Alfred."

"What'd he see?"

"Best as I can make it out—he's only six—Alfred saw the gas meterman at that residence this morning. The kids were hiding in the bushes next door. It's a game—stalking the metermen. Indians. Didn't you play that as a kid, Sarge?"

"Metermen wouldn't come down into our quarter of New Orleans. Have your station phone the gas company. Check it out."

"Right away."

The patrolman trotted off for his radio, and Murtaugh strolled up to the youngster, who was now using orange chalk to depict what Dixie's house had looked like in the throes of the explosion.

He glanced up at Murtaugh, his eyes still evasive.

"Hello, Alfred."

"Hello."

"Is that the house that went boom?"

"Yeah."

"Did it scare you?"

"Yeah."

"Boy, it scared me, too. Will you talk with me now?"

Alfred shook his head from side to side, then went on drawing.

Riggs began at the water heater, which had been sheared in two. But the jagged edges of copper and sheet metal were curled inward, which indicated to him that the heater had not been the source of the blast. That was much more reason to believe that it had not been accidental.

He then followed the gas line to the meter, which looked like it had sustained a direct hit from a rocket-propelled grenade. On the concrete pad directly beneath the demolished meter was a radiation pattern. "All right . . . all right." This could only mean high explosives, but he knew he had only a dim hope of finding any visible trace of the HE.

Instead, he turned to the facing wall of the next-door dwelling. The shanty was abandoned. Otherwise, any occupants would now be riddled by glass—there wasn't a single window left intact. In fact, it was amazing no one had been hurt; reportedly, panes were cracked and knick-knacks toppled from shelves for a radius of three blocks.

Against the foundation, Riggs's eyes picked up something that would have been overlooked even by the arson investigator, unless he'd served in Nam: an uninteresting-looking strip of shiny paper, coiled, scorched at the edges.

"Well, hello, Mr. Boom," he whispered. "I believe I've got your number—and it's M-112. Correct me if I'm wrong."

The military's M-112 block demolition contains a pound and a quarter of C-4 plastic explosives. More than enough for a little slum clearance like this morning's. One surface of the puttylike chunk is covered with a pressure-sensitive adhesive. This tape is protected by a layer of shiny paper that the blaster peels off immediately prior to slapping the demolition onto something like a gas meter.

Military explosives. Riggs didn't like it. The standard California bomber used commercial stuff, straight dynamite or even home-doctored ammonium nitrate. C-4 was hard to come by; its brisance, or high-destructive power, and light weight put it at a premium on the black market. Anybody interested in silencing a southside working girl would opt for the economy package and use a black powder pipe bomb—not a costly block of plastic explosives.

"Okay, Mr. Boom, tell me more about yourself . . ." Once again, Riggs studied the radiation pattern on the concrete, which helped him visualize that first instantaneous expansion of gasses. Then he walked purposefully for the next-door garage, which was detached and at the weedy back of the lot. It looked like it had been strafed by fighter aircraft, the termite-weakened wood riddled by pieces of Dixie's house.

Inside the garage, Riggs almost let out a whoop when he found what he'd never hoped to—a piece of fist-sized debris, actually an assemblage of things welded together by a flash of heat. If hung in the window of a Rodeo Drive boutique, it would probably go for ten grand as a kinetic mobile executed by the genius sculptor Martino. But Riggs saw another value in it: The tiny radio receiver component and the pearls of mercury still lodged in the recesses told him much about the people that Murtaugh and he were up against.

These people were not bush league.

"Know thy enemy," Riggs chuckled to himself as he scanned the growing crowd of onlookers for Murtaugh. "This could really get fun."

"You got a gun?" Alfred asked.

"Yes, I do." Murtaugh parted his coat so the boy could glimpse his holstered revolver.

"You shoot black folks?"

Murtaugh laughed helplessly. "Honey, *I'm* black folks."

"You a cop?"

"Yes."

"Mama says cops shoot black folks."

Rolling his eyes, Murtaugh decided to change the subject. "Alfred, the man you saw earlier this morning, the man who checks the meters . . . do you know what I'm saying?"

He nodded indifferently.

"Was he black like us?"

"Shit no."

"Honey, that's no way to talk."

"I hear you before. You say shit to the doctor when he touch your hands."

"Well, then I was wrong. But back to the white man you saw this morning."

"He wasn't no white man."

"Okay . . . do you know what a Mexican-American is?"

"No."

"Was his skin light brown like this?" Murtaugh picked up a tan piece of chalk.

"No."

"Like this?" Lemon colored.

"No."

"Well, you pick out the color here that reminds you of the man who fixed Dixie's meter."

"None of this." Alfred's eyes darted to the clear plastic case in which the pieces of chalk had come. "Like this."

"Great, we're looking for Plastic Man," Murtaugh muttered under his breath, wishing that the other children who'd been here hadn't been carted off by their sitters and grandmothers in the minutes after the explosion. Then he smiled again. "All right, here's what I want you to do for an ice cream, Alfred. I want you to draw me a picture of the man you saw. Okay?"

"Okay."

The shadow of a patrolman fell between Murtaugh and the boy. "Sarge?"

"Yo?"

"Station phoned the gas company like you asked. Nix on a service call to this address this morning."

"What about a meter read?"

"None scheduled until next month."

"Good work, thanks."

Then Riggs hunkered down beside Murtaugh, grinning happily.

"What've you been messing with now, Martin?"

In silence, he handed Murtaugh a piece of debris, which the homicide sergeant was going to ridicule until he realized what it was—or had been prior to the blast. "Sweet Jesus. This thing was radio-command detonated."

"That's not all." Riggs ran a chewed fingernail along a seam in the twisted metal. "What's this look like to an old Green Beret blaster?"

"Quicksilver, ain't it?"

"Right, mercury."

Then Murtaugh was hit with a second jolt: "Mercury switches."

"Damn, I wish I had a cigar for you."

"The bastard slapped some anti-tilt shit on it just in case our bomb squad got a crack at dismantling the mother. Dirty no-good prick."

Alfred glanced up reproachfully. "You be saying shit again."

"Sorry, honey," Murtaugh mumbled. Then his eyes widened. "Good Lord, Martin, the bastard could've been watching us troop up to Dixie's house from a remote location!"

"I'd almost bet on it. This is all too elaborate just to snuff poor old Dixie. I'd also guess our blaster hit the transmitter button a little early, just so he could have the pleasure of watching us splattered all over the lawn. Lucky for us, the main force of the blast didn't vent in our direction."

"But if this is all so, he had to be on to us, our movements this morning."

"Right," Riggs said gently. "We're being watched, Rog."

"My *home* . . . they might be on to my *home*."

"This be him," Alfred announced.

Riggs and Murtaugh glanced aside at each other: The figure, although garbed in a gray, short-sleeved uniform, had bright pink eyes.

"Honey, were his eyes really *pink* like this?"

"Yeah."

"And his hair all white?"

"Yeah."

"Was he an old man then?"

"Uh-huh—like you."

Murtaugh ignored Riggs's snigger. "And what's this on his arm?"

"It be pained."

"Pained, pained . . ." Riggs shrugged to Murtaugh. "What the hell's he saying?"

"Sssh. Alfred, was it painted?"

"Yeah."

"Like a tattoo? Do you watch Popeye? Was it a tattoo like Popeye has?"

"Wait, here—" Riggs rolled up the long sleeve of his cambric shirt, revealing the Marine Corps globe and anchor. "Like this, son?"

"Yeah." Alfred's eyes lit up, then dimmed slowly again. " 'Cept no."

"Draw it for us, Alfred, please."

For three agonizingly slow minutes, they watched the boy hunch over his scribblings on the cement, his tongue protruding slightly from the corner of his mouth. At last, he sat up.

Riggs couldn't make it out: two crossed rockets, perhaps, and an upright sword. All over a big number twenty-two. "What are these?"

"Arrows," Murtaugh said, his voice hushed. "It's the Special Forces crest, Martin, for my old outfit. *De Oppresso Liber.*" Dazed, Murtaugh came to his height. "Come on, I've got some hard questions for someone in Pacific Palisades."

CHAPTER 11

RIGGS FOUND A small terrace where the upscale friends of the Michael Hunsaker family couldn't gawk at his singed hair and sooty clothes.

Most of the guests were now thronging the buffet table that had been set out by Filipino stewards on the putting green one level above him on the bluff. He could hear their subdued chatter but was unable to see them over a hedge clipped into crenellations. Of course, he could see Hunsaker's castle from nearly wherever he wandered on the grounds. The earl himself was standing behind the tinted French windows to his study, surveying the well-groomed idlers who'd come to pay their final respects to Amanda Denise Hunsaker—and have some lunch catered by La Scala while they were at it.

Roger Murtaugh was standing at Hunsaker's side, but the distance was too great for Riggs to catch his partner's expression.

Turning, he gazed over the stone parapet and out to the sea. There was a breeze, so the sky was clear. In the cove to the north of the estate, a helicopter was hovering, spalling the surface into ever-widening circles. Not just any chopper, but an Aerospeciale, a joint French-German job as sleek-looking as an attack bird like the Cobra.

Riggs was asking himself why it was lurking in the neighborhood when the pilot suddenly banked and headed out into the channel toward an offshore oil-drilling rig, which he was probably servicing. Riggs thought nothing more of it.

Two Yuppie types came tripping down the slate steps to the terrace, holding hands and laughing merrily, probably in the sure and certain hope of the resurrection of low interest rates. But they looked disappointed when they noticed that Riggs had beaten them to the secluded spot. Then their expressions—especially the young debutante's— turned haughty, as if that would be enough to make this disreputable-looking man move on.

"Go play stink finger someplace else," Riggs told them.

"God, it doesn't seem possible," Michael Hunsaker said after taking a nip of brandy. "I close my eyes and I can see her plain as day, tearing around Bragg. Raising cain. MPs phoning me to do something about her. Even the colonel on my ass. She was always a pistol, wasn't she?"

Murtaugh gave a noncommittal shrug.

"And she was always drawn to you. I'll bet you're a damned good father. I just never had the knack, Rog. Oh, my heart's in the right place. But it's a gift, I think, being a competent father. Two girls, two different mothers—and somehow I've failed them all. I've failed everybody." His eyes misted briefly, but then quickly cleared. "Well, I want to thank you for dropping by today. It means a lot to me."

"There's more to it than that, Mike."

"Oh?"

"Amanda isn't dead because of something *she* was into."

"Good—you're on to a lead then?"

"Yes. And it tells me she's dead because of something *you're* involved in."

Hunsaker held up his hands as if he were completely bewildered. "What?"

"My partner and I were down on the southside this morning. Trying to interview a prostitute who witnessed Amanda's plunge."

Hunsaker took another sip; the steadiness of his hand seemed labored. "What'd this bimbo have to say?"

"Nothing."

"Wouldn't talk?"

"Couldn't. As Riggs and I were walking up to the front porch, her house went to pieces. In case you didn't notice, my eyebrows are a little thin this afternoon."

"You mean it exploded?"

Murtaugh nodded.

"Jesus! Are you guys all right?"

Murtaugh ignored the question. "You called last week because you were going to blow the whistle."

"On whom?"

"You tell me. But I can figure this much—you were going to spill your guts. So they sent somebody to kill Amanda. Tell me I'm wrong."

Hunsaker drifted over to the desk as if in a trance and sank into the executive chair.

"Talk to me, Mike."

The Aerospeciale had looped around the drilling rig and then returned to shore. It was hovering a hundred feet above the cove again, and Riggs thought he could see the copilot checking out the Hunsaker mansion with a pair of binoculars.

"Who the hell are you guys?" he asked himself, wishing he had brought along Murtaugh's Bushnells. There appeared to be a big piece of apparatus in the rear compartment of the craft. A television videocam? Had some news crew gotten their wires crossed and somehow believed Amanda Hunsaker's memorial service to be a celebrity wedding?

Unconsciously, Riggs patted the extra clip of 9-mm ammunition he'd tucked in the back pocket of his Levi's.

He glanced at the French windows again. Only Murtaugh was visible now. He was stabbing a finger in the air as he talked. Things were heating up inside. Maybe they weren't such great buddies, after all.

"Mike, they paid a hooker to poison your daughter. You've got to talk to me!"

"I can't, Roger. I just can't."

"Why?"

"Because I've got another daughter!" Hunsaker shouted, then shut his eyes tightly. His voice was low and hoarse when he finally spoke again. "Don't you see? They've got me right where they want me."

"We'll protect your girl. We've got a special detail that does nothing but that."

Hunsaker laughed pathetically. "You don't know these men. And if you cross them so as they find out, you'll be busy enough protecting your own family. You just don't know them." Then he buried half of his face in the brandy snifter. "Or maybe you do."

"Acquaint me."

When Hunsaker opened his eyes, they were calculating. "I'll talk only if it goes no further than you. I've got to have that guarantee first."

"Mike, I'm a cop. I'm part of a department."

"I didn't ask you what you planned to be, Roger, that day I packed you back to the LZ. And the medic aboard that Huey said you would've drowned in your own blood in another five minutes without his care. You owe me, for chrissake!"

"I paid that debt in full."

"How's that?"

"I never followed through on reporting your war crimes to the inspector general."

"War crimes?" Hunsaker laughed viciously.

"That's how I saw it. And I think the IG would've seen it that way, too."

"Oh, friend—who do you think took over our group? A brigadier general from the inspector general's command, that's who. He wound up with a bigger collection of ears than I did!"

Murtaugh looked away from Hunsaker's face—for fear he'd punch it.

"So nobody was going to buy your bleeding heart crap. You were damned lucky you got hit when you did. Believe me, this general would've had you for breakfast. Hell, he shit-canned his aide for not shooting a bound and gagged prisoner!" Hunsaker fell silent for a moment, then smiled strangely. "Do we still have an understanding, Roger? Please tell me we have an understanding."

"He's the one behind this, isn't he? That brigadier."

"Jesus!" Hunsaker seethed. "Will you wise up? I'm trying to keep you out of this!"

"Then why'd you phone?"

"Let it drop, Roger. Things have changed since last week. It's a different game now."

"And it doesn't matter how they played it with Amanda?"

"Of course it does. But they've upped the stakes, and I've got to fold for this hand. I'm a realist."

"No, Mike, you're a—" But when Murtaugh looked him square in the eye to tell him that he was a coward, he found himself facing a Walther PPK. It was fitted with a silencer.

"Stand away from the windows," Hunsaker demanded, rising.

"Easy, Mike." Before stepping back into the middle of the study, Murtaugh tried to catch a glimpse of Riggs below, but instead his eye was drawn to a helicopter just as it dipped behind the north face of the bluff.

"Fast now, do as I say. Keep your hands out in front of you like that. Where's your partner?"

"Outside."

"You can do better than that."

"I'm not sure exactly. He tends to wander."

Hunsaker hurried to the windows and scanned the grounds, but apparently was unable to catch sight of Riggs either. He inclined his ear toward the whine of the retreating chopper for a moment, then turned back on Murtaugh with a smile that was full of contempt. "You wanted to know, Rog. So now I'm going to tell you . . ."

From Hunsaker's almost giddy tone of voice, his sudden willingness to talk, Murtaugh realized that this speech would be punctuated at its conclusion with a bullet from the PPK. He made up his mind to go for his revolver before the moment—and instantly if Hunsaker tried to disarm him. He had already survived one severe wound in his lifetime. He told himself that he could survive this one, too. He would make it for his family's sake. He would refuse to die. "I'm listening to you, Mike."

"Okay, here it is in a nutshell. The fall of Saigon put a lot of mercs out of work, Special Forces people who'd stayed in-country and not gone back to be dumped in some stateside airborne unit. Well, a lot of these guys shifted operations from Nam to Thailand, working part-time for the CIA, part-time for themselves."

"How's that?"

"Well, they'd fly arms and materiel out to anti-Communist guerrillas in Laos and Cambodia. They had a whole fleet of DC-3s at their disposal. Pretty soon, it occurred to an entrepreneurial type—a first sergeant you'd know if I told you his name—that it made no sense to dead-head a cargo plane out of the Golden Triangle."

"So they started flying raw opium back to Bangkok."

"You got it." Hunsaker couldn't help but grin at the cleverness of it all. "Things were going so well, this entrepreneur asked his buddy if he wanted a piece of the action. And this buddy asked his buddy. Before you knew it, half our old outfit was involved and organizing along military lines. It was beautiful back then. The efficiency."

"How'd they get their hooks into you? Were you working for the company in Thailand?"

"Oh hell, no—I was right here in Pacific Palisades at the bank. Loan officer. Hardscrabbling for a piece of the American dream like the rest of the slaves."

A sweep of Murtaugh's eyes took in the rosewood-paneled study, the shelves filled with rare books and ancient Roman artifacts. "Looks to me like you wound up with the plantation. How'd that go down?"

"Simple. The consortium was making so much money they ran into laundering difficulties. So they turned to me. My bank has branches in over thirty countries and its own air courier service. And I did so well with this assignment, the old man— "

"The brigadier?"

"Bingo. He gave me responsibility for the consortium's portfolio."

"Venture capital," Murtaugh said wryly. "Are you involved at all with the enforcement end of this thing?"

"No, I swear it. Strictly the finances. And most of them are legal now."

"Then why'd you start sweating it lately? It sounds to me like you'd just get richer and richer by keeping your mouth shut. Juggling a few books can't be that dangerous."

Hunsaker's smile vanished. "The *sums*, Roger. You can only hide so much. The sums have become enormous because of the scope of this thing. Hell, hundreds of mercs are under contract. And not just former berets like at the beginning. IRA Provos, Basque separatists, even fucking Arabs. There's a heroin-processing lab in Macao that's bigger than the Bonaventure Hotel. It's just a matter of time before some sharp accountant gets on to me. I figured this for a quick kill. In and out with a few million. But it didn't turn out that way."

"So Mike Hunsaker got cold feet. He asked the good general if he could be honorably discharged. The general said no. Mike then tried to get a hold of a cop he felt he could control, thinking maybe he could slip it to the consortium on the sly. Feed LAPD enough information to arrest most of the principals. And get himself off the hook. But the general caught wind of Mike's plan and gave the order for Mike's daughter to be snuffed. He couldn't kill Mike—the consortium needed his financial expertise. But what's a man's daughter? Especially when *billions* of dollars are at stake?''

"Nobody ever accused you of being stupid." Hunsaker shifted the PPK to his other hand. He'd been clutching it so tightly he had to shake a cramp out of his right hand. "Now you know, Rog. You know way too much."

"Not quite yet." Murtaugh was still waiting for Hunsaker to take his eyes off him, if for only a split second. "When does the next shipment come in from Macao?"

Riggs could hear the Aerospeciale coming in low along the surf. He was just leaning over the parapet to have a look when a blast of turbulent air half blinded him and the copter roared up the face of the bluff. The compartment door slid open, revealing something Riggs had never expected to see again in his lifetime: a 7.62-mm minigun.

"Shit!"

He drew his pistol in the same instant the door gunner, a bruiser with closely cropped white hair, opened fired.

"Shit!" Riggs rolled flush against the parapet as the terrace flagstones became alive with white sparks, each of them a ricochet. He was trying to squeeze off a round at the gunner when the Aerospeciale soared up toward the mansion so swiftly he was left with no shot.

He could hear screams from the gathering as the minigun opened up once again. Glass could be heard shattering.

Not taking the time to surmount the flight of steps, he crashed through the hedge, thrusting his pistol out in front of him, and belly flopped on the grass beyond.

The Aerospeciale was banking back toward the sea, flickering directly behind the guests lined up at the buffet table. With his sights, Riggs tracked the craft across a tableau of black dresses and charcoal suits, but knew he couldn't pull the trigger.

Somewhere up near the house, a woman shrieked, "My God! Help! Help!"

"Shit!" In a rage, Riggs ran back down to the parapet and fired his 9-mm automatic at the impossibly distant helicopter until the slide snapped back and the last empty casing clinked onto the flagstones.

"The arrival of the next load from Macao is imminent," Hunsaker said, sidestepping to the windows as the approach of the helicopter became louder and louder.

"How big?"

"Let me put it this way—it'll be the biggest thing to hit L.A. since the Long Beach earthquake."

"Not if you and I tear down this consortium first."

"No way. That's no longer possible."

"It is if we team up, Mike. And something this hot, the department will pull out all the stops, throw everything and everybody available against this renegade general. He can't kill every cop in California, can he?"

"I wouldn't put it past him."

The chopper noise was now deafening, and Hunsaker turned his face to look outside.

Murtaugh knew it would be his only chance. A green light came on in his head, and he drew his revolver with the intention of killing Mike Hunsaker.

But at that instant the glass panes disintegrated around the man.

In those first seconds of complete shock, Murtaugh thought that it had been a blast—the shards of glass seemed to implode toward the center of the room. But then he realized by the way Hunsaker was being pummeled and lashed by an invisible force that it was automatic gunfire of ferocious intensity.

Murtaugh dived behind the desk. And, when he glanced back toward the French windows, Hunsaker was being jerked and twitched on the carpet by the final shots of the massive burst.

He did not bleed much. His heart had been demolished too quickly to pump much blood through his numerous entry and exit wounds.

The housemaid threw open the door, and her scream frightened Murtaugh almost more than the gunfire had. "My God! Help! Help!"

Outside, Rigg's pistol could be heard cracking against the retreating chopper.

By the time Murtaugh stepped over Hunsaker's corpse and opened one of the jagged-edged casements to slip out onto the balcony, the helicopter was no more than a dot skimming over the ocean.

Riggs turned and caught his eye. "Shit, this is war!"

"Mr. Joshua," the Aerospeciale pilot said over the intercom. "The general wants a disposition."

Touching a hand to his headset receiver, Joshua frowned as he tried to formulate a way to break this bad news. The green swells of the channel slipped past the open door unseen, as he considered how to put as good a face as possible on this failure. The general did not tolerate failure, and it was unlikely that Joshua's flawless track record would absolve him from the lapse. "Patch the general in, Gomez."

Joshua took a deep breath and released the trigger grips of the 7.62-mm minigun.

"Good afternoon, Joshua," the resonant voice came through the headset.

"Good afternoon, sir."

"Are you clear for debriefing?"

"Yes, sir."

"Proceed."

"We went airborne as soon as Forward Observer One confirmed that Sergeants Murtaugh and Riggs had entered the estate grounds."

"Did they have time to converse with Hunsaker before you neutralized them?"

"They did, sir."

"Elaborate."

"The two police officers split up upon their arrival. Murtaugh entered the house to speak with Hunsaker. Riggs took up a defensive position on the grounds. Only after approximately ten minutes were we able to observe Murtaugh and Hunsaker in the latter's study. We attempted to neutralize Riggs on the terrace—"

"*Attempted*, Joshua?"

He paused. "Yes, sir, Sergeant Riggs survived our attack."

"And the others?"

"Hunsaker is a confirmed kill. Unknown on Murtaugh."

The silence at the other end of the radio connection seemed eternal. "This is extremely disappointing, Joshua."

"Yes, sir. I accept complete responsibility for the failure of the mission."

"Indeed you shall. We must now assume that the police are privy to our most sensitive intelligence. You are to return to base for further orders."

Joshua knew that it was a breach of acceptable conduct toward his absolute superior, but he felt desperate enough to ask, "May I inquire as to the nature of those orders, sir?"

The general chuckled mirthlessly. "Don't worry, Joshua. I'll give you the opportunity to redeem yourself. You shall personally undertake an offensive to minimize the damage caused by this afternoon's blunder. I will acquaint you with the targets upon your return."

"Yes, sir, thank you, sir. Airborne!"

"Airborne."

Joshua grinned as he slammed the compartment door shut.

It had been a reprieve, and the general didn't hand out many of them.

CHAPTER *12*

RIANNE WAITED UNTIL he had drawn her panties all the way down to her knees before she whispered, "No, Mark."

"Please." He touched her tenderly, and she came close to relenting.

"My father'd shoot you."

"Some things are worth dying for."

She laughed under her breath, but still said, "No, baby. Not this way. Not in a car."

"What's wrong with a car?"

"It's just not *right*."

"But what about that other time?"

"That was then. Besides, we were drinking."

"Well . . . I can get somebody to buy for us."

"That isn't what I meant."

"What do you mean then, Ri?"

"I love you."

"Besides that."

Glowering, she pulled up her panties and scooted away from him. "There's not supposed to be anything besides that." She stared over the front seat and out the windshield, hoping to see the city lights again. They'd looked so pretty, so Christmasy before. But the windows had steamed over in the past hour. Where had the time gone? Her digital watch read nine-thirty.

Mark grunted softly as he buttoned up his Levi's. "You getting close to your period?"

"No." Resting her chin on her hand, she considered this for a moment, then said, "Why, whenever I try to tell you how I really feel, do you ask me if I'm close to my period?"

"Because . . ." But then he crawled over the front seat and slumped behind the wheel. "Never mind."

"Hand me my purse," she said from the back seat.

"Why?"

"I need fresh lipstick before I face my mother."

All at once, the car rocked from side to side. "Jeez," he said.

"Are we having a quake?"

"Feels like it. I'll take a look outside." Mark flicked up the lock button on his door. Long ago, Rianne had been warned by her paranoid cop-father to lock all the car doors if a boyfriend and she parked someplace remote "to talk."

At the same moment Mark opened his door, bringing on the overhead light, Rianne rubbed a circle in the fog on her window, then screamed.

A pallid face leered at her from the circle, the eyes pinkish and inhuman.

She turned to warn Mark, but he was already being yanked out of the car by his long, blond hair.

"Rianne!" he cried, as if he were falling down a very long ways.

Murtaugh had Riggs take the corner at Trafficante's Pool Palace at a snail's pace so he could get a thorough look through the front windows at tonight's customers. "No," he finally said, his voice low with disappointment. "Drive on, Martin. Make a U-turn here, then head on down Avalon."

"Who were you looking for in there?"

"A drifter named Junkyard. Used to be a damned good

informant of mine. He'd put us on to why Dixie's latest pimp disappeared.''

"Well, you want to go back and shake down the joint anyway? Maybe somebody'll talk.''

"Naw, Trafficante's is the heart of that pimp's turf. These people know better than to talk to us. He may not be dead. Keep heading south along the boulevard. We'll come across some working girls with different loyalties. They'll talk.''

As they passed under a streetlight, Riggs glanced down at the copies of a booking photograph on the seat between them. Murtaugh had borrowed them from Southeast division vice. A ferret-faced pimp with one robbery conviction, two-drug-related arrests—no convictions, naturally. Conspicuously absent from his usual haunts since last night. "I'll bet he's somewhere out in the Mojave right now, vacationing under two feet of sand.''

"Me, too," Murtaugh admitted. "But whoever struck a deal with Dixie had to go through him. And we need a link to this consortium—fast.''

"What about that one-star Hunsaker told you about?''

"I phoned the department's contact with the army's criminal investigations division while you were cleaning up. According to them, this brigadier just dropped out of sight after his last command. A total vanisher.''

"So old soldiers do fade away. Where was he last posted?''

"Korea. Ranger outfit.''

"Do you think Hunsaker was blowing smoke about the mercenary muscle involved in this operation?''

"Maybe, but I don't think so. I believe the consortium is as high-powered as he said. Shit, we had our hands full today just with their air wing.''

"Have you got CID checking on any old names from your old outfit?''

"You bet, and I'm running them through the Department of Motor Vehicles, too.''

"May as well run Amelia Earhart for a current address—these heroes don't exist on paper. Trust me."

Murtaugh sighed. "I know. But we've got to start someplace."

Riggs nodded after a pensive moment, the store front lights flickering across his stubbly face in different colors. "Yeah, you're right, I guess."

"What time you got?"

"A little after midnight. Where's your watch?"

He glared at Riggs. "It wasn't *waterproof*, Martin."

"Well, shit . . ." Riggs unstrapped his watch and handed it to Murtaugh. "Take mine, you fucking crybaby."

As Murtaugh studied the timepiece, his lips slowly formed a scowl. "My watch was Swiss. Twenty-four-carat case. Eighteen-carat flexband. More jewels than Queen Elizabeth can lay claim to. And you offer me in return a Timex with a cracked crystal and an imitation lizard strap?"

"It's the thought that counts, Roger."

Riggs was strolling down the sidewalk when it came to him: He'd gone all day and not once—until this moment—had he suddenly remembered, *she's gone and I'll never see her again*.

The knowledge still felt like being bayoneted in the heart. But he was consoled to realize that this was the first time today since awakening.

The job.

It was wonderful. It occupied him completely and kept him from thinking. He would stay on duty until he dropped.

And Murtaugh was finally coming around as a partner. After this afternoon's air show at Pacific Palisades, he'd filled Riggs in on everything he'd been sitting on—including how Michael Hunsaker had saved his life in Nam, something Murtaugh could have kept to himself and Riggs would've been none the wiser.

Riggs found himself agreeing in principle with Roger about jerks like Hunsaker, big heroes who'd killed indiscriminately over there. More than just being vicious, it was plain stupid: You needed intelligence from the villagers to keep from getting your own ass in a sling. Bust caps at everything that moved and this life-saving intelligence dried up and was swept away like dust before the monsoon winds.

Murtaugh wasn't really a bad grunt—for having been in the army.

Like most marines, Riggs felt that Special Forces owed its inflated reputation to a popular song. And he'd even told a grim-faced Murtaugh that wearing the vaunted forest green beret meant only that a dog face was field-qualified to serve as a PFC in a marine rifle company. But, despite the trading of barbs, Riggs was beginning to enjoy working with the man, who at this moment was canvassing the whores loitering on the other side of Avalon Boulevard.

They waved to assure each other that all was well, then Riggs approached a woman sitting on a bus bench, taking advantage of the brash light of a billboard to show off her legs. "Hey, mama."

"Hi, baby."

He flashed his shield.

She shot to her feet. "Motherfucker—"

"Wait, wait, I can't bust you for just saying hello to me, can I?"

"You got that shit straight, fool."

He took the mug-shot photocopy out of his shirt pocket and unfolded it. "Know him?"

"Maybe."

"No maybe—we both know the man, baby. I'm trying to find out why he left the planet so suddenly." He slipped her a five spot borrowed from Murtaugh's lunch money.

She switched her chewing gum to her other battery of molars, then checked carefully over each shoulder. "This is all I can say: Your man here took over where Tyrone the Bone left off. And he ain't coming back to the boulevard either."

Riggs nodded thoughtfully. Murtaugh had also filled him in about Dixie's former pimp, repeatedly shot by a white mercenary type who'd accepted his sentence to Chino without sounding a peep about his heavy-dealing confederates. "You acquainted with any of these chuck dudes?"

"That's it, Jack. I mean it."

"You sure?" This time he waved a ten-dollar bill before her eyes.

"I'm sure. Good night."

"Okay, thanks for that much."

She was smirking. "Say, what happened to your hair? You burn it trying to frizz yourself up a nap?"

"No, I moonlight up at Trader Vic's—Hawaiian torch dancer."

"Hawaiian fucking *what*, baby?"

"Torch dancer. It happened when some fat chick tried to slip a twenty in my breech cloth."

Riggs left her guffawing. He continued down the sidewalk, checking for Murtaugh, who was now a block ahead of him, talking to a cluster of street hoods—a sight which quickened Riggs's pace.

Murtaugh flashed four fingers at Riggs to tell him that he was code four, all right.

"It's your neck, man." Riggs stopped in front of a small Salvation Army store to light a Winston.

Then the sound of tires made him drop the smoke to the sidewalk. New tires, barking slowly over the asphalt, when everybody on this side of town was running on rims at no less than fifty miles per hour.

His right hand darting to his shoulder holster, Riggs spun around and faced a black El Dorado, which was weighing low on its springs as if with armor plating.

Three silhouettes were inside, two in the front, one in the back. The rear passenger window facing Riggs's was gliding down as the Cadillac continued to roll slowly forward in approach.

Riggs fired in the same instant a sawed-off shotgun bellowed twice from the rear window. He would have hit the towheaded man in the back seat except that he was driven back—smacked in the chest as if by a wrecking ball—as he squeezed off his controlled burst.

By the time he crashed through the plate glass of the Salvation Army store, he was thoroughly disoriented. He thought that he was tumbling down into a swimming pool; the sprays of glass looked like water curling up around his body.

Then his vision grayed out.

Very far away, a universe or two away, he could hear a car accelerate, and then three rapid shots echoed down to silence.

Benign silence.

"Ain't no wisdom in that approach, see?" the tough explained on the Avalon street corner.

Murtaugh frowned at the youth's earrings, which were only slightly smaller than Lena Horne's. While assigned to southeast patrol, he'd arrested all three of these gang members numerous times. It felt like old home week. "How's that?"

"There be no way to best the man aboveboard, see? And that's what Tyrone tried . . ."

"And that's why Tyrone died," one of his buddies finished the couplet for him.

Checking on Riggs's progress down the other side of Avalon, Murtaugh saw him barreling down the sidewalk to assist. Quickly, he held up four fingers before the gang members found themselves gnawing pavement—or worse.

"Okay, okay, gentlemen, what's the connection between these dudes and—" Murtaugh saw it in the shocked eyes of the youths before the actual gunfire reports reverberated down the boulevard. He turned in time to see Riggs hurled backwards through a storefront.

A black Cadillac veered sharply to make a mid-block U-turn and swiftly built speed northbound.

Murtaugh fired three times at the car. But, at a range of more than a hundred meters, all three rounds missed their mark. He could make out no plate number: The license lightbulb had been extinguished. A late-model black El Dorado—that's all he had on the bastards.

Dodging traffic, he sprinted across the boulevard, coming close to vomiting as he visualized the sight that awaited him inside the Salvation Army store window. Behind him, he could hear the gang members making tracks: Innocent of involvement or not, they weren't about to stick around in any locale where a cop had just been blown away.

Murtaugh skidded on the soles of his oxfords up to the smashed window. His revolver plopped down to his side.

"Oh, brother . . ."

Riggs was half buried in the piled clothes of an overturned rack. His shirt front was peppered with pencil-thick holes—it looked like he had taken all three blasts of double-ought buckshot in the torso.

No blood. An instantaneous death. Some consolation.

His shoes crackling over the broken glass, Murtaugh stepped inside and knelt beside Martin Riggs. He didn't know if it was grief or fear or his adrenaline let down—whatever, he couldn't breathe. He was hyperventilating, and he realized that his hands were very cold. He'd never lost a partner. "Oh, man . . . this is no way for things to wind up."

Although it seemed hopeless, he pressed his fingers against Riggs's neck in search of a carotid pulse.

Then a dead hand darted up and clamped onto his wrist. "Faggot."

Murtaugh recoiled, bowling over backwards into a wooden box filled with old shoes. "You son of a bitch!"

Riggs was chuckling, but quietly, like it hurt him.

His hands fisted, Murtaugh sprang up again. "I'm going to kick your ass, Riggs!"

"I've just had my ass kicked."

Murtaugh blinked at him a moment. "Are you wearing Kevlar?"

"No, I'm a fucking alien, Roger. Just give me another two minutes and I'll be completely healed."

Murtaugh tore open Riggs's ruined shirt, revealing the

thin bulletproof vest. "Since when did Mr. Devil-May-Care start wearing body armor?"

"Since I saw that minigun's muzzle flashing at me today."

"I'm impressed."

"What do you mean, *you're impressed?*"

"This marks a definite shift in attitude."

Riggs winced.

"You sure you're all right, Martin?"

"Well, now that I got my wind back, things are looking much better, thank you. Of course, tomorrow my chest is going to look like I slept on a Chinese checkerboard. Other than that, great. I take it you missed?"

"Hey, man, that thing was booking. A regular war wagon, too."

"Tell me about it."

"Did you get a look at the joker who nailed you?"

"Yeah, the door gunner in the chopper. Looks like Mr. Lurch on a bad morning. Real pale blond hair. Ring a bell with you?"

"No, but a shit-pot load of troopers rotated through that outfit after I was sidelined."

Riggs rose on his elbows and groaned. "Well, one thing—we don't have to go looking for them anymore. They're bringing the war to us express. Help me up and let's get out of here."

"No, wait—" An idea brightened Murtaugh's eyes, which then fixed on the telephone atop the counter. "Stay down. I'm going to roll my people on a homicide. I want you leaving this scene in the back of the coroner's wagon with a blanket over your face."

"Roger, I know you're slow sometimes to catch on to shit, but I *survived* this."

"I know that, but the consortium *doesn't*. And from this point on, we've got one chess piece on the board they don't know about."

All at once Riggs grinned. "You know, that is inspired!"

"Don't patronize me, Martin."

• • •

The deputy coroner parked his station wagon on a dark side street, then got out and unlatched the rear door. Riggs climbed off the gurney and eased his chukka boots down onto the pavement, still a bit stiff from the shotgun blasts.

"What's it like being dead?" the deputy asked him.

"Kind of like watching TV during a power failure."

"I'll have to think about that one."

"Don't bother."

Riggs skidded in beside Murtaugh, who had an odd look on his face as he clutched the radio mike.

He started to ask Murtaugh what was wrong, but the man waved him off before transmitting, "Listen, control, I'm down in southeast. I can't copy two-king-four's traffic. Will you relay?"

"Affirmative, standby, king-seven."

"What is it?" Riggs tried again.

"Homicide. A vehicle parked up in Verdugo Hills."

"So?"

"Hang on, dammit. Our on-duty dick sergeant up there wants to talk to me—urgent."

"Two-king-seven," the dispatcher finally broke the uneasy stillness in the car, "king-sixty requests the following information: Are you related to a Rianne Tritia Murtaugh, DOB of 3-16-70?"

Murtaugh couldn't speak. He just stared out the windshield, his eyes slowly glazing over as if he were dying.

"King-seven, copy?"

Riggs pried the mike out of Murtaugh's paralyzed hand. "That is affirmative on Rianne Murtaugh. Give us a status on the subject *now*."

"Stand by, I'll try to get one."

"Don't try—do it, dammit."

"King-seven," the dispatcher said prissily, "the communications sergeant advises you are not conforming to radio procedure."

"Fuck the procedure. And this is M. Riggs not conforming."

Riggs didn't hesitate or balk. He reached out and held Murtaugh's hand.

Nothing showed in the man's eyes, but he squeezed back desperately.

Both men were startled when the radio came back on: "King-seven, be advised, subject Rianne is not present at the scene. No further information."

"Copy that she is *not* the victim?"

"That is affirmative. Her purse was found in the vehicle. Information was taken off her DMV learner's permit. Does king-seven request that we telephone his residence as to whereabouts of the subject?"

Murtaugh seized the mike from Riggs. "Negative!" His breath was seething back and forth in his throat like the surf. He sounded as if he were on the verge of suffering a heart attack. Riggs moved to loosen his tie, but Murtaugh batted his hand down. "No one is to phone my wife!"

CHAPTER **13**

THE ORDER WAS clear: All inquiries concerning the shoot-ing death of Detective Sergeant Martin Riggs were to be trunked to one desk. Behind the desk slouched Detective Burke, who'd been dragged out of a roaring Christmas party in a Winnebago parked in the underground lot for this harebrained assignment.

For the first time in an hour, the phone rang. "Robbery/homicide, Burke speaking."

"Hi, KTLA news. We're trying to confirm a shooting incident in the Watts district around midnight. Have you got anything to give us on that?"

"Uh, yeah, I've got a prepared statement from detective headquarters. You ready to copy or record?"

"Shoot."

"All right . . ." Burke cleared his throat twice, trying to buy a little more time for the phone company crew to trace the origin of the call. "At approximately 0027 hours this date, Detective Sergeant Martin Riggs, while assigned to a special anti-street crime task force in South Los Ange-les, was shot and killed by an unknown assailant, or assailants. He is the third Los Angeles police officer to be killed in the line of duty this year. No further details are available at this time. The chief of police will convene a news conference concerning Sergeant Riggs's death at Parker Center, room 187, 1030 hours this date.''

"Can you tell me this: Was he declared dead at Martin Luther King Memorial?''

"Uh . . . no. At the scene. He was a mess, but that's off the record.''

"Sure . . .'' Then the alleged newsman said, sounding sincere as hell, "Isn't this the shits?''

"It's a dangerous job,'' Burke intoned, swilling down the last of the spiked punch he'd brought up from the Winnebago in a coffee thermos. "But somebody's got to do it. I didn't catch your name—''

But the caller had hung up.

"Buh-dee, buh-dee . . . that's all folks.'' Burke laid his face down on the desktop and tried to catch a few winks.

Joshua replaced the receiver in its cradle, then hurried out of the booth and onto the curb.

The rear door to the Mercedes swung open to admit him, and he quickly got inside.

"Disposition?'' the general asked.

"Sergeant Riggs is out of the picture.'' Joshua was beaming. "His body was a mess, according to robbery/homicide.'' But he sobered when he saw that the general wasn't joining in the moment of celebration.

I've got a lot of respect for Marine Corps discipline and motivation. And let it be said that this man was a *marine*.''

"Yes, sir,'' Joshua said, hoping he sounded sufficiently reverent. "He certainly went down fighting.''

The general leaned forward and tapped the driver on the shoulder. "Drive for ten more minutes—say, into Westwood. Then find another booth in a dark location.'' Sitting back again, he told Joshua, "We can expect them to trace all calls involving this from now on.''

"Instructions for the next call, sir?''

"Advise the Murtaughs that we are in possession of their daughter. She is alive and well at this time, but will remain so commensurate only to how her parents behave during this unfortunate incident. Sergeant Murtaugh is not to apprise his department or any allied law-enforcement agency, such as the FBI, of the abduction. Make it clear that this is not a kidnapping for ransom.''

"What exactly are we after, sir?"

"Murtaugh. In the flesh." The general suddenly frowned. "Are you sure those were undercover officers he was standing with on Avalon Boulevard tonight?"

"Yes, sir. They all seemed quite fraternal."

"Damn—it would've been an excellent opportunity to abduct him."

"Given the conditions, sir, we could have neutralized him. But not taken him alive. Does the general consider the window to now be closed on Murtaugh's abduction?"

"Negative. We still have to determine how much he knows and how much he has revealed to his department before we take any positive action. During the call, indicate to him that we're willing to trade his person for his daughter's.'' The general's expression became pensive. "An exchange no decent father can refuse. And he's certainly that, according to our intelligence. I just wish we had more good family men on our staff. That way, our ideals would be carried into the future and not die with us.''

Joshua waited a respectful moment before asking, "Time and location for this trade, sir?"

"That will be revealed to him within twelve hours— unless it becomes evident that he has violated our instructions by revealing the abduction to the authorities. In that case, we shall mail him a map, indicating where he might find his daughter's body for purposes of Christian burial.''

"Sir?"

"We are soldiers, Joshua, nor barbarians."

The car hadn't come to a full stop when Murtaugh bailed out and raced up the walkway to his house. He forced the front door with his shoulder rather than fumble for the right key on the blacked-out porch.

Riggs had insisted on taking the wheel in South Los Angeles for fear Murtaugh would wrap them around a telephone pole in his panic to get back to Glendale.

Perhaps to ward off his growing despair, Murtaugh had gotten it in his head that Rianne's boyfriend, Mark—the confirmed victim of a strangulation—had driven her home from school, and she'd forgotten her purse in his car.

"I know she's okay," he kept repeating, his voice quavering like he had the chills. "She's home, otherwise Trish would've phoned me earlier. She phoned me the last time Rianne pulled this stunt. Rianne's going to be in bed. I just know it, Martin."

"Me, too, buddy. Everything's going to be okay."

"Can you drive a little faster?"

Riggs didn't say anything: He was already doing over a hundred on the Glendale Freeway, stitching in and out of the sparse traffic. He considered it a minor miracle that the highway patrol had failed to materialize in a blaze of red and blue lights anywhere along his route.

Now he jogged up the walkway in Murtaugh's wake, noticing how the man's shoulder had shoved the hardened-steel throw of the deadbolt lock completely out of the doorjamb.

Trish appeared at the top of the stairs, looking petrified. She noticed Riggs first, standing in the small foyer. "Martin, what is it?" But, before he could answer, her eyes flickered toward Murtaugh, who was shuffling back from Rianne's room in a daze.

Trish didn't have to be told. She saw it all in her husband's face. "Oh my dear Lord Jesus . . . I knew it . . . I just knew it . . ."

Riggs turned away, unable to bear the sight of them clinging to each other, crying. He took a deep breath, then massaged his sore chest as he slowly exhaled.

The phone rang on the tripod table beside him. Riggs started to reach for it.

"No!" Murtaugh shot down the stairs, rage evaporating his tears as he ran. He picked up the receiver, his fist trembling. His voice cracked from the strain of keeping it level: "Murtaugh here." Expressionless, he listened to the faint squawk at the other end of the line, seemingly forever, then whispered with what Riggs realized to be enormous self-control, "Yes, I understand. I'll be waiting."

When it was finished, Murtaugh just let the receiver drop to the floor. His gaze floated around the foyer, then lit on Riggs's stricken face. "They got my baby, Martin. The bastards got my baby."

Riggs sat on the couch, watching the late late show with Nick under one arm and Carrie under the other.

Once in a while, he could hear Roger and Trish's exhausted voices drifting from upstairs. But mostly, he tried to tune them out and concentrate on the screen. After a long while, it occurred to him that he had no idea what movie he was watching. He couldn't even name the actors, although they looked intensely familiar.

The kids had fallen asleep, perhaps for good this time.

Somehow, it gratified him to have Murtaugh's children snuggled up against him. Injured creatures sense who they can trust, and these children had been injured by fear tonight. Even more than infectious hepatitis, it was the most repulsive thing a cop could bring home with him from the job—fear.

He kissed them both atop the head, then he began weeping. He wept in silence for more than an hour—and never really understood why. The world, maybe.

He clung to Murtaugh's children more than they did to him.

Murtaugh came down the stairs one at a time. The man and wife counsel was finished.

Trish wanted him to tell the department. She begged him to tell.

Like most cops' wives, she had been conditioned through

the years to believe that the chief of police was among the exalted of the earth. He could make things *happen,* impossible things for ordinary men. He could raise men up and lower them down. At promotion time, he could fix the stars in the firmament or make the sun stand still in the sky. He could even create men in his own image: Murtaugh could think of a half-dozen clones without even trying. They were called deputy chiefs.

But, despite all this, he tried to explain to Trish that Rianne would die if he told the chief. The chief would try to rescue their daughter within the parameters of the law. And that just wasn't good enough.

She didn't believe him, and he cut short their agonized discussion before his arguments might damage her love for him. Forever.

Reaching the bottom newel post of the stairs, he turned like a robot toward the family room, homing in on the glow of the television set.

Riggs was sitting there, sheltering the sleeping children under his arms.

Murtaugh felt a burst of affection for the man, but found himself mumbling inanely, "Trish tried to phone tonight . . . when Rianne was late. The department said I was out on a homicide. So she said not to bother me."

"She didn't know. Nobody knew."

"Yeah." Murtaugh sank into his easy chair. "You want a drink, Martin?"

Riggs brought a finger to his lips. "Sssh. No, I'm fine."

"You sure?"

"I'm not drinking until we get Rianne back and kill every last one of those cocksuckers." Then Riggs went back to watching the movie.

So this was it. Murtaugh could summon all the resources of one of the largest and most professional police organizations in the world—and they would do him no good in this situation. He knew with a chilling certainty that he needed to strike fast and deadly if he had any hope of saving his daughter. The bastards were going to kill Rianne just as they had murdered Amanda and Mark and all the others.

If he turned to his department's brass, they would advise patience and caution. But patience and caution would put his baby in her grave.

Murtaugh needed a lethal weapon on his side, and there he sat, smoking a Winston as calmly and confidently as if he'd been plunked down on that couch by God Himself. Yes, *God* had loaned this crazy soul to Roger Murtaugh in his hour of need. And Murtaugh thought this without feeling prejudice toward Riggs's condition, for he now realized that a man can be no crazier than the world in which he tries to live.

"You're a good friend, Martin," he forced himself to say after a while, his voice choked by emotion.

"Fucking A," Riggs said, not taking his eyes from the screen. "What's the name of this goddamned movie?"

"I . . . I don't know, Martin."

"Take a guess."

At first light, which came grayly and overcast, Trish and Riggs made breakfast while Murtaugh went upstairs to bathe and shave.

There was something in the sizzling of bacon and hash browns on the griddle that seemed to calm Trish a little, perhaps the normalcy of it.

Riggs sat at the table grating cheese, a cigarette dangling from the corner of his mouth.

Ten minutes earlier, Trish had tried to say something conversational but had immediately broken into sobs. "Don't try to talk, babe," Riggs had told her softly. "Sometimes it just can't clear the lump in your throat. Know what I mean?"

She nodded fiercely.

But now, after ten minutes of cooking, she felt more in control of herself. "Martin?"

He'd nicked a knuckle on the grater and was sucking it.
"Yeah?"

"I'm sorry about your wife. Roger just told me last
night."

Riggs went on grating the cheese.

"Do you mind talking about her?"

"No." He snubbed out his smoke into his coffee cup.
"I guess not."

"Do you think you'll ever get over the *hurt?*" She
suffered a relapse and had to press her fingers against her
lips momentarily. But then her face smoothed out again.
"I know it's probably awful to ask you so soon—"

"No, it's a good thing to talk about." He shrugged as
he thought about it. "Maybe it's what I've been waiting to
talk about."

"Good . . . I'm glad then."

"No, Trish, I'll never get over the hurt. I don't want to.
Feeling no hurt would be like saying she meant nothing.
She meant as much as one person can mean to another. So
I always expect to feel that pain. I just hope it eventually
won't take my breath away each time it comes." Riggs
suddenly pointed at the hash browns. "You're burning
those bastards."

She spun around with the spatula in hand. "Did she
handle your job well?"

"On the surface, maybe. But she had a weak heart.
And I think my job shortened her life." Riggs held up a
hand to keep Trish from crying again. "Hang on, babe.
This is not guilt trip. I think I'm finally getting a grip on
it. See, I'm a grunt. Even now. A cop's just a soldier who
can't rely on artillery to get him out of a jam. And I've
been a soldier ever since I was seventeen, shaking in my
skivvies and crying in my rack at bootcamp down in
Diego. I mean, can you honestly see me managing a
Burger King? Shit, within a week, I'd be pressing some
loudmouth's mug against a hot grill."

Trish chuckled briefly.

"No, my wife knew the score about me. I think she

admired the way I am, too—sort of. And me, I came back from Nam pretty messed up in the head. I came back to everybody questioning what we did over there. Well, I needed something tangible to fight for. Someone to protect. And she and I together—we made sense. I had the brawn. She had the heart, a way of looking at things that helped me from going over the edge.''

''But the job, the danger, the endless stress you fellows—''

''Yeah, the stress . . .'' He nodded sadly. ''She wanted me to quit and didn't want me to quit. I wanted to quit and couldn't. We must've looked at that riddle a thousand times—from a thousand different angles. Not angrily, mind you, not bitching at and blaming each other. Just searching for a solution.''

''And you never found one?''

''No, Trish, we ran out of time first. Maybe it's selfish, what I'm thinking these days. I mean, she's gone. So it looks like the job won out. But I'm starting to see it in another light. You know, maybe love is its own solution. It's what you have when you run out of solutions. And there wasn't a day when we didn't have love.''

Trish turned away again quickly.

After a few seconds, Riggs went back to grating cheese.

The wall phone rang.

They glanced at each other, then Riggs shouted, ''Roger!''

Within seconds, he could hear feet coming down the stairs to the extension in the foyer. ''Murtaugh here.''

Listening, Trish stared right through the griddle and the bacon, which had shriveled to black curls. She started at the sound of Murtaugh hanging up—it had come unexpectedly soon. As if a death message had been delivered, and there was nothing more to discuss.

Murtaugh appeared at the swinging door, holding a towel around his waist. ''She's still okay.''

''Oh, thank God.'' Trish clenched her eyelids shut.

Murtaugh looked to Riggs. ''They want to meet with me.''

"When?"

"Noon today."

"Where?"

"The low desert. I'm to come in my family car. No undercover unit. No radio. No wire. Directions are—Interstate 10 to the Chuckwalla exit ramp. Then down a dirt road they'll mark with a cairn of stones."

"Good."

Murtaugh's eyes narrowed at Riggs. "Pardon?"

"I trained for recon out in that country—Twenty-nine Palms Marine Corps Base."

"I'm supposed to arrive alone."

"You will arrive alone." Riggs stood up from the table. "If it's okay with you, I'm going to borrow your unit again."

"Now?"

"Now."

"Where are you going?"

"Home, to throw my gear together. I'm also going to dig up the topographical maps on that hunk of desert. You might toss a blanket or a tarp in the back of your station wagon." Riggs glanced at the Timex that Murtaugh had refused. "I suggest you shove off in the next hour."

"It's only about a hundred and forty miles from here. They said *noon*."

"I know, but I want you to shake off the tail they're going to put on you, for sure. Drive over half of Southern California if you have to. Just make certain nobody's behind you when you pick me up at eleven."

"And where will that be? Your place?"

"No, Cabazon exit on the freeway. The gas staion with the big dinosaur for the tourists. Know where it is?"

"Yeah. The kids always look for the damn thing when we go to Palm Springs." Murtaugh came close to smiling.

But Riggs had turned to Trish. "I hate to ask this, but do you own a wig?"

"Yes . . . why?"

"Go get it for me—and one of your long coats. Roger,

why don't you get some clothes on and pull the unit into the garage. Put the door down as soon as you're inside. But look cool—you have the knack.''

''Why are you doing all this, Martin?''

''I don't have time to explain, Trish.'' He didn't want to tell her that the house might be under surveillance, and he needed a cover to drive away from it. He was confident he could lose anyone trying to tail him within a few blocks.

Murtaugh hurried upstairs, but Trish remained standing in the kitchen, looking at Riggs with pleading in her eyes. ''Martin, I have to believe that this is going to work. I just have to believe.''

''Don't you trust me?''

''It's not that.'' She firmly touched her fingertips to her forehead.

''I understand. And here's my answer. The biggest reason I couldn't quit—even though I knew what it was doing to her—is this, Trish. *I'm the best.* Oh, Roger's a better man than I am. A smarter man, too. But he doesn't even come close in this game. The killing game. That's taking nothing away from him—your man is a tough son of a bitch with enough balls for ten men. But nobody gives war like Riggs does. Nobody comes away as clean. Nobody.''

''Please, Martin, don't get my baby killed.''

''You know I won't. Deep down, you know that.''

CHAPTER **14**

THE̲Y̲ H̲A̲D̲ B̲E̲E̲N̲ *kids*.

The revelation stunned Riggs, and it was some time
before he could put away the snapshot. He'd been digging
through his old footlocker, its lid caked with dust—an
offense worthy of a million or so push-ups in another
lifetime—when he found the small vinyl pouch. He probably hadn't opened it in ten years. Inside it were some
military decorations—a tarnished silver star, two bronze
stars with oak leaf clusters, the Republic of Vietnam cross
of gallantry, three meritorious unit ribbons—and a few
photographs. Three to be exact. Two tours, and he had
three crinkled pictures to show for it.

And then it came back to Riggs: He'd believed at the
time that he was never coming back. Fatalists don't take
pictures.

He finally had to laugh at the youthful faces, his own
and those of his buddies. Kids. Babies. One year away
from prom night, five years from wondering how to put a
jockstrap on the right way. How ever had they gotten the
job done? By investing their own blood, he supposed.

As far as he knew, only two in the photograph were
still living—Benitez and himself. And the last he'd heard

some years before, poor Jesus was trapped in the revolving door of a V.A. mental ward. Six months inside on Thorazine, then six outside on vodka. He was probably dead by now, another delayed-fuse KIA.

They hadn't had a youth—any of them. They'd had Nam. The whole nine yards. Down to the Dear John letters, postscripted *a la* sixties, *Why are you guys killing babies?*

Is that what's wrong with me? he asked himself. Am I still trying to prove that I want to save babies, not murder them?

He slipped the photographs back in the vinyl pouch. It felt a little like stuffing those marines in their body bags, putting them back in their graves.

There were two sets of camouflaged fatigues in the bottom of the footlocker: one for jungle and one for desert. He took out the desert cammies and put them on slowly, with the deliberateness of a senior quarterback suiting up for his last game. His mind was racing ahead to the kickoff, but his fingers took care with each button.

This was a championship game, and it would be easy.

On the way home from Murtaugh's, he had stopped off at a sporting goods store and picked up the topographical map for the Chuckwalla quadrangle. Immediately, he surmised that the consortium would use the dry flats of Alkalai Lake for their confrontation with Murtaugh. They would want to be out in the open where a LAPD SWAT team or two couldn't set up on them. There was little cover and no high ground within miles of the sun-baked mud of the lake bed.

Riggs would have his work cut out for him: These people knew how to play the game as well as he did.

Passing the quietly murmuring television, he made his way down the length of the trailer to the spare bedroom in the front. There, he patted the covered sewing machine almost as if it were an animate being, then stooped in a corner of the room and lifted the vent grate off the floor. He set it aside.

Reaching down into the subflooring space, he grabbed a two-foot-long gun case and dragged it out. The rifle it contained—with all its accessories—weighed nearly twenty pounds. Twice as much as an ordinary rifle. Three times as much as a carbine. But there was a reason the Heckler and Koch PSG-1 long-range sniper rifle weighed almost as much as a machine gun, although its rate of fire was only semi-automatic. It was designed to accurately hurl a 7.62-mm round across seemingly impossible distances.

Next, he went to the utility room and slid aside Cato's bed basket and removed the vent plate beneath it. The canvas bag he removed from there looked like it was filled with oranges, but when Riggs undid the drawstring an assortment of grenades was revealed: tear gas, smoke of all colors, American and Soviet fragmentation jobs, a few surprises of his own manufacture. The anti-personnel grenades he had confiscated over his years as a cop, but failed to turn over to the department. Had the brass ever found out, it would have been instant dismissal and then prosecution on federal statutes.

But somehow, Riggs had always known that this day would come. And, to honor it now, to keep it pure, he didn't pack his bulletproof vest.

When his duffel bag was stuffed with all the gear he would take, he lashed open the back door so Cato could come and go at will. If Riggs didn't survive the next twenty-four hours, well—Cato was a handsome Labrador. Someone would steal him. Riggs, as always, put his faith in human frailty.

He looked at the television screen for a moment, then around the living room before resting on the dog. "Well, Cato, we've had the best of times and worst of times in this tin box. And if I don't come back, just remember— its' a far, far better place I got to. Now, stay inside while I drive away, dammit."

But Cato jumped the back fence and chased the car all the way out to the refinery before turning back.

• • •

Joshua took his cue from the general and bowed his head.

"Lord," the general said softly, "bless this food we are about to receive. And smile upon the enterprises we undertake this day in Your Name. Amen."

"Amen, sir."

Joshua waited until the general reached for the Tabasco sauce before he touched his own breakfast of steak and eggs.

The two men sat alone in a corner booth of the silent nightclub, although a Korean waiter stood just out of earshot, waiting attentively to provide for the general's smallest need.

"All right, Joshua, let's go through the checklist."

"Yes, sir—airborne, sir."

"Convoy?"

"Both vehicles fueled and ready."

"Troop count?"

"Nine men, sir. Nine automatic weapons."

"Air support?"

"Minigun pods fully loaded. The chopper will form up on the convoy at San Gorgonio Pass."

The general frowned. "Why not sooner?"

"It is believed that the Aerospeciale will draw undue attention to the convoy while the vehicles negotiate the freeways through the greater metropolitan area, sir."

The general patted Joshua's arm. "Good thinking."

Joshua knew then that he'd been tested. "Thank you, sir."

"That's what I like—strict adherence to the Five Ps."

Joshua realized this to be a cue. "Yes, sir—prior planning prevents piss-poor performance."

The general chuckled while grinding a hunk of filet mignon between his back teeth. "Yes indeed." Then something new occurred to him: "What about the shadow on Sergeant Murtaugh?"

"In position several blocks away from the sergeant's residence, sir."

"Right—should he have been so foolish as to inform his department, I don't want any of our people taken prisoner. We can't afford the risk of being compromised at this point. In another few months, it will be a different matter. We will have consolidated our political assets to deal with this sort of thing."

"Yes, sir."

"You see, my boy, it's the great lesson I took away from Vietnam. Arms are not power enough. You must also have money to bring about political and moral change. Now, I have no great affection for the narcotics trade. But it's far too profitable to be ignored as a source of revenue. So we find ourselves in the position of the Viet Cong during the late war—trafficking but never indulging in the stuff in order to finance our efforts. Of course, one cannot discount the big side benefit of this sort of program."

"Sir?"

"Look at those who are debilitated by these drugs—the very hedonistic ethnocultural elements of society that threaten our way of life, my boy."

The car-jammed lanes of the Foothill Freeway bleared in and out of focus. Murtaugh rolled down his window for some air, trying to keep a clear head. His feelings of exhaustion were so intense they had begun to frighten him that he wouldn't make it. He wouldn't have the energy to save his daughter's life when the critical seconds arrived.

He had kept a wary eye on the rear-view mirror since leaving the house, but with so much traffic moving at the same moderate speed it was impossible to tell if he was being tailed or not. Near the Santa Anita Race Track he abruptly switched lanes, and a dark blue BMW sedan with two occupants promptly did the same maneuver several vehicles behind him. But Murtaugh had had no reason to believe that it was anything but coincidence.

He struggled to cope with his terror. It was draining him. He felt as if he'd just run a marathon on two hours' sleep. He needed to relax, to save something for what lay ahead.

He glanced at the mountains. Only half of them showed under the thick marine overcast; the summits were obscured. He flicked on the radio, but music was so upbeat he quickly fumbled for the off button. He then made do with the white noise of the breeze gushing in through his open window.

Once he grew nauseous, but was able to keep from vomiting by taking deep breaths. And by ordering himself not to get sick.

The BMW was still behind him by the time he approached the cloverleaf with the San Gabriel River Freeway. On a hunch, he decided to head south along this route. He could pick up the San Bernardino Freeway in five miles or so and continue east.

Waiting until the last possible second to veer into the exit ramp, he sharply spun the wheel and bounced across the dividing hump into the curving lane.

The BMW swerved wildly to follow.

"Motherfuckers!" Murtaugh shouted. "Come on! The more the merrier!" His hand was tight on the grips of his revolver before he calmed himself. He thought of Rianne, and his rage melted into fear once again, leaving him light-headed. "Come on, man, keep yourself in one bag. Do it for your baby. You can do it."

He glanced in the mirror once again.

The losers had crew cuts and and wore mirrored sunglasses. Murtaugh started to laugh contemptuously, but stopped when it promised to trigger a gag reflex. He would have killed for a cigarette during those first moments alongside the parched, rocky bed of the San Gabriel River, and he hadn't smoked in twenty years.

The BMW eased back and tried to blend into the traffic again.

"Yeah, man, you're just as cool as fresh shit."

Then Murtaugh settled down to thinking. Riggs had been insistent: Murtaugh had to shake off the tail before the rendezvous. He sifted the network of freeways through his mind and realized that the stretch he was presently on was one of the few with a gravel median strip instead of a concrete barrier dividing the opposing lanes. And a mile ahead he could see where the barrier began again on the far side of an overpass, running indefinitely south from that point on.

"Okay," he said to himself, "Simon says, change lanes." Smoothly, remembering to use his blinker, Murtaugh crossed over into the far left lane.

After a moment, the BMW did the same.

"Good. Now, Simon says, give her a little more pedal." Murtaugh pressed it down to the firewall. His eyes shot to his mirror: The BMW's tailpipe was laying down some steely blue exhaust as the driver accelerated to catch up.

"Now, go fast, stop, and turn around real fast." Murtaugh pressed down on the pedal until the speedometer needle was vibrating on ninety—about all the family station wagon could be expected to do. Then he braked hard, nearly overturning the sluggish car as he skidded sideways across the gravel median. The Ford came to rest within inches of the concrete buttress of the overpass.

Yet, looking back through the pall of dust, he saw the BMW roar past. Its taillights were shining, but the driver had reacted too late—he was already through the overpass and locked onto the barrier-flanked portion of the freeway, where he had to stay until the next exit—two miles ahead.

"Oh, you fucked up." Murtaugh restarted his stalled engine and pulled onto the northbound lanes of the freeway. "I didn't say *Simon says*."

Riggs threw his duffel bag in the back of the station wagon, then took the passenger side of the front bench.

His eyes red-rimmed, his facial skin tones more gray than brown, Murtaugh was hunched over the wheel, looking up at the plaster dinosaur. "Things haven't changed much since back then, have they?"

"Nope. It still pays to be the nastiest lizard in the

swamp." Riggs was wearing a white sweat shirt over his camouflage shirt. "Anybody tail you?"

"A BMW until Duarte—where I shook it off my rear bumper."

Riggs studied him for a moment. "You doing okay?"

Murtaugh hiked his shoulders slightly, then shifted the wagon into reverse and headed back down Interstate 10.

A hard wind was pouring down the pass, keeping the overcast from spilling out into the desert. The sky was deep blue with no paler band of blue resting on the horizon. Fifty-mile visibility, except where the sand was being raised.

"You ready to go over it?" Riggs asked.

"Yeah."

Over the next ten minutes, Riggs outlined how he thought it should go down. Murtaugh listened attentively but said nothing even when Riggs asked him for input. Finally, Riggs interrupted himself with an exasperated grunt and said, "You got problems with this mission profile, Roger?"

"No."

"Then what's with the silent treatment?"

"Nothing, I guess."

"Bullshit."

"Get off my fucking case."

"I'm not on your fucking case. I asked a simple question."

Then Murtaugh slammed his fists against the steering wheel, "It's my daughter, for chrissake!'"

"I understand that."

"The hell you do! You're rattling on like it's war games or something! It's my kid, Martin, and if we fuck up, it's her life! It's my baby's life!"

Riggs stared out the window for a few seconds. Most of the traffic was taking the Palm Springs turnoff. "If I sound enthusiastic, it's only because I believe this is going to work. I know we'll get Rianne back. Unharmed."

"I'm scared, Martin. I've never been so goddamned scared in my life."

Riggs clenched Murtaugh's shoulder and kneaded it for a moment in his hand. "Me, too. But it can't get in the way. You know that."

"Okay, okay . . ." Murtaugh's attempt at a smile failed. "That's behind us. Sorry. So get on with the briefing."

Riggs took an olive-drab grenade from the thigh pocket of his fatigue trousers and dropped it in Murtaugh's inner coat pocket. "Here."

"Oh, Martin, I can't be chucking a frag with Rianne close by!"

"Understood. Consider it just an attention-getter. A negotiating tool. Pull the pin, *then* start your talking. Meanwhile, I'll be scoping the scene, waiting for our opening. Keep your revolver on you."

"What about a frisk? They're bound to shake me down."

"Nobody's going to get within five meters of you. Promise."

"Damn, I wish we had a way to communicate."

"We do—one way. At least I'll be able to hear you."

"They said no wire. They'll look for a wire."

"Who needs one? It's too bulky." Riggs took a pair of silver wings from his pocket, then leaned over and clipped them onto Murtaugh's handkerchief pocket.

"What's that?"

"Your paratroop wings."

"Where'd you get them?"

"Trish, while you were outside this morning."

"Why?"

"First off, let them think you're playing for sympathy. Bringing up the old days. Old comrades. Airborne and all that crap. I think you should play up that angle—if only to buy time for me to study the ring they've thrown around Rianne." Riggs reached for his pack of cigarettes. "But that's not all . . ."

"Give me one of those evil things." Murtaugh inhaled hungrily when Riggs lit it for him. "What's not all?"

"I borrowed a miniature radio-transmitting bug from my

division and glued to the back of your wings. Don't lose the damned thing. It's got a price tag of twenty grand."

"Fuck their twenty grand."

Riggs grinned. "I knew you'd finally come around, Roger. Time for me to get under wraps in the back."

"Want me to stop?"

"Nope." Riggs snuffed out his smoke and crawled over the back. "As of this moment we don't stop for nothing."

"All right, Martin, here's the cairn of rocks. I'm turning onto the dirt road. No vehicles, no personnel in sight anywhere."

Riggs's voice was slightly muffled coming from under the canvas tarp. "What about the dunes?"

"Dead ahead. But they ain't much—the highest is maybe ten feet. A few clumps of saltbush here and there. Wind's fucking fierce."

"According to the topo, this road snakes through the sand before straightening out again across the lake bed."

"That fits what I see. Man, there're dust devils spinning all over that dry lake. I hope you can see to shoot."

"I always rise to the occasion."

"I mean it, Martin, the air's more grit than air."

Riggs sighed in the semi-darkness under the tarp. "I can do it."

"We're in the dunes now."

"Wait until they hug the road good."

"We're coming to a place like that now. Fifty meters away."

"Don't slow down and don't stop."

"That's affirm." Then Murtaugh said, "Do it *now*, Martin."

Riggs reached out from under the tarp and cracked the rear swing-up window. Dust immediately billowed inside. "Bye." He tossed his duffel bag outside, then rolled out behind it.

●   ●   ●

"God speed, Martin." Murtaugh continued out onto the lake bed. The wind-driven sand and dust closed on the windows and sizzled against the glass. It was like driving through a snow flurry. The strange light. The sense of isolation and detachment. It felt like being dead.

Whenever the clouds of grit momentarily cleared, he looked around for some sign of the consortium. Nothing. No vehicles. No advancing skirmishes.

It occurred to him that this was part of a monstrous joke. While he waited out in the middle of the desert, they were burying his daughter elsewhere. Or even abducting Trish and his two remaining children. He'd left his old hideaway .22-caliber pistol from his patrol days with her, but she'd only fired a weapon once in her life. And then she'd cringed so bad as it went off she'd missed the entire paper target.

He fought another attack of nausea. His fear and hate were so strong they were sickening him.

Riggs found his place in a low clump of brush in the cleft between two intersecting dunes.

There, he quickly got to work.

He unpacked his Heckler and Koch rifle, unfolded its tripod stabilizer, and seated the twenty-round magazine. The cap covers to the Hensoldt 6x-power scope he would keep on until he needed to fire, otherwise the flying sand would score the glass.

"Listen to it . . . shit."

The wind was whistling over the crests of the dunes. He could hear nothing else, which bothered him. He knew all too well that a sniper mission calls for a two-man team, one on the rifle and a trusted buddy to provide security for him. Sniping requires so much concentration the shooter can't keep glancing around to make sure someone isn't sneaking up on him. He must meld his spirit to the reticle, the system of luminous dots or cross hairs that is his only guideline. He must let nothing distract him from the single, split-second opportunity he will have for success. If he fails, he will have no other.

And Riggs was alone.

He placed his Beretta atop the duffel bag, where he could grab it in an instant.

Then he donned his face mask. It was made of expandable, dun-colored netting and did away with the need for camouflage paint.

Finally, he lay down with his monocular range finder in hand. He leveled it on the yellow Ford station wagon, which was tiny in the distance now. It was still slowly cruising across Alkalai Lake, flickering in and out of the choking clouds.

Riggs checked his reading: nine hundred meters.

"All right, Roger . . . let's not overdo it."

As if on cue, the taillights twinkled through the blowing dust. The wagon stopped, and the lights went out.

Murtaugh got out of the vehicle and stood forlornly on the flats, his hands in his pockets.

One thousand meters.

Riggs put away the range finder.

He rested his chin atop his fist.

He watched.

CHAPTER 15

A WHINE CAME out of the distance, direction unknown. Murtaugh thought for a moment that it might be a high note of the wind, but then it failed to fade when a hard gust receded. Cupping a hand behind his ear, he tried to determine where it was coming from.

He could discern a rhythm in the sound.

Then he realized: It could only be the approach of the Aerospeciale whose minigun had riddled Michael Hunsaker.

Shielding his eyes against the blasts of sand with his forearm, Murtaugh turned completely around, carefully scanning all points of the compass. Nothing.

Half convinced that he had only imagined the sound, he was facing west when it suddenly roared out of the dust behind him, ten feet off the lake bed, forcing him to hug the ground. The Aerospeciale banked, climbing steeply, and vanished into the sun.

"Pecker."

Riggs had not really expected to see the Aerospeciale here.

The area was restricted to military air traffic. If the jet helicopter showed up on radar, attack choppers would scramble and converge on it from the marine base at Twenty-nine Palms. But the Aerospeciale's pilot was playing it smart: staying below five hundred feet as he swooped down on Murtaugh.

Gritting his teeth, Riggs waited helplessly for it to turn into a strafing run. The bastards on board were going to put Murtaugh out of the picture quick and clean with a squall of 7.62-mm bullets.

But then the Aerospeciale swept past the tiny figure without its minigun opening up, the crew apparently content only to have Murtaugh taste some dried mud.

"Pecker," Murtaugh's breathless voice came over Riggs's headset.

"Ditto," he whispered, although he knew that Murtaugh couldn't hear him.

Then, quickly, before the Aerospeciale completed a wide turn in his direction, Riggs reached inside his duffel bag for a camouflage tarp, which he unfurled with a snap and wrapped around himself before burrowing deeper into the low brush.

He uncapped his scope. He watched Murtaugh rise to his feet again in the illuminated cross hairs of the rifle with the impossible reach.

The two vehicles ventured onto Alkalai Lake from the dunes to the south, a Dodge pickup with camper shell followed by the black El Dorado Murtaugh had last seen speeding up Avalon Boulevard.

The Aerospeciale flew directly overhead, providing cover with its door gun.

The sight filled Murtaugh with anger. "Yeah, I'm a big threat standing out here alone. Bring on the air cavalry."

He strained for a glimpse of Rianne, but only men were sitting in the cab of the truck. Three of them. And several heads were visible in silhouette inside the Cadillac, but he couldn't pick out hers. If she still lived, she was inside the El Dorado, he told himself.

He started trotting toward the slow-moving convoy, but then forced himself to stop.

"I don't know if you can see them, Martin," he said with his mouth close to his jump wings. "But here they come out of south-southeast. Three heavies in a pickup. I can't see inside their pimp mobile. They've got a combat air patrol topside. Be careful."

When they were within a hundred meters of Murtaugh, the two vehicles formed a kind of battle line, and the chopper split off to resume its sweep of the area.

The pickup stopped, and then the Cadillac halted slightly to the rear of it in echelon. No one moved to get out for a few minutes.

"Yeah, check it out," Murtaugh muttered. "We got ourselves one crazy nigger here. Maybe he's got a switch-blade. Break out the tactical nukes."

Defiantly, he slipped his hand inside his outer coat pocket and kept it there.

The three men in the Dodge were first to bail out.

The driver remained standing behind his opened door, keeping it at a slant to deflect any rounds Murtaugh might so foolishly throw in his direction—he was holding an M-16 at port of arms, and his two partners were quietly flanking Murtaugh with Ingram submachine guns in their gloved hands. These two men stopped just when Murtaugh was thinking of ordering them to do so: He couldn't let them surround him. He needed to keep an open back door.

They regarded him as if he were a bug. Their faces were expressionless, except for a vague look of boredom. If they were the least bit apprehensive, it didn't show.

Murtaugh was seized by his anger once again—their unruffled manner had done it to him. "Which one of you fuckheads was issued a tongue?" he shouted.

No one responded.

The wind fluttered their trouser cuffs around their legs. One of them dabbed a piece of grit out of the corner of his eye.

A few moments later, a rear door to the El Dorado yawned open, and a polished shoe gently touched down.

Murtaugh had expected a middle-aged West Point type, but instead a lean young man with sloped shoulders eased out of the car and started approaching. Cautiously but smiling nonetheless. His Roman collar did not quite complement the Thompson submachine gun with drum magazine he was brandishing.

He stopped ten meters shy of Murtaugh. His smile turned into a full-blown grin as he squinted up into the noon sun, then back down into Murtaugh's face. "Afternoon."

"You a *priest?*"

"*Oh Lord, no, Sergeant dear . . .*" He had an Irish accent and a high, almost sweet voice. "*But it's a lovely disguise to use on the police the world over. Except in your Moslem countries. And in the orange side of Belfast's fair city, of course.*"

"*I want my daughter now.*"

"Or?"

"Or there'll be hell to pay!"

The mercenary chuckled. "Spoken like a free-born man. God will bless you for such courage. But lowly men as ourselves will only kill you for it. Now, most fools would ask you to slip your hand out of your pocket there . . ."

Murtaugh clenched the grenade even tighter.

"But I'm no fool. You see, years and years ago, my brother captured himself a lad from the Ulster Defense Association. Had his hand in his pocket just like yourself here. My brother ordered him to take his hand from his pocket and quickly now, too. The Orangeman complied. But when his bloody hand came out there was a revolver in it . . ." The pleasant face turned so grim it no longer seemed to be the same countenance. "And he drove my darling brother's blue eyes through the back of his head. So, keep your hand in there, Sergeant. The moment it comes out, I'll send you to heaven on a benediction of lead."

Murtaugh's jaw muscles hardened. These people were good. He was afraid *too good*. He damned himself for having believed in Riggs. Just the two of them would never be able to pull this off. There was only one way it might even remotely succeed: Murtaugh would have to sacrifice himself so Rianne could get away in the station wagon.

"I pray you've followed our instructions?" the Irishman asked.

"I'm here. What more do you want?"

"That is open to negotiation."

"I don't understand."

"The general can use a lad in your position. It's a lovely constabulary, the LAPD, as far as constabularies go. And we should all be friends, don't you agree?"

"I won't discuss shit until I see Rianne."

The mercenary exhaled deeply, but then smiled again. "I understand. She's colleen and a half, truly."

"Yeah, fucking Black Irish. Get her out here—*now*."

The next figure to emerge from the El Dorado—some minutes after the joker in the priest's garb had tripped out—was the man who had dumped Riggs through the Salvation Army store front, leaving him with a bruise-mottled chest that was still sore.

Riggs's trigger finger twinged. It ached to send a bullet into that distant head.

But so far, there had been no sign of Rianne. He would have to wait until he had a fix on her before doing anything. He wondered if she was even in the Cadillac, but then put the unsettling thought out of his head. She *had* to be there.

The wind had slacked off a bit in the last few minutes, but it was still gusting hard. He would have to time his shots between the surges, which was more difficult than simply accounting for a steady blow.

Riggs listened to the voices that were coming through his headset again:

"Murtaugh. My name is Joshua. Let's cut the bullshit."

"I'm ready. Where's my girl?"

Murtaugh thought the man calling himself Joshua was one shade away from being an albino. The pinkish eyes struck him as being obscene, even when they seemed suddenly to smile.

"The wings," Joshua said, "they look good on you. I'm glad you wore them today. It says something to me."

"I'm proud of them."

"You should be. We fought a good war."

"Some of us."

A corner of Joshua's mouth twitched. But, otherwise, he ignored the barb. "But the war isn't over. We should all pull together. Continue fighting for the things we believed in back then."

"I've never stopped doing that."

"Good. Then what are we arguing about?"

Murtaugh's voice became a growl: "You bastards took my baby. How's that for starters?"

"Don't worry, she's fine."

"Prove it."

Joshua snapped his fingers without looking back at the Cadillac.

Riggs sucked in a breath and held it as Rianna was brought out of the El Dorado.

"Shit . . ."

From this angle, her face was almost directly in front of the mercenary's. He was holding a survival knife to her throat. Riggs had less than two inches of clearance to drop him without hitting her. Impossible at a thousand yards. In a capricious wind, too.

Wait, he told himself.

But the terror in her face made it tough to keep looking at her through the scope. He wanted to start pumping rounds into the mercenaries who had formed a semicircle around Murtaugh.

"Come on . . . come on . . ." He thought he could hear the Aerospeciale in the distance behind him, but couldn't take his eyes away from the sight picture for even an instant. "Please . . ."

For several seconds after Murtaugh first caught sight of Rianne, he was blinded by tears.

"Daddy!"

The way she cried out made Murtaugh want to run to her. But he forced himself to stand his ground. "It's okay . . . everything's going to be okay, baby . . . you stay calm for your daddy . . . please." He thought to tell her that he loved her, but realized that she would recognize these to be words of final parting—that he was going to die here. She might not run for it then. He tried to say everything with his eyes: his love, his hopes that she would live a long time and always be a decent person, a person with compassion for others. Nor did he want her to be obsessed with revenge. There was so much he needed to say.

"Here's the deal, Murtaugh," Joshua said. "You come with us. And she drives away. She'll be home in a couple of hours. We won't move against her or the rest of your family. I give you that assurance. On our honor."

"You don't know what honor means. And that's why there'll be no deal."

Joshua chortled as he gestured at the array of automatic weapons facing Murtaugh. "Well, you got my curiosity aroused—just what do you plan to do here?"

"This." Murtaugh brought his hand out of his pocket.

The Irish mercenary was raising his Thompson when he saw the grenade—and froze in the same instant Murtaugh yanked the pin and tossed it away.

"Don't shoot!" someone else cried. "It's an M-26!"

"The hell it is." Joshua swung an Uzi submachine gun out of his jacket. "It's a dummy."

"Look, Joshua, olive drab with yellow markings!"

"It's a goddamned spooker! He wouldn't kill his own daughter!"

"Guess again." Slowly, Murtaugh took three strides forward—to make sure everyone was well within the grenade's kill radius. All but Joshua started inching back. "I'm a cop. Been one for fifteen years. Seen everything. I've got no illusions about what you got in mind. And I didn't come here because I figured I could save my daughter's life. You're not going to let us live. Never planned to. Can't afford to." Murtaugh grinned with outrage at each of them, one by one. "No, I came here so I could take some of you with us. And shoot me or not—this baby goes off the minute my hand lets go. A dead hand lets go just as good as a live one."

"Liam." Joshua motioned with his Uzi for the Irishman to advance. "Take him down. The general wants him alive at this point."

"I don't know, Joshua. He has a certain daftness in his eyes. I think she's set to blow."

"Christ." Joshua had taken two steps forward when Rianne screamed.

Murtaugh's eyes swept to her in the same instant the report of Riggs's shot rolled out of the dunes.

The knife tumbled out of her captor's fist as he sank to the ground. Riggs's glancing bullet had torn away his forehead, revealing the front lobes of the brain.

"Rianne—run!" Murtaugh cried as he pitched the grenade toward Joshua. "Take a car! Any car! Drive!"

Then he drew his revolver and fired twice at close range on the Irishman, who was stumbling backwards in expectation of the blast. Struck in the chest, he let go with a burst from his Thompson, but the rounds splattered a few feet in front of his shoes as he landed heavily on his haunches, then toppled to the side with his eyes rolled back up into his head.

Joshua, meanwhile, had dived away from the grenade and was assuming the textbook position: feet toward the blast, hands over ears, mouth open.

Murtaugh tried to shoot him in the back. But at that second, the grenade detonated.

Riggs had no time to congratulate himself for the fine shot he'd just made on the mercenary holding Rianne. The opportunity had come in the split second Murtaugh lobbed the grenade; the man's head had moved a full foot away from Rianne's as he desperately sought cover.

But now he had other targets in need of killing.

And the harmless green smoke billowing out of the grenade was not helping matters.

He no sooner drilled the man crouching behind the door of the pickup—the thin sheet metal no match for his high-velocity round—than he heard Murtaugh shout to Rianne over the headset, "Take a car! Any car! Drive!"

Riggs realized the same thing Rianne apparently did as she cringed behind the El Dorado—the family station wagon was too far away. With all the firing going on, she'd never make it.

Riggs swung his reticle onto the Cadillac's windshield. He squeezed off two shots about eighteen inches apart. Because of the sun's glare on the glass, he had no idea if he'd scored a hit until Rianne crawled around the side of the car, threw open the door, and tugged on a coat sleeve with all her might. A body tumbled out.

"You can do it, girl . . . that's it . . . get in the fucking car . . ."

Rianne's face was twisted by revulsion, but she jumped in behind the wheel and slammed the door in the same instant a pistol-toting mercenary tried to force it open again.

Riggs bent him double with a neck shot.

It did not take long for the green smoke to clear.

And when it was finally shredded apart and wafted away by the gusts, Joshua was still standing, firing from the hip with his Uzi.

Murtaugh lunged for cover behind the station wagon.

But, even before he struck the ground, he knew he'd been wounded. He clutched his left shoulder. It was warm and moist to the touch. He could not see the entry wound, but the fabric of his coat wasn't badly torn. A nice clean 9-mm parabellum wound, he hoped as he waited for the pain to come.

Still, he was smiling: He had seen Rianne drive away in the El Dorado.

His daughter was going to live.

Bullets were thunking and ringing off the sides and windows of the station wagon. It was being peppered with round after round after round. Trish is going to shit when she sees her car tonight, he thought. But then it occurred to him with an almost paralyzing sadness that he wasn't going home—not unless Riggs started dropping more mercenaries than he already had.

"Come on, Martin," he said into his silver wings, then saw that they were missing.

He cracked open the cylinder to his revolver and inspected the cartridges—one undented primer.

A mercenary raced around on Murtaugh's flank, firing short bursts as he came.

Murtaugh rolled away from the station wagon and pulled the trigger sharply in his haste to get the shot off before he himself was struck.

He missed, then hurled his empty handgun at the man, who held his fire, smirking.

"Where are you, Riggs?" Murtaugh whispered between stabs of firelike pain, his eyes dazed. "I trusted you, man. You said it would work."

Then, struggling to his feet, clamping onto his shoulder to stem the flow of blood, he staggered toward the dunes. They were a thousand miles away.

Suddenly, the lake bed sprouted little geysers of dust in long streams on both sides of him.

He collapsed to his knees, and the firing died away.

Footfalls approached him from behind.

"What happened, Martin?" he kept repeating. "You promised."

Riggs had Joshua's upper torso squarely in his cross hairs when a boot stepped on his Beretta laid out beside him.

He started to turn, but an M-16 dented his cheek and prevented him from seeing the man who was holding the rifle.

"That's it, son," a dignified voice said. "Remain as you are for the moment. Do you have any other weapons on your person?"

"A knife."

"No problem, just don't touch it. I'm going to take off your face netting now."

With a yank, he removed Riggs's mask.

"Roll over now—slowly."

Riggs did so, and the man laughed with more amusement than contempt. It was a face with presidential lines and crags. "Well, this *is* a singular honor."

Riggs shrugged. "I'd call it a fuck-up."

"No more so than our assuming you were dead, Sergeant Riggs. Body armor?"

"Right."

"Good show."

"And now may I ask you a professional question, General?"

"Certainly."

"How'd you spot me from the chopper?"

"Infrared scanner picked up your body heat. Otherwise your camouflage was quite adequate. And it took me nearly ten minutes to close on you. The wind helped. Where's your sniper's assistant?"

"His mother wouldn't let him come."

The general paused. "You know, Riggs, I can really use a man like you."

Riggs held the man's gaze. "No, you can't."

"Oh . . . well, that's a shame. Truly a shame."

And from the general's tone of voice, Riggs knew that the offer would never be made again.

Rianne recalled that the interstate lay somewhere to the north. She raced across the lake in that direction, the wind whispering through the two jagged holes in the windshield.

In Indio, or Palm Springs even, she would summon the police and lead them back here. This was the only reason she had left her father behind—to return with enough force to save him.

Something warm trickled down her face. She wiped her fingers across a cheek. Tears. She hadn't known she was crying. But she stopped. She would hang on, do whatever she had to do—to save her father.

Sitting very straight, she took a firm grip on the wheel— hands at ten o'clock and two o'clock, as learned in her driver's education course. Compared to her classmates, she had learned to drive late. Her father had resisted as long as he could, afraid she would wind up in a grisly accident like the hundreds he'd seen as a cop.

God, what garbage am I thinking about? she suddenly reminded herself. Find a cop! Or get to a phone!

The speedometer read ninety, but she didn't quite believe it. The big vehicle was rolling along so smoothly.

Then the windshield seemed to fill with the helicopter.

Her shoe darted to the brake pedal, and the El Dorado became a carousel, spinning around and around on the lake bed. She let go of the wheel and flopped down across the seat, waiting for the car to overturn.

But it didn't. The Cadillac remained upright, although the engine had stalled.

She tried the ignition, but it wouldn't catch and she was afraid the grating noise was damaging something. Then she remembered to depress the accelerator twice prior to making another attempt.

The engine rumbled to life, but before she could shift the lever from park, the dust began to boil up around the car. It was like being trapped inside her mother's Cuisinart, everything spinning in a blur—except for the helicopter strut, which wobbled down and then came to rest on the hood of the car with a loud clunk.

She could hear someone jump onto the roof. Two deep bulges showed through the vinyl headliner. The butt of a rifle began smashing out the window beside her. Her lap was filled with broken glass.

She closed her eyes and screamed.

CHAPTER 16

RIGGS STARED DOWN at the inexplicable.

He was sitting naked in a half-filled bathtub. The porcelain was streaked with red. Rust stains. Or were they blood? He tried to lift his eyes, but they wanted to shrivel back into the sockets: an overhead light, as glaring as the sun.

"Welcome back from the dead," a voice said from behind him.

"Where am I?"

"The first level of hell. We have many more to explore, Sergeant Riggs."

Riggs tried to touch the ache issuing from his cheekbone, but his right hand made it only halfway to his face before being jerked to a dead stop. Then he saw that both of his hands were manacled and chained to eyebolts anchored in the concrete floor. On a burst of anger, he pulled against his bonds, but succeeded only in slopping the water back and forth in the tub.

"Save your strength," the voice said, coming around the tub. "You'll need it in the next hour. Believe me."

Riggs tried to focus on the pale blurs. There were six of

them, revolving crazily in a circle. Gradually, they slowed and gathered in a single face. Joshua's.

"Why don't you get some sun?" Riggs muttered.

"Not good for the skin. You should check with your dermatologist."

Riggs started to speak, but then his head began bobbing and his chin sank down again his chest. He closed his eyes.

"Looks like I got you pretty good with the scatter gun."

Riggs grunted.

"Didn't think you'd be wearing a Kevlar vest. You're supposed to be such a loony troop. I hear you were a recon marine."

"Yeah . . . LURP."

"Long-range reconnaissance patrol. Get any into Laos?"

"No, we went deep into Australia. Kept tabs on fucking kangeroos coming in and out of Alice Springs."

Joshua's voice hardened. "Just trying to get along, Riggs."

"Sorry . . . I have this recurring hallucination that somebody just beat the shit out of me. Must have been a Chinese thumping. Half an hour later—and I've got the feeling I'm about ready for another one. Where's your helper?"

"Kwak is Korean, not Chinese. Learned a thing or two while serving with the Republic of Korea Special Forces. He's right here in the corner, rigging up some boffo interrogation gear."

Riggs remained silent. He dipped his face in the water, but it was too warm to refresh him.

"Now, Sergeant Riggs, let's continue where we left off. Do you often take such sudden naps?"

"Narcolepsy."

"Tell me how your narcotics unit is set up."

"Listen, I'll give you a phone number. There's a captain downtown. Does nothing but handle public information. God knows, he isn't smart enough to put together a bust. But he'd be tickled to field any questions you have about our operations and methods. He knows more about what we do than we do. Just ask him. Captain Hingejaw's his name. No, wait—it's Meehoff. Captain Jack Meehoff.''

Joshua shifted the overhead light so Riggs could make out the Korean in the corner of the concrete chamber. ''Can you see Mr. Kwak?''

''Barely. Something seems to be wrong with my eyes.''

''Well, let me keep you abreast of current developments. He's wiring a big sponge to a car battery. Ever had a Korean sponge bath?''

''No, a basket job in Hong Kong once. Does that count?''

Joshua backhanded him hard.

Riggs's mouth went coppery with the taste of blood. ''I guess it doesn't count.''

''Last chance—what are you doing linked up with a homicide detective sergeant? The truth.''

''It's a special detail. Orders came down from detective headquarters.''

Joshua paused for a moment. When he spoke again, his voice was calm. ''All right, that's better. How many men are committed to this detail?''

''Just Murtaugh and me.''

''And—in accordance with the mission set down by your headquarters—what are you working on?''

''Nothing.''

Joshua slapped him again, harder.

''I'm serious. It's a bullshit detail. A showboat to prove that the two divisions can get along.''

Joshua fell silent.

Riggs could hear the blood dripping off his chin into the water.

''What do the names Tyrone Fontaine and James Cleveland mean to you?''

''Uh . . . backup singers for Neil Diamond?''

Riggs's head snapped back and forth as Joshua repeatedly pummeled it.

''How about pimps in South Los Angeles, Riggs?''

''That was my next guess.''

"Why were you and Murtaugh working the streets, asking questions about them?"

"Okay . . . okay . . . you've got to understand something about our procedure . . ." Riggs's vision grayed out for a few seconds, but then he found Joshua's pinkish eyes again. "What we were doing is routine . . . just routine . . ."

"I'm listening."

"Fontaine's murder was never fully solved. It's believed more suspects were involved than the joker who took the rap for it."

"What do you think about that?"

"Bullshit. The hitman worked alone. But every so many months, the sergeant has to submit follow-ups on all his open homicide cases. And he just can't put down *no new leads . . . case still under investigation*. He has to make it look like his unit's still working these cases. For the brass. We heard Cleveland is missing. Cleveland and Fontaine were buddies. So Murtaugh thought maybe we could work that angle for one of these bullshit follow-ups."

"Oh, Riggs," Joshua sighed. "I tried to help you. Vet to vet, I really tried. Now, we're going through the same questions one more time. Except first we're going to clear your head with a little electricity. Mr. Kwak, proceed."

Riggs steeled himself with a deep breath. He tried to find a place deep inside his brain where the pain couldn't find him.

It did no good. The third jolt made him scream.

But he felt himself soar up on that long scream into clouds. Dark monsoon clouds breaking against his face, leaving it cool and moist.

When Murtaugh was a very small boy, he saw in a magazine a photograph of a black man who'd been lynched in Georgia. The rope fibers must have cut the man's throat a little, for blood had dripped down his bare chest and the whites standing by had covered his neck with a handkerchief.

The night after seeing this photograph, Murtaugh had terrible nightmares. He dreamed that he was the lynched black man. And, although dead, he could hear the hushed voices of the white men who had just killed him.

Now, he felt trapped in that nightmare once again as he listened to the soft, Caucasian voices around him:

"Should we go to something else, sir?"

"No, they don't take well to the sophisticated methods. They go hysterical on you. Completely out of their heads."

"Do you think he can sustain another series of blows?"

"Oh yes, they have an amazing cranial resilence. Look at the punishment to the noggin their prize fighters can take."

Murtaugh wanted to laugh, but his mouth hurt too badly.

"He's coming around again, sir."

"Put on your sap gloves, but stand by for a few minutes. Let's see if I can make any progress with him first."

Murtaugh felt his face being gently lifted by the chin. He tried to squirm away, but realized once again that he was tied to a wooden chair.

"Sergeant, can you hear me?"

"Yes."

"Is your flesh wound hurting you?"

"I don't know."

"You mean it's numb?"

"I mean . . . everything hurts."

"Of course, and we'd sincerely like to stop this. We'd like to arrange for some medical attention for your gunshot wound. But first, we need some answers to some rather troubling questions."

Murtaugh tried to will himself to black out again. But he remained conscious.

"Why'd you call on Mike Hunsaker?"

"Condolences and . . ."

"Yes?"

"Business."

"What manner of business, Sergeant?"

"His daughter's suicide."

"Did you personally investigate her suicide?"

"As unit supervisor."

Murtaugh felt his shoulder being patted tenderly.

"Okay, son. Tell me this then: Were you and Mike Hunsaker pretty close?"

"No."

"Why not?" The voice suddenly edged with surprise.

"I didn't like him."

A chuckle. "Me neither. He was a chameleon. I mean, he displayed all the right colors in the war environment. But back home he turned soft with pastels. Liked his comfort too much. A soldier can't be infatuated with comfort. Tell me, what did Mike and you discuss the afternoon he was terminated?'

"A reason why Amanda would want to kill herself."

"And what did Mike come up with?"

"Nothing. That was the sad thing. He didn't know his own daughter. He knew nothing about her."

"Yes, that is sad. Particularly from your point of view—a man who cares so deeply for his daughter."

Riggs soared over the misty, jungle-clad mountains.

Strange, he knew he had to be airborne in a Huey, but when he reached out he couldn't feel the bubble. There was no Plexiglas between him and the monsoon. The sky poured around him like wet velvet. And below—trees, trees, trees. The leaves glistened with rain. And then he was down in the midst of those trees. In the perpetual twilight. Somehow, he had been inserted into the jungle. But where was the rest of his team? Had he been sent out alone on a recon mission? He lay perfectly still and listened. After a while, he felt vibrations coming through the dark, moldy soil—footfalls. The NVA were coming down the trail. And after a few minutes he could hear them talking low. But what was this? They were whispering in English:

"Your opinion, Mr. Kwak?"

"He has either an extraordinary capacity to block pain or he knows nothing about the shipment."

"That resolves nothing. Which is it?"

"I fear we won't know that unless I take him to the brink of death."

"Do it."

"And should he fall over that brink, Mr. Joshua?"

"Than it's obvious—he doesn't know. I'll leave it to you, Mr. Kwak. I have more promising POWs to interrogate. Proceed as you see fit."

Riggs could hear a steel door open and close. It confused him: a door out in the jungle. But then the agony was clinging to his flesh once again, and he quickly retreated back into the dripping trees—gratefully and without question.

"That's it," the general said, exasperated. "I give up. Send for Joshua."

"Here, sir." A door clicked shut. "What seems to be the problem?"

"The man refuses to be swayed by reason. See what you can do with him. Then join me in my office."

Then there was some whispering Murtaugh couldn't overhear."

"Yes, sir—airborne, sir!"

"Carry on, my boy."

Murtaugh knew that he would lose consciousness with the next blow to his head. He looked forward to it. He wanted to goad them into it. "Come on, hero—kill me! Then you can go to the merc conventions and talk about what a bad-ass you are! You beat a fucking cop to death with your bare hands!"

Joshua came close to Murtaugh's ear. "I can't accomplish my mission by killing you at this point. Your daughter's a different matter."

"Damn you, cocksucker!" Murtaugh hissed before he could gain control over himself again.

"And if your daughter's death doesn't work, your wife's might. Or Nicholas's. Or Carrie's. I can't threaten you in regards to Sergeant Riggs. He's already dead. And he might have saved himself with just a few polite replies. Simple answers to simple questions.''

Murtaugh lowered his head, his eyes tightly shut. Shame nearly choked off his words: ''What questions?''

''Why'd you and Riggs go to Dixie Monroe's house?''

''She was a witness to Amanda Hunsaker's death.''

''So what?''

''We needed to interview her.''

''Wasn't she questioned at the scene in Century City?''

''Yes.''

''Then what made you suddenly decide a second interview was necessary?''

''Nothing special. Routine follow-up.''

''No, no,'' Joshua chuckled. ''I've just been down this path with Riggs. And it ended with him bleeding from the ears. Do I make myself clear?''

Murtaugh laughed drunkenly. ''It's the truth . . . what I'm saying about Dixie.''

''Okay, I'll let Dixie pass for a minute. Let's move on to Michael Hunsaker.''

''What about him? He was an asshole.''

''I'll second that. Did he happen to mention how he got so filthy rich on a bank vice-president's take-home pay?''

''Playing the commodities market, he said.''

Joshua laughed. ''Yeah, sure—pork belly futures. Come on, Murtaugh, you can do better than that.''

''It's what Hunsaker told me.''

''Sure. What about narcotics?''

''It crossed my mind as he showed me around his place.''

''But you didn't go any further with your suspicion?''

''No probable cause. I can't bust a man just because he's successful.''

''What about Special Forces vets in Asia?''

''We talked some about old times.''

''No, vets in the East *now*, Murtaugh.''

''I don't know what you're talking about.''

''Macao. What do you know about Macao?''

Murtaugh struggled to keep his face expressionless. There was absolutely no remaining hope for survival: The consortium wasn't about to divulge its most sensitive secrets to him and let him live. But he still felt he had to buy time in the hope Joshua would make a mistake. Murtaugh couldn't bring himself to throw in the towel. "Macao?"

"Yeah."

"Portuguese colony near Hong Kong. Never made it there. I got hit before I was eligible for R and R."

"The shipment, you black son of a bitch!" Joshua exploded. "What did Hunsaker tell you about the shipment?"

Murtaugh kept his voice as level as he could. "I don't know what the hell you're talking about."

But then Joshua unfisted his hands and slowly grinned. He backed away, and Murtaugh lost sight of him in the shadows at the far end of the room.

A few moments later, he came forward again with someone at his side. Someone much shorter than himself. They stepped into the ring of light that fell over Murtaugh.

"Baby . . ." Murtaugh began choking on his tears.

Clad only in her bra and panties, Rianne was blindfolded, her hands bound behind her. "Daddy?"

"It's okay, baby. I'm here with you. I'll always be with you."

"What's happening? What are they doing to us?"

"Listen, baby . . ." He fought down a sob. "There are some parts of us they can never touch. Those are the good things. And they can't be harmed, ever—"

Joshua laughed again. "You really didn't spend much time in Nam, did you? Well, let me fill you in. It's too late for this daughter. And you're responsible, Murtaugh. You and your shucking and jiving. Now it's up to you if you want to save the rest of your family."

"I'll kill you! I'll kill every one of you!"

"Sure. If you'll let me continue . . . I asked around how many of the guys were double veterans."

"No, no, no," Murtaugh began moaning.

"It turns out three troopers were still cherries in this

department. They're waiting out in the corridor. You'll be given a ringside seat. When they're finished, I expect a full rundown on your chat with Hunsaker. Otherwise, your wife is next.''

''No, no, no.''

''Daddy?'' Her frightened voice broke through the roar of his own pulse in his ears. ''What is he talking about? What's a double veteran?''

He bit his tongue until it bled.

He could not tell his daughter that a double vet earned this sobriquet by having sex with a woman, then murdering her.

CHAPTER **17**

RIGGS WAS SLUMPED forward across the surface of the water, his face submerged. A train of tiny bubbles was issuing from one of his nostrils—not like a man breathing, but like one in the final stages of death.

Kwak touched the sponge to Riggs's back one last time. Nothing. No writhing. No spasms.

He felt for a pulse at the wrist, then frowned when he detected a dim throb. "We will give you one minute more, my friend. Death is a ladder. And it is often descended one step at a time."

Kwak duck-walked around to the front of the tub so he could look directly into the slack face. Riggs's eyelids were drooping over his milky-looking pupils, and his skin was now like gray flannel. "A shame, my friend. You knew nothing. You had nothing to trade for your life. Always keep something. Well, let us check now . . ."

He took Riggs's limp hand and began to turn it over to expose the inner wrist. But, all at once, there was a chopping sound on the water as if a fish had broken the surface. And Kwak saw in horror that the prisoner's chain was looped tightly around his own wrist.

Riggs was glowering at him, the agony in his eyes now

replaced by cold rage. "I'm feeling much better, thank you."

Immediately flattening his right hand into a blade, Kwak snapped back his forearm to deliver a blow, but Riggs gave a heave on the chain, spinning the man partly by his own momentum.

Kwak fought to regain his balance, but a second, harder yank sent his forehead crashing against the edge of the tub. Eyes dazed, he reared up—a gash exposing the pale blue color of his skull. He was reaching for the commando knife on his belt when Riggs coiled the chain around his neck.

"You!" Kwak gurgled, both hands clawing at the links. He threw a quick look in the direction of the steel door, as if hoping someone might rescue him.

"Fat fucking chance, Mr. Electrodes," Riggs said, then dragged the empurpled face down into the water.

After a minute, a bulging eye hemorrhaged, and blood began curdling the water. Only then did Riggs ease up on the chain. He pulled the body by the hair halfway into the tub. "I never trade when I can just take, *my friend*."

Inside one of Kwak's pants pockets, he found the small key he needed. But it was several long seconds before he had the strength to unlock his manacles and climb out of the tub.

When the mercenary unhitched his web belt and let his fatigue trousers slide down to his ankles, Murtaugh lunged for him. But he only succeeded in overturning the chair to which he was tied, nearly knocking himself out on the concrete floor.

Through the loud buzzing in his head, he could hear Rianne screaming for him to help him. He prayed for it to be possible for him to burst out of his body. To roll forward like napalm and incinerate these animals. Then he would find Joshua and the general—wherever they were in this building—and delight in their death screams. He would cremate every last member of the consortium with the white phosphorous heat of his rage.

But it was no good. His avenging spirit was trapped in this exhausted body.

He stopped fighting his bindings and lay still on the floor. He closed his ears to Rianne's pleas. He waited for his heart to explode. He waited for the blackness.

Then the door was thrown back against the wall with a boom.

Murtaugh's first thought was that someone else had come to join in the fun. But then a naked white body flashed across his bleared vision. There followed a man's scream.

Murtaugh raised his head in time to see the mercenary who had lowered himself before Rianne on his knees suddenly arch his spine. He was trying to twist away from the knife Martin Riggs was driving into his back.

The man's two partners let go of Rianne's arms and started going for the pistols in their belt holsters.

Riggs tried to yank free the knife, but it was imbedded in bone, so he turned on the two men without benefit of the blade. Keeping his chin tucked low, he caught one of them in the mouth with the top of his head, then spun aside to suddenly squat like a cossack dancer. He used his legs like pistons to kick the other mercenary's feet out from under him.

Falling, the man threw up his hands to brace himself, and his pistol skimmed across the floor. Murtaugh quickly covered it with his chest.

"Shook him, Mick!" the mercenary cried, then landed hard.

His partner spat out a wad of blood and tooth chips, but held on to his handgun despite the pain his shattered mouth was giving him. "All right," he seethed, swinging the muzzle on Riggs, "you want to fuck with—"

From less than an arm's length away, Riggs drove the heel of his hand into the base of the man's nose, which remained squashed and formless against his cheek. He was dead before he had completely sunk to the floor, the bridge of his nose shoved like a spike up into his brain.

The pistol dropped from his hand and clattered against the floor.

Staying close to his prey, Riggs smashed an elbow into the surviving mercenary's larynx, which gave with a hollow-sounding pop.

"Mind if I borrow these?" The man was still gagging to death when Riggs reached down and ripped off his trousers, donning them for his own use. "I forgot to mark mine with a laundry pen before I came to camp. Mom warned me."

At the moment of death, the mercenary loosed his bowels, and Riggs grimaced.

"What kind of fighting was *that?*" Murtaugh asked hoarsely. Rianne had crawled across the floor and was clinging to him, whimpering like a small child.

"I save your ass and that's all you can say?"

"I've never seen any martial arts like it."

"It's called jail-house rock. Came out of the prison system. I learned it from an ex-con. Good for places where you can't leap around like a ballerina." Bracing his foot against the body, Riggs was finally able to extricate the knife, which he then used to cut free Murtaugh.

"Where the hell are we, Martin?"

"Back in L.A. someplace."

"You could see out of your blindfold?"

"No, but I kept track of how long we were on the road. And the traffic outside this building didn't sound like Kingman, Arizona." Riggs winked at Rianne. "Keep it together, babe. We still have to get out of this joint."

"I'm okay," she said quietly.

Murtaugh chambered a round into the pistol he'd just concealed under him.

Riggs found the other handgun and inspected it for damage. "Browning 9-mm. It'll do in a pinch." He went to the door. "I suggest we surprise them before they do the same to us. How's your shoulder, Roger?"

"I'll make it."

"You sure? You look like hell."

"Just lead the way, for chrissake. Do we have to argue about everything?"

Riggs led them at a run around a bend in the corridor and right into a bus cart being wheeled by a Korean in a steward's jacket. The waiter made a startled cry that wasn't much different from Rianne's. But then, recovering his presence of mind, he reached inside his red jacket, revealing a shoulder holster.

Riggs fired first.

The shot to the breastbone sent the man bouncing against the wall and then sprawling across the dinner dishes on the cart.

"Wouldn't you know it?" Riggs asked. "Just when we finally get some room service around this place, we've got to leave."

"Yeah, well, let's go European plan this time and skip the meals." Then Murtaugh winced and gripped his shoulder all the tighter.

"Hell, that hole isn't even really coagulating yet."

Murtaugh motioned tersely with his pistol for Riggs to go on.

At the landing above a long flight of stairs, Riggs went down on one knee and watched below for a few seconds. Music was welling up the darkened incline. Very mediocre rhythm and blues. An accordion would have made it complete. When Riggs glanced back quizzically, as if to ask where the hell they were, Murtaugh whispered, "Can't be no black club."

Riggs started down the steps first.

Murtaugh and Rianne followed fifteen feet behind him.

Then, without warning, Riggs crouched low—his buttocks almost resting on a step—and extended his pistol between his knees, aiming downward. He fired three shots that lit up the staircase and blotted out Murtaugh's view of the figure below.

He thought that Riggs had gotten his man, but wasn't sure. Nevertheless, he seized Rianne's hand and said, his voice quavering as they ran, "This is it, honey. Don't stop. Whatever happens, even to me, don't stop."

"I love you, Daddy."

"I love you, too, baby."

Riggs was shooting again.

This time Murtaugh clearly saw the mercenary. He was just opening up with an Uzi when Riggs's bullets hammered into his chest. He reeled in agony, his finger frozen to the trigger. His burst went high, chipping concrete off the ceiling of the staircase and showering Murtaugh and Rianne with dust.

The mercenary had no sooner thudded hollowly against the hardwood floor than Riggs grasped his submachine gun and began ransacking his pockets for spare magazines. He found two and tucked them in the thigh pockets of the fatigue trousers.

The empty pistol he tossed aside.

From behind a pair of swinging doors came screaming and shouting. It sounded like a large crowd.

Reloading the Uzi, Riggs smiled at Murtaugh. "Shall we do it?"

Murtaugh shrugged. "Why not? I'm sure as hell not going back the way we just came."

Then Riggs barreled through the doors first. Murtaugh, dragging Rianne, went through close on his heels.

They found themselves in the main lounge of a large nightclub. The place was packed with a mixed crowd of Orientals and whites, most of whom were shrieking and squirming under their tables. Even the band members were chucking their instruments aside and scrambling for cover.

Across the smoky room, standing between parted velvet curtains, was Joshua. The mouth of his Uzi was flashing as he swept it back and forth like a fire hose.

Swinging his arm behind him, Murtaugh threw Rianne to the carpet.

Riggs was leaping from table to table, his bare feet

crunching over glassware as he advanced, trying to get a clear shot at Joshua.

"Crazy bastard," Murtaugh muttered. Then he saw a mercenary throw open the kitchen door with the butt of an M-16 rifle and glare out across the tables in search of a target. He had just fixed his eyes on Riggs when Murtaugh shouted, "Don't shoot—the general's out here! He's been hit!"

The mercenary hesitated, then turned his face in the direction from which Murtaugh's voice had come. "General, sir?"

Murtaugh's pistol barked twice, and the mercenary was blown back into the kitchen, where the lights quickly went off.

After directing one final burst at Riggs, Joshua backed through the door behind the reservation desk, reloading as he withdrew.

Riggs signaled Murtaugh that he was going out after him.

Murtaugh nodded. He was so winded he could barely stand. His shoulder felt like it was on fire.

Holding herself in her arms, Rianne seemed aware for the first time that she had nothing on but her underwear. She was trembling. "I'm afraid, Daddy."

"Me, too." Murtaugh found a mink stole draped over the back of a booth and put it around her shoulders. "Come on, we've got to stick with Martin. We've got to stay together."

Outside the wide boulevard was a four-lane parking lot—Christmas shoppers adding to what Murtaugh realized was the evening rush hour. Horns were indicating the frustration level, and the exhaust of all the idling engines was turning the cold air silvery.

He realized that they had been captives for little more than twenty-four hours, although it had seemed a lifetime. And this was Hollywood Boulevard. The streetlamps were decked out with shaggy manes of tinsel, from which Christmas lights winked on and off.

Riggs was standing on his toes, peering down the crowded sidewalk for a glimpse of Joshua.

"Did you lose him?" Murtaugh asked, pleased to hear the caterwauling of police sirens in the distance.

"No, he just tried to hijack a car. But then he got a look at this traffic. I can catch him." Riggs was trotting backwards as he asked: "You okay?"

"Go ahead. I'll wait here with Rianne for the cavalry."

Bare-chested, holding the Uzi down at his side, Riggs started running. The pedestrians quickly parted for him, giving him all the sidewalk he needed. Murtaugh was reminded of Moses, the way that sea of humanity was cleaved by Riggs.

Softly, he started singing an old spiritual, but then stopped after a few bars. He sagged against the dirty plaster wall of the nightclub and clasped Rianne's hand tightly.

Riggs had left bloody footprints behind on the pavement.

After a couple of blocks, Riggs heard the tune of a carol in the air. "White Christmas" by Elvis Presley was coming over the P.A. speakers atop the streetlight poles. Softly, Riggs hummed along as he scanned both sides of the boulevard and into the glass storefronts.

He was half convinced that Joshua had ducked into a shop when he caught a flash of white hair far ahead— under the bright marquee of a porno theater.

The mercenary started to turn his head to look back. Riggs ducked behind a fat old woman, who quickly sidestepped away and growled that she had no money.

"Merry fucking Christmas to you, too, mom."

Joshua then jaywalked the boulevard mid-block, stitching among the grid-locked vehicles toward the other side, using bumpers as catwalks when he had to. Every several seconds, he glanced back.

At last, he spotted Riggs. He opened fire with a three-shot burst that skimmed over the tops of the cars and took out most of the plate-glass front of a jewelry store. The burglary alarm startled jangling. There were screams from the sidewalk, but they were from fright, not pain.

Riggs didn't return fire, although he picked up his pace.

Elvis continued to croon about sleigh bells ringing.

The black-and-white had to drive on the sidewalk to reach the entrance to the nightclub. And the redheaded senior patrolman took one look at Murtaugh—half dressed with hamburger for a face and a trickling shoulder wound— and shouted, "You there! Keep your hands in sight! Turn around slowly!"

"Murtaugh . . . robbery/homicide," he mumbled, realizing for the first time how badly swollen his lips were.

"What'd he say?" the two-striper asked his partner without looking askance at him. Both of them continued to leer down their sights at the half-dressed black man who was able to loft only one hand in obedience to their instructions. He needed to keep the other one on the wall to maintain his balance.

"He said something about robbery/homicide."

"You a cop?"

Murtaugh bobbed his head. "Sergeant . . . homicide."

"Who's your deputy chief?"

Murtaugh told them, then sighed as one muttered to other: "Is he right?"

"Fuck if I know. What do I care about detective headquarters? A bunch of prima-donna jerk-offs. But I do know homicide has one Negro sergeant."

"Don't you read fucking memos? We're not supposed to say *Negro* anymore."

"Then what?"

"Let's skip it." The two-striper raised his voice again: "Sergeant, where's your badge?"

Murtaugh hooked his thumb toward the nightclub.

The patrolmen lowered their wheel guns, and Murtaugh waved for Rianne to come back to him out of the crowd.

Expecting this little ritual as soon as he'd seen the two white faces in the approaching cruiser, he had tucked his pistol in the deep pocket of Rianne's borrowed fur stole and ordered her to stand out of harm's way.

She now hugged him protectively and glared at the patrolmen.

Switching from siren to horn to clear the pedestrians, a second unit crept up the sidewalk to the nightclub. And then a third car.

"Don't go in there," Murtaugh told the blue-suiters, "until you've got plenty of backup."

"Well, it's on the way," somebody said. "Listen."

It sounded like every cat in Los Angeles County was in heat.

Taking Rianne by the elbow, Murtaugh led her to the nearest car and sat her down in the back seat. "You stay right here."

"Where're you going?" Her eyes were still enormous with fear.

"Got to help Martin."

"Daddy . . ." She started crying.

"Listen—no time. You've got to understand. Martin helped us. He risked his life for our family."

After a moment, she nodded, then said in a voice that was hauntingly like Trish's, "Be careful."

A patrol sergeant trotted up behind Murtaugh, his keys jingling. "Roger Murtaugh? Is that *you?*"

"Rex?"

"What the shit's going on, buddy?"

"My daughter will explain. But two things quick. Get a hold of Glendale PD. Have them secure my house. ASAP. My family's in danger. Next, put it out to responding units—we have an undercover man in foot pursuit westbound." Murtaugh was already hobbling down Hollywood Boulevard as he shouted the last: "It's Martin Riggs! He's armed with an Uzi!"

"Riggs is in on this?"

"Yes, and he has no shirt! Like me!"

"Submachine gun . . . no shirt . . . foot pursuit." The Hollywood division sergeant shrugged at Rianne. "Who else could it be but Riggs, or that Dago kid with all the muscles and the bent lips?''

Riggs skidded to a stop on the still bleeding soles of his feet. Carefully, he stepped beneath a brick arch and into a small arcade of specialty shops.

In the last block, he had lost sight of Joshua on the sidewalk.

A low planter bright with poinsettias stood at the center of the little plaza. Riggs thrashed through them to come flying over the top, his Uzi held at the ready in case Joshua was hiding behind.

He wasn't.

The arcade was a dead end. The shops that didn't depend on the Christmas trade were already darkened. But the last place in line was still throwing a rectangle of light out into the plaza.

It proved to be a gourmet boutique. From the edge of the window, Riggs looked at copper pots dangling from ceiling racks, piles of pot holders and, standing with his arms crossed behind the cash register, an indignant-looking clerk with a beard he probably trimmed with depilatory cream instead of a razor.

Riggs sensed it in his expression: The clerk had just observed something he hadn't liked. Something fishy. He was reaching for the phone when Riggs caught a faint reflection on the glass of a metallic glint in the background—up high along the roof line on the other side of the arcade.

Riggs didn't hesitate. He made a rolling dive through the window and landed hard on a display of omelette pans. But he quickly hugged the wall because Joshua's spray of bullets was chiming against the copper pans overhead.

Oblivious to what was really happening, the clerk cried, ''That does it! I'm phoning the police right now!''

''Get down, you stupid fuck!''

''Why?''

''We're being shot at!''

The man sank to the floor so swiftly, Riggs wondered if he'd fainted.

There was no time to find out. He went back out through the smashed window and tried to glimpse Joshua's fleeing silhouette above. He couldn't see anything but heard shoes drumming down the far slope of the roof.

Sprinting out through the brick arch, Riggs rounded the next corner onto a side street and caught sight of Joshua spider-crawling down off the ledge of the one-story building. He was returning fire even before his shoes touched pavement.

Riggs kept shooting—but rolled into the gutter and used the curb for cover as Joshua's bullets snapped like electricity against the concrete around him.

Then, waving his arms, the mercenary jumped out in front of a slow-moving car. The Dodge Aspen hadn't come to a complete stop before Joshua opened the door and yanked the middle-aged woman down onto the pavement by the hair.

He accelerated past Riggs, sitting low behind the wheel, his door cracked open a few inches so he could fire back as he made his escape away from Hollywood Boulevard.

Riggs was able to blow out a taillight with a parting burst. But that was it.

"Shit!" He turned. "You okay, mom?"

Murtaugh had reached the edge of the sprawling night-club building when something down the alley caught his eye—the reflection of headlights on a stucco wall. A car was coming out of a smaller alley that connected to the one Murtaugh now hurried up.

He popped the clip out of the Browning pistol to see how many rounds he had left, then slapped it back in. Seven. A lucky number. Yet, he decided that if the car contained well-armed mercenaries, desperate to be on their way, he would let them go. He would live to fight another day.

But then, coming around the corner and into the side

alley, he saw—over the glare of headlights—the general sitting beside a grim-faced driver in a cargo van.

Murtaugh knew that he could never let the general get away. Not after everything that had happened.

He hoisted the pistol and fired.

The windshield sprouted holes, but they appeared in the space between the general and his driver, who reached outside with his own handgun and opened up at Murtaugh.

"Come on!" Murtaugh shouted. He took more time with the next two shots. His bullets snapped back the driver's head as if his neck had been broken. He had been speeding up to ram Murtaugh when struck, and now his dead foot remained heavy on the pedal.

The general, seeing that only a collision with a stucco wall lay ahead, tried to leave the vehicle through his side door, but the alley was too narrow to allow this. He slammed the door again, his eyes furious.

Murtaugh squeezed the trigger again and again until the slide jerked back after the last round. But he had no idea if he'd scored, for in that split second it came to him that the van was going to run him down. He flattened himself against the wall, but sensed that it would do no good.

He was going to die. And, curiously, he didn't care—the general was going to die, too.

But the van deflected off the wall as it roared onward once again, and then rode up the bricks on its right-hand wheels. The driver's mirror left deep scratches on Murtaugh's chest as it streaked past, but at that point the van was canting away from him as it overturned.

It skidded the last yards on its side, trailing big fountains of orange sparks, then plowed head-on into the wall. A cloud of radiator steam hissed up, and when it finally cleared the cab could be seen crumpled back into the cargo section. No screams came from this compressed ball of wreckage, even when flames began worming up through the mangled sheet metal from the engine.

Small arms ammunition began shooting off. Then a different kind of percussive report echoed down the alley.

Louder than pistol cartridges. Blasting caps or like military detonators—Murtaugh couldn't quite tell which, but he ran with everything he had left for the edge of the loading dock at the end of the alley.

This, he realized, was the vehicle that had hauled Joshua and his blocks of C-4 down to South L.A. to blow up poor Dixie Monroe.

Murtaugh was still running when the high-explosive blast rolled up on him from behind like the sun grazing the earth.

Riggs was within sight of the nightclub when it started to snow on Hollywood Boulevard.

The horde of onlookers pressing against the yellow-taped police line, the jaded-looking shoppers coursing behind them, lifted their faces to the fine white flakes that were sheeting out of a clear winter sky. And they smiled like children. They opened their mouths to catch the stuff.

Riggs let some settle on his hand, then transferred it on a moistened fingertip to his mouth. "Shit . . ."

His eyes slowly enlarged as he tried a second taste, not believing the first. *"Holy shit!"*

Murtaugh staggered out of an alley, and Riggs jogged up to him. "Do you believe this?"

Murtaugh gazed up into the swirling powder. "Yes, I do."

"The blast I just heard?"

"Right. The general just went *airborne*—along with the big shipment from Macao." He looked back at Riggs questioningly. "Joshua?"

"Got away. If I'd had a rifle instead of this burp gun, he'd be a goner. Of course, if he'd had a rifle, I'd be the goner. So it goes. Rianne all right?"

"With a patrol sergeant, I trust."

"Good, let's get to Glendale."

They took the first black-and-white they found. Flicking on the wipers to clear the white powder off the windshield, Riggs shook his head. "Another ten minutes, every hype in Southern California will be here, licking the sidewalks. Switch on the siren down there, will you, Roger?"

CHAPTER 18

A FULL MOON shone down on the Glendale Police black-and-white, but it was so paled by smog the patrolman working the *Times* crossword puzzle had to use the high-intensity lamp jutting out of the dashboard.

His partner, sprawled sleepily on the shotgun side of the front seat, bent the light his way by wrenching the tensor arm. He checked his wrist watch.

"Give me the lamp back."

"Fuck you."

They said nothing again for ten minutes. The only sound in the parked car was the drivel coming over the radio, a series of momentous-sounding codes that really only meant that a dog was barking, a purse was missing, a husband was drunk again.

Both patrolmen had been at the job for ten years. Neither had done well on the most recent written promotional exams for detective and sergeant. Neither was chipping away at a college degree in his spare time. And they were slowly but surely getting fitted for a jacket by the brass—adequate for field duty when closely supervised, but completely lacking in self-motivation. Blue-suiters until retirement or early death from cardiovascular disease. Ordinary cops.

And they'd been together on the night shift for six years. They didn't realize it, but they now talked to each other in the same tone of voice they used on their wives.

"Give me seven letters for an Italian cheese. Fourth letter's an *o*."

"Ricotta."

"Jeez, how'd you know that?"

"I'm not stupid, Walt."

"Did I say you were fucking stupid, Mario?"

"No, but you think it. I can tell sometimes."

"Hey, leave the lamp alone. Why don't you buy yourself a watch that lights up?"

"I don't want a new watch. This one belonged to my dad. It made it back in one piece—twenty-five missions over Europe."

"Was that Wop air force? No wonder it's in such good shape. Wop planes never got out of the hangar."

"Fuck you."

"Fuck *you*."

Another ten minutes of silence followed, then the dispatcher announced the top of the hour before asking the two patrolmen if they were still alive and well at their location.

"We're code four here, Glendale."

"Ten-four, Paul-seven."

Walt yawned and set aside his puzzle. "You ever get the chance to ball her?"

"Who? *That* dispatcher?"

"Sure, what's wrong with Claudine?"

"You'd have to pay me. A face like Brando's in *The Godfather*."

"Yeah, but the tits."

"You can't fuck tits . . ."

This started an argument that lasted until 2140 hours—when they suddenly shut up. A pedestrian was approaching on the sidewalk, a newspaper folded under his arm.

"Big mother, ain't he?"

"Fill out an FI card on him."

"Why field interrogate him? He looks like a stockbroker, for chrissake."

"Because we ought to put something on the log. Make it look like we're doing something here."

"Why *are* we sitting on this house? What good is it doing?"

"Sarge said it's a professional courtesy. Security blanket for a brother officer from an allied agency and all that crock. But we're *here*, and that's all what matters."

"Then you FI him. I'm out of cards."

"Sorry I asked, Mario."

Walt stepped out of the car and slid his nightstick into its ring on his Sam Browne belt. "Pardon me, sir—"

The large blond man dutifully halted. "Yes, officer?"

"May I see some identification please?"

"Is there some problem?" He turned toward the brightly lit house. "Are the Murtaughs all right?"

"You know them?"

"Sure, I live just around the corner. We're in the P.T.A. together."

"Everything's swell with them."

"Then why are you people out in force?"

"We're not *in force*, sir, it's just the little old two of us."

"Oh." The man began fumbling through his wallet. "Oh, dear, I hope I didn't leave my license at home. Well, it's not like I'm out driving, is it?"

"Aw, that's okay, sir. Just checking." Walt waved him on. "Sorry for the interruption. Enjoy your walk."

"Thank you, officer."

Mario smirked at Walt as he got back inside the car. "This one's going to bitch you."

"The hell you say."

"I know the type. He's already working up a little steam under the collar. The nerve of his fucking cops to hit

him with a bunch of questions fit only for colored folks
and *pachucos*.''

''I think I handled it real professional. Did you hear him
thank me?''

''The complaint filers always say thank you. That's
what gets them rolling, remembering how mousy they
acted. Believe me, he's going to bitch.''

''He *loved* me.''

''He's going to—''

Then Mario's face took on a funny, thoughtful expression as if he'd suddenly recalled the worst thing that had
ever happened to him.

The interior of the car had somehow filled with the
stench of smoke. And there were all kinds of noises.
Louder than the strange clattering sounds coming from
outside the car were the clangs of metal bouncing off metal
inside.

Before the tensor lamp shattered and winked out, Walt
looked over at Mario one last time: He was amazed to see
his partner of seven years jerking and squirming like he
had a case of Saint Vitus's dance. And, all at once, there
was blood everywhere—on the inside of the windshield,
twining down the Remington shotgun that was still locked
in its holder, dripping off the face plate of the radio.

Through Mario's open window, two hands could be
seen clutching a stubby-looking automatic weapon. It was
still firing.

Walt was reaching for the microphone when he felt a
blow to his neck like he'd been struck with a baseball bat.

He immediately knew that it had been a bullet. He
realized that from his first day at the academy he had been
expecting this to happen. His dreams had warned him that
this would happen.

And now he almost wanted to laugh.

He'd been wearing a Kevlar vest summer and winter for
five years faithfully.

And when he finally gets it—it's in the neck.

It was his last thought.

• • •

The yelp siren stopped being a siren. It became a fist hammering on the roof of the patrol car in which Riggs was hurtling down the freeway toward Glendale.

Murtaugh was on the radio, trying to find out from Glendale's communications division through LAPD's communication division if that department had responded to his house. And, as usual, something was being lost in translation between the two law-enforcement fiefdoms. Murtaugh was getting no clear answer. His raspy voice was on the verge of completely giving out.

Riggs, keeping his eyes on the thick holiday traffic, snatched the microphone from Murtaugh's hand and shouted, "I don't care if you have to get our fucking chief to phone their fucking chief—give us a status on Sergeant Murtaugh's family ASAP! And yes, control—I know I'm not conforming to radio procedure!" He tossed the mike on the seat between them.

Pressing a handkerchief to his shoulder, Murtaugh leaned back and shut his eyes. "This nightmare just goes on and on and on . . ."

"Hang in there. It's just about over."

"After just one more shooting?"

Riggs shrugged. "Probably."

Murtaugh laughed helplessly, then had to bite his tongue to keep from losing control. "You must have the all-time record for shooting incidents in a single work week. How many SIs as of this minute? Five? Six?"

Riggs was tight-lipped for a moment. "One more than you know about."

"What are you talking about?"

"You heard me."

Murtaugh stared out the windshield. He didn't cringe when Riggs used the narrow emergency-parking lane to pass a tractor-trailer on the right: He was too exhausted to feel fear anymore. "I was trying to make a joke, Martin. A shitty little joke. And now what are you telling me?"

"Any of your guys working a double homicide way

down south? Two jokers in a fancy van conversion on Pacific Coast Highway?''

''The dick assigned to Harbor division drew the initial investigation, but yeah, we're going to help follow-up on it. When we get the damn time.''

''What do you know about it?''

''Kind of a Robin Hood caper. Witnesses say this bozo saved them from being abducted.''

''I did it.''

Murtaugh lifted the handkerchief off his wound. He inspected the bloodstain carefully as if he didn't want to meet Riggs's eyes. ''Was it a righteous shooting?''

''Yes.''

''Then why didn't you report it?''

''I don't know.''

''Why'd you flee the scene?''

''I just didn't give a fuck.''

''That isn't good enough, Martin.''

''Maybe I was looking for a way out that night. Nothing matters when you're looking to die. I don't know.''

''And the *next* morning you did that number on the sniper?''

''Right.''

''Jesus, you have had a busy week.'' Then Murtaugh clammed up. After a while, he started flexing his jaw muscles, but he refused to speak, even though his eyes were glistening.

The traffic came to a standstill for an accident, and Riggs took to the surface streets for a few miles before getting back on the freeway. Finally, he had to ask, ''Well, what are you thinking?''

''Nothing.''

''I mean it, Roger, please.''

''Does it matter?''

''Yes.''

''Why are you laying this shit on me *now?*''

''Because I've got some strong vibes. Never had them like this before. Not even during my worst times in Nam.''

"Vibes?"

Riggs smiled sadly at him. "Your family—everything's going to be okay. I just know it. But I'm not going to make it. Tonight's going to be it."

"How can you be so sure?"

"I just am."

Murtaugh got gooseflesh from the resignation in Riggs's voice. The man was fessing up so homicide could clear the case—a final favor for Murtaugh. "Don't talk this way, Martin."

"Why not?"

"Because you're my motherfucking partner, that's why!"

"You don't have to bring up my personal habits, Roger."

"Can the shit, Riggs!" Murtaugh hurled the bloody handkerchief at him. "Do you hear me, loser? You're my friend!" Then he lowered his voice and glanced away. "My best friend."

"Okay." Riggs looked surprised. "I hear you."

"And I started out this gig trying to nail your ass."

"What do you mean?"

"Remember that day you sneaked up on me atop the overpass? Well, I was talking with the department shrink. She asked me to help put together a jacket on you. Enough to pension you out on a stress disability."

"Christ." Riggs paused, his jaw slack. "Do you honestly think I'm nuts?"

"Yes . . . no . . . I mean, I don't know. Just drive, man."

Riggs kept his mouth shut until they were nearly to Murtaugh's house, then asked as he reached down to kill the siren, "If I happen to live through tonight, are you going to tell the shrink what I just said? And tell the department everything else?"

"I'm not sure." Then Murtaugh slowly turned and met Riggs's eyes, which seemed evasive all at once. "Wait, wait—do you *want* me to tell?"

"I'll leave it up to you, Roger. See, I guess I trust you. And I don't trust nobody. Other than my wife, I mean."

Riggs was humming softly as he took the corner of Murtaugh's street on what felt like only two wheels. "I'll be damned. Another entire day—and I forgot."

"Forgot what, brother?"

"Ah, you know."

"No, I don't."

"That she's away."

Murtaugh studied him closely. "She's not away, Martin. She's gone. You have to accept that."

"Why?" Riggs grinned, almost defiantly.

"Because you're still here. And there's people here who care a whole lot about you." Then Murtaugh held his breath as his house came into view.

Everything looked normal: the Christmas lights shining, the skateboard left wheels up on the walkway, Burbank visible through the parted living room curtains, arching his spine atop the camelback sofa—undoubtedly at one of the kids for manhandling him.

And parked squarely in front of the house was a black-and-white.

"Bless them," Murtaugh laughed with relief. "I will never badmouth Glendale PD again for as long as I live!"

"I wouldn't go that far."

Murtaugh bailed out first and trotted up to the patrol car. He leaned over to talk to the blue-suiter on the shotgun side, then stumbled backwards as if he'd been struck and cried, "Martin! They're dead!"

Riggs rolled out of his door with the Uzi in hand. Taking cover behind the engine block, he caught a glimpse of a silhouette in one of the second-story windows.

"Look out, Roger!" he shouted the split second before Joshua fired downward, right through the glass, showering the lawn with glimmering shards.

Then, as Murtaugh dived over the hood of the Glendale car, Riggs drove Joshua away from the upstairs window with a burst that quickly gave out. He had been careful to keep the fire selector on semi-automatic as much as possible, but still the Uzi was bone dry.

He chucked it aside.

Crawling across the front seat, hugging it to stay low, he hit the shotgun release button and yanked the Ithaca twelve-gauge out of its dash holder. With his left hand, he seized the microphone and put out a code 999, officers down, carefully transmitting Murtaugh's address twice.

Then, firing, hopefully keeping Joshua's head down with a salvo of double-ought buck to each of the three second-story windows, he charged for the front door. Out of the corner of his eye, he could see Murtaugh running for the back of the house.

As soon as Joshua had riddled the two patrolmen sitting out front, he slapped a fresh clip into the grip of the Uzi and turned up the walkway for the house.

The front door was unlocked. All for the best. He didn't want Murtaugh's family to file out the back. He wanted to get them all. He wanted this to be remembered as a massacre.

The living room was empty, except for a cat, which he kicked aside when it tried to twine around his legs.

A television was on somewhere in the back of the house, and he worked toward the sound by cutting through the kitchen. The oven door was warm; he opened it on a clove-studded ham that was baking. The skin around his pinkish eyes crinkled in a smile. *They were still here.* And now they were all going to die for Murtaugh's sins against the consortium. And, over twenty years of continuous warfare, Joshua's emotions had been rearranged in such a way that nothing was sweeter than revenge.

He threw back the swinging door and advanced into the family room, shooting from the hip. The television screen shattered, and its electronic guts spewed sparks onto carpet. The fabric of the couch burst and stuffing flew around the room in tufts. The panes of a Tiffany lamp tinkled as they tore through the Christmas tree like grapeshot, overturning it. The only illumination remaining in the room flickered from the gas logs in the fireplace.

Yet, as his forefinger slid off the trigger, Joshua gave a second, longer look around the room and cried, "No!"

He took the stairs four at a time and drummed down the hallway to the master bedroom. Kicking in the door, he let go on the king-sized bed with a burst.

But no one was in the room. Nor in the adjoining bathroom.

"Come out! Come out and die with dignity!"

Then he noticed the bullet-torn slip of pink paper on the bed:

> *Roger—*
> *Detective Norris of Glendale PD is tak-*
> *ing us to Parker Center to await you*
> *there. He thinks this will be safer than*
> *trying to guard us here.*
>
> > *I love you,*
> > *Trish*

"Bitch! Don't think you're safe now! Don't think—!"

Then he heard a car brake sharply in front of the house.

He darkened the master bedroom by smashing the night-stand lamp against the wall, then gazed down onto the street.

The dim moonlight reflected off his front teeth as he slowly bared them in a grin. "There is a God—oh yes, there is indeed a God."

Joshua took his last magazine from his coat pocket and kissed the cold metal before inserting it into the subma-chine gun.

CHAPTER 19

RIGGS CROUCHED IN the foyer at the foot of the stairs, listening.

He heard the sliding-glass door in the family room rumble open—Murtaugh slipping in through the back, he had to assume.

The inside of the house reeked of smokeless powder, plus the residue of some kind of electrical fire. He hoped Murtaugh wouldn't go berserk when the obvious occurred to him: There had just been gunfire in his house—Joshua would let no errors of anger slip past unpunished.

Riggs decided to circle back to the stairs after making a search of the first floor. Keeping in a crouch, he passed through the kitchen and paused at the swinging door to the family room.

He prepared himself for what he might see on the other side, then pitched himself headfirst through the door, staying low as he hit the carpet.

Murtaugh pivoted on him with his pistol, but held his fire, as Riggs had trusted he would.

Riggs pointed at the stairs. Murtaugh nodded that he understood, but his eyes were wild as they swept over the shambles of a room. Riggs could tell that he was aching to call out for his family. But that would never do. Not with a man-eater on the premises. Murtaugh had understood: This was no longer his home. It was now the jungle. A free-fire zone.

His bare feet sifting noiselessly through the debris on the floor, Riggs made his way back to the newel post and hunkered down behind it. After a few seconds, Murtaugh joined him there and instinctively began providing protection to the rear, keeping an eye on the foyer and the door that connected to the garage.

The house was silent, except for the something sizzling in the oven.

Riggs filled his lungs with air, then started up the stairs.

He had climbed three steps when he suddenly recoiled. He fired the shotgun twice, then pushed himself off the wall with his legs, crashing through the wooden banister and landing in the middle of the family room on his back.

"Jesus!" Murtaugh lunged away from the stair opening the instant after Riggs—to evade Joshua's hail of bullets that ricocheted into the foyer and splintered the front door, taking out its amber pane of glass with a crash.

Then Joshua came bolting down the stairs. And before Murtaugh could shoot over the top of the newel post at him, the mercenary barreled through the gap in the banister and began grappling with Riggs for the shotgun.

"Stand clear, Martin!" Murtaugh shouted as the two men rolled as one back and forth across the carpet. "Give me a shot! Stand clear of him!"

But then Murtaugh slowly lowered the pistol to his side.

In a blinking, Joshua had ripped the Ithaca out of Riggs's exhausted grip. The muzzle was pressing deeply into Martin's throat.

"Airborne!" Joshua exulted.

Riggs looked up at Murtaugh with that unsettling smile and said, "Waste the son of a bitch, Rog."

"Drop it!" Murtaugh ordered, suddenly raising the 9-mm pistol again and drawing a bead on Joshua's head. "You drop it right now!"

"Bullshit," Joshua sneered. "Drop yours or Riggs does his thinking separate from his body from now on."

"Go ahead and dust him, Roger." Incredibly, Riggs was now chuckling. "Blow a rib roast off this bastard. You can wrap this thing up with one shot. You can set the world right again by pulling the trigger."

"I can't . . . I can't just watch you die, Martin."

"Smart man," Joshua said. "Toss that pistol outside and you'll both live."

Murtaugh hesitated a moment, his face twisted. Then he pitched the handgun out the open sliding-glass door.

It bounced across the patio and into a row of Boston fern.

Joshua laughed contemptuously.

"What's so goddamned funny?" Murtaugh asked.

"I lied." Joshua pulled the trigger.

"No!" Murtaugh roared so loudly he almost missed the *snick* sound that came from the Ithaca instead of a deafening blast of double-ought buck.

The top of Riggs's head was still were it belonged. And he was grinning. "I lied, too." Then he bashed his elbow into Joshua's face, reeling the man backwards.

Both men scrambled to their feet and widened their stances into ready positions for fighting.

Joshua's eyes were shining as he gestured at his street clothes. "With your permission?"

"By all means."

Joshua kicked off his shoes and hurriedly stripped down to his briefs. "I'm going to butcher you with my hands, Riggs."

"I sure don't want to be you when all this bad karma comes around again."

They both laughed.

And Murtaugh began inching toward the hallway and his study at its end.

"Stay where you are, Roger," Riggs insisted. "Keep away from your gun collection. This is between me and this loser."

Murtaugh could still hear no sirens in approach. "Use your head, Martin."

"No, I'm going to use my *rage*." And Riggs spun forward without his eyes giving warning. He delivered a high roundhouse kick that hung a whooshing sound in the air.

At first, Murtaugh thought that Riggs's kick had missed its mark, but then he saw that half of Joshua's ear was folded over, torn away from his head. Bright red blood began trickling down his neck and across his back.

"Nice—you're more limber than you look." Joshua flew back at him with a blur of fists. Riggs parried the first fist blow, but the second caught him in the cheekbone. The mashed spot on his face remained slightly depressed, and Murtaugh realized that the bone had been broken.

Yet both men were grinning at each other as they spun apart and assumed defensive stances while recovering their wind.

"To the death then?" Joshua asked, something obscene about his eagerness. It seemed lustful.

"Let me check my calendar." Riggs tried a quick, bayonetlike thrust with his hand to the abdomen, which Joshua blocked downward.

"Good move—reach up inside my chest cavity. Then show me what my heart looks like."

"I'd have to make do with a lung," Riggs seethed, dancing on the balls of his feet. "You don't have a fucking heart."

Joshua barked a laugh, then loosed such a furious side kick his foot plowed through Riggs's deflective blow and found ribs.

Riggs cried out but—as he reeled away—his knuckles sank into the side of Joshua's mouth.

The mercenary spat out a molar.

"Just had it crowned, I bet." Riggs investigated his ribs with his fingers and winced.

At last, Murtaugh could hear sirens. One, maybe two miles of winding suburban streets away, which meant that the patrol cars were still at least three minutes from arrival. An eternity in a fight this ruthless. Yet there was a side of Murtaugh that was fascinated by the variety of styles used by the two men: military combative moves, judo, karate, Brazilian jujitsu, even testa—a desperate form of African martial arts concocted to deter slave traders. And just when the fighting would begin to seem predictable, one of them would throw in the monkey wrench of a new discipline.

Ignoring the pain of his fractured ribs, Riggs came at Joshua with a feint and then the flat knife hand, which the mercenary deftly snagged at the wrist and elaborated into a downward twist lock. At the same time, he struck Riggs behind the knee with his heel and toppled him.

Riggs lay still for a second, then lifted his head only to take Joshua's roundhouse kick full in the face.

"Too soon." Joshua said aside to Murtaugh. "I was afraid he wasn't rested enough for this caliber of match." Then he extended both thumbs like claws in preparation of gouging out Riggs's closed eyes.

Murtaugh started forward. "Martin!"

His thumbs still outstretched, Joshua was leaping in the air—his knees drawn together to batter Riggs's chest as he landed—when Riggs suddenly rolled under the walnut coffee table. He sprang back up, using the table as a shield and then as a ram to drive Joshua into the confines of a corner. The mercenary's head struck the wall so hard it left a pock in the thick sheet rock, but the man quickly shook off any promise of being dazed.

"You son of a bitch!"

"Shouldn't tilt your aggression on people," Riggs was gasping. "Bad karma."

Joshua then counterattacked with such crisp, focused blows the table was splintered to kindling that fell in a heap around Riggs's legs. Martin took at least three lightning blows to the abdomen before he caught a punch with a hooking block and wearily pinned Joshua to the corner again, this time with his head instead of the coffee table.

He continued to butt Joshua in the solar plexus with his head.

Joshua reached down for one of the broken wooden legs, which he then hefted as a club.

Riggs seemed too spent to knock it out of the man's hand. His eyes looked drunken and sleepy, perhaps only because they were swollen half shut. He was beginning to rock from side to side like the losing boxer in his final round. A knockout seemed imminent.

Yet, just when Murtaugh was sure Riggs would collapse, the man started hammering Joshua with those constrained moves he had described as jail-house rock. The club slipped out of the mercenary's grasp. He appeared unable to deal with this tight little atmosphere of violence in which it was impossible to extend his arms or legs to deliver a blow. But he hung on, and Riggs gradually weakened.

Then Joshua brought him down with an old-fashioned hip throw.

Riggs did not try to get up again. He was struggling hard enough just to breathe.

Pushing off the walls of the corner, Joshua stood over him, triumphant, but his predatory eyes sought Murtaugh's. He gave a grin, his teeth bloody, then gloated down at Riggs again.

"You lose."

"Let Murtaugh go."

Joshua shrugged. "Sure, why not."

"You're lying again."

"Yes. What can you do about it?"

Riggs's eyes seemed to clear again, and there quickly followed the most startling and improbable acrobatic movement Murtaugh had ever witnessed.

Using his shoulders as a base, Riggs unfurled his body straight up into the air and, while still crazily inverted, spun around to lash Joshua with a full front kick that broke the man's clavicle. A sliver of the smashed bone protruded from his pasty skin like the tip of a lance.

The mercenary was still dropping to the floor when Riggs followed up the kick with a pressure-point strike to the groin. And he was winding up a perfectly integrated fist for a death blow to Joshua's heart when Murtaugh cried, "No!"

Riggs halted his trembling fist an inch from Joshua's breastbone. "Why not?" he asked, not meeting Murtaugh's eyes.

"I don't really have to tell you, do I?"

Riggs reared back his arm again, then hesitated. He smiled to himself, then shook out the fist.

Murtaugh realized that two patrolmen were standing in his foyer, holding their revolvers at the ready.

"Code four!" he shouted. "We're cops!"

"Good God!" one of them cried, still not lowering his gun. "What's going on around here? We've got two of our guys dead in the unit out front!" The man was close to tears.

"Here's the son of a bitch who did it. I'd double cuff him between you."

The patrolmen promptly did so, each connecting one of Joshua's wrists to one of his own. Then, angrily, they dragged him to his feet. He said nothing, his pinkish eyes reduced to slits that still seemed menacing.

Riggs remained huddled on the floor. Murtaugh patted him on the shoulder, then went out onto the patio to recover the 9-mm gun from the Boston fern. He was trudging back through the sliding-glass door when he saw Joshua stir and slowly grin.

Then the mercenary delivered a short downward strike onto the forearm of the blue-suiter standing on his left. This gave him enough freedom of movement to reach across himself and rip the revolver from the holster on the cop to his right.

Howling like an animal, his eyes seeming to distend from his pale, sweaty face, he directed the muzzle of the .357 Magnum toward Martin Riggs's back.

But the hammer had not fully cocked back when Murtaugh shot him once in the face and twice in the chest.

CHAPTER 20

RIGGS HAD FORGOTTEN where he was headed through the early morning fog until he saw the refinery loom out of the grayness on the side of the highway. Then he recalled that, after telling security to get fucked and simply walking out of the hospital, he had come to the decision to go home—as opposed to camping out again at Jake's bar.

His ribs were taped. Half of his face had been bandaged, although he'd chucked the dressing out the window somewhere along the Harbor Freeway. He really didn't feel up to enduring the hard wooden bench in one of Jake's grimy booths.

He parked close to the porch of his trailer and turned off the engine.

The windshield slowly misted over as he sat there, working up the herculean energy he'd need to get inside, only to flop down into bed again.

The fog absorbed the sound of the distant surf. The stuff was dense but not thick enough to start dripping off telephone lines and the live oak trees. He rolled down his side window and tried to feel the stuff with his fingers. Clammy as hell, he thought. It gave him a shudder.

The quiet was unsettling.

Then his face paled around its deep bruises.

"Oh, no . . ."

Gnashing his teeth against the pain, he bolted out of the car and hobbled up the steps. He unlocked the front door but hesitated before entering.

No sounds came from within. No sounds from the television.

He crept into the living room and realized in a glance what had happened: Cato had snagged the cord while sniffing around behind the unstable stand.

"Oh no."

Riggs knelt before the overturned television. He touched all ten fingertips to the darkened screen, which crackled softly from a final snap of static electricity. Then the set went dead and cold, reduced to chrome and glass and plastic once again.

"No, no, no . . . babe."

He sensed a presence behind him. Cowering, Cato was crawling across the rug toward him, twisting his muzzle to the side in a gesture that begged forgiveness.

"Do you know what the hell you've done to me?" Riggs was going to strike him, but then he buried his fists in his armpits and began quietly sobbing instead. "You've set me free, dammit."

After a while, the dog wriggled into his arms.

Riggs clung to him.

Murtaugh stood at the sliding-glass door, watching the droplets spangle on the patio. "A rainy Christmas." He tried to get his arm comfortable in the sling intended to immobilize his shoulder. "Shit."

Trish sat with her feet under her on the couch. Her eyes frowned as they passed over the yet unrepaired dents and bullet holes in the walls. Even the Christmas tree looked like it had been violated. "Stop worrying about it, Roger."

"Worrying about what?"

"He'll show."

"I don't know. Maybe the rain got him down. I was

sure he'd phone yesterday. Or the day before. Or the damned day before that. What's with that man?"

"He'll be here any minute."

Nick appeared at the gap in the banister, looking disgruntled as he spun around once in a wool suit. "This okay, Mom?"

"I said the *blue* shirt, young man, not the yellow. And find socks that match."

"Aw, Mom. I don't see why we've got to go. We ain't been in three years."

"We *haven't*—"

"Because we're going!" Murtaugh exploded. "Now get your ass up there and do what your mother says! Now!"

Nick shot up the stairs.

Murtaugh touched his hand to his eyes and groaned. "I shouldn't have done that—not on Christmas morning. Not when we have so damn much to be joyful for."

"You're upset," Trish said gently.

"Yeah, I'm real upset. I was so sure he'd show. But I guess he can't find it in his heart to forgive me."

"Maybe it's not that at all."

"No, honey, it's that. I finked."

"He all but asked you to tell."

"I know. And the bastards damn near drooled when they realized they finally had enough juice to pension out crazy old Martin Riggs. That shrink looked like she'd just been voted Rose Queen. Thanked me again and again. Told me how responsible I am. Maybe that's what makes me feel so sneaky."

"You told the department because you care for him, Roger. He knows that. It's a big adjustment being retired when your entire life has been LAPD. Try to imagine how you're going to feel about it in fifteen years. Maybe he just needed these past days to work it out for himself."

"Whatever—let's get in the car. I promised those folks I'd show."

"No," Trish said. "I think we should give him another few minutes."

"Honey, let's forget it. He's not going to—"
"He'll show, Roger, because he said he would."

The *Times* headline read: *Hollywood Heroin Ring Smashed after Bloody Shoot-Out*. But Riggs ignored the story as he tented the paper over his head and dashed for the big pepper tree in the middle of the old graveyard. Still, the shoulders of his new K-Mart suit got wet during those urgent strides.

Two days after she was gone, he had walked numbly through several modern cemeteries but went away from each thinking it to be a U-rent body storage center. Oh, they had immaculate and spacious lawns uncluttered by tombstones; but somehow this made them seem even more desolate. Then he recalled the pioneer graveyard in Sierra Madre, a small town on the fringe of L.A.'s suburban sprawl with enough surviving Victorian homes to be quaint. A throwback to a quieter California she would have probably preferred.

Years before, on one of his rare days off not spoiled by court, they had wandered through the irregular rows of this cemetery. She'd read somewhere about tracing monument inscriptions onto paper and wanted to give it a try. She was always reading things in women's magazines and wanting to give them a go.

Riggs had brought along a six-pack to kill the time while she traced, but even he finally agreed that it was an agreeable and peaceful place, as far as these places went. There was no grass, but families had planted shrubs and trees around their loved ones, and over the decades these had mushroomed into a kind of forest. The light that filtered down through the foliage onto the marble stones was all soft and dappled.

Of course, when he inquired on the third day after her passing, there had been no available plots. None since the forties. But Riggs asked the caretaker for the names of any living owners. And one old man, who'd inherited his space from a shirt-tail relative, gladly parted with it for twenty grand. He planned to be cremated anyway.

In the maintenance yard in the far back, where monuments toppled by vandals were patiently repaired by an aged Mexican stonecutter, Riggs found a piece of weathered dolomite. It had been the pedestal to a slab that was stolen one Halloween night long ago. The stonecutter agreed to shape it into her marker. Riggs didn't want glistening new marble: That would stand out in the old cemetery, and she had never liked to stand out. She was comfortable only when she was woven into other things, other lives.

And now, wistfully, he smiled down at this piece of stone that bore her name, the years that had enclosed her brief time. "I . . ." He looked up again, fighting to keep his voice level and his eyes clear. A breath of rain-chilled air helped. "I won't be coming here again, babe, anytime soon. See, I didn't realize it until these last couple of days, but there're two good-byes to this thing. The first one—well, it just blew me away. Left me half crazy. Not caring about anything. That's the one that still scares me because I haven't been maintaining so good. The booze again. I'm a powerful man, but sometimes I'm not very strong. But you always knew that—and you still loved me. So maybe I can accept it, too." He shrugged as if in apology, and then the trembling in his voice came to his lips. "Now it's time for another good-bye. This one doesn't mean I don't love you any less. You're everything, babe. It's just that I have to go on alone. Or not at all. And I've got a feeling what you'd want me to do . . ." Riggs kissed his fingers, then touched them to the stone. Turning quickly, he started for the car.

He never looked back, but he sat a long time behind the wheel before starting the engine.

Murtaugh threw back the front door with his free arm.

"Merry fucking Christmas, Roger," Riggs said, his arms full of presents that, obviously, had not been professionally wrapped. Some were done with newspaper.

"Where the hell have you been?"

"I'll explain after the kids open their shit."

"No time, they can go at them in the car. We're late." Murtaugh turned and hollered up the stairs, "Everybody in the car—*now!*"

As soon as they were on the freeway, Riggs began passing around his packages. Trish and Rianne got perfume they both realized to be hyperexpensive, but Riggs waved off their thank-you kisses by pointing to his yet empurpled face. Carrie received another Cabbage Patch doll, and Murtaugh a Swiss watch comparable to the one that had been ruined in the Bel Air swimming pool.

"You been drinking heavy, Martin?" he asked after Riggs unwrapped it for him.

"Not a fucking drop in three days."

"Martin!" Trish snapped.

"Sorry, ma'am."

"Then where've you been? I wore out my finger dialing your house."

"I can only explain with this." Riggs handed a present to Nick, who—thinking he'd been forgotten—smiled for the first time in several minutes.

"Wow!" the boy cried. "A Rambo suit!"

"Not a Rambo suit—Special Forces fatigues, for chrissake."

"And pilot wings!"

"Not pilot wings. Don't you explain anything to this kid, Roger? They're *paratroop* wings. And not just any trooper's wings. They're your dad's."

Murtaugh slapped the steering wheel with his free hand. "Is *that* where you've been?"

"Yeah . . . on my hands and knees sifting over every inch of that miserable dry lake. Also, they wouldn't let me retire unless I found that fucking radio-transmitting bug."

"Martin!"

"Sorry, ma'am."

"Mom," Nick asked, "can I wear them inside? Please?"

"Ask your father."

"Dad?"

"I don't know. It's up to your mother."

The portly minister at Temple Baptist Church glowered down on his congregation. "I must confess, brothers and sisters, that I was sorely tempted . . . yes, *tempted* now . . . to change this morning's message when Brother Roger Murtaugh telephoned me a few days ago. For I was then torn between two topics, the birth of our Lord on this happy day—and the parable of the lost sheep. For, truly, I figured that Brother Roger had gone to Glendale and left God behind!"

There followed a smattering of grumpy-sounding amens, and Rianne looked past her mother to see her father squirm a little at his end of the pew. Riggs poked him hard in the ribs.

"But I rejoice at Brother Roger's return to the flock and hope to see him right there with his lovely family . . ." The minister's tone of voice brightened, but his pointing finger was accusatory. ". . . this coming Sunday . . . and every Sunday henceforth."

"Amen," Riggs said loudly.

Rianne saw her mother try to scorch him with a glance, and he mouthed, "Sorry."

"And now, Brother Roger, will you make your introduction so we might conclude the announcement portion of our service?"

"Thank you, Reverend Cowley." Murtaugh rose, his knee joints cracking.

Rianne thought he looked handsome, but a little frightened, too.

"I would like the people of this congregation to meet Detective Sergeant Martin Riggs, Los Angeles Police Department, retired . . ."

Rianne realized that her father had said *po*-lice, something he hadn't done since they'd moved from Compton to Glendale. It was then that she realized how terrified he really was. He hated to speak in public, more so than she had ever imagined. Here he was with a bullet hole in his shoulder, but his hands were shaking not because of this injury, but only because he had to stand up and say a few words in church.

"Starting right after the holidays, Sergeant Riggs can be found at the Avalon Boulevard Boys's Club as a martial arts instructor . . ."

There was some polite applause.

"And I should mention that he'll be there full-time as a non-paid volunteer."

Louder applause.

Riggs stared down at his thumbs. He was slowly twirling them.

"Now, some folks might say, why do we need martial arts in a community already plagued by so much fighting among our young people? What do we need karate for when we already have street gangs warring each other day and night?"

"Amen . . . amen."

"Well, I asked Sergeant Riggs this same question . . ."

Rianne knew this to be a fib: Her father had promoted the entire idea from the start. Riggs had gone along with it, but had also made it clear that "none of those little dipshits" was going to get in his face.

"And Sergeant Riggs told me, 'When a young man is confident he can defend himself, he doesn't need to attack somebody else.' "

"Amen . . . amen, brother," another set of voices started up.

She saw it in her father's eyes: He was finally warming to his task. "He can afford to turn the other cheek!"

"Hallelujah!" an old woman shrieked from the back, the church nurse going over to check on her because she'd slumped forward with her chin resting on her lace bodice.

Rianne looked at her father again.

"He can become a peacemaker in his community!"

Looking uptight, Trish gave his coattail a furtive tug—a

warning that he was getting carried away. She had been raised an Episcopalian and had never cared for this church.

Murtaugh became self-conscious once again. "So, Brother Martin, stand up and say something."

Riggs stood, turned stiffly, and peered out into the sea of black faces. He opened his mouth but no words escaped. The seconds ticked by in silence, except for the rustling of clothing as people leaned forward in their pews to have a better look at the battered white man.

"Hi," he muttered at last. "Nice to meet you." He quickly sat again, the heat of the moment showing only in his neck—the rest of his face was too bruised to register his embarrassment.

"We welcome you, Brother Martin," the minister said, "and thank you for the commitment of time and self you are freely making to the people of South Los Angeles." But then he frowned again. "Still, I must remark on one thing. Please don't take offense now, but by the looks of your face this morning . . . well, it seems you can use a few lessons yourself."

Murtaugh laughed louder than anyone.

Rianne was mortified.